Hidden at the crossroad
human

To the outside world, Ava Matheson is a successful travel photographer from a privileged background. But Ava's spent a lifetime battling voices in her mind she can't understand, and her fractured family has convinced her she'll never belong.

Malachi is an Irin scribe, descended from an angelic race and sworn by blood and magic to defend humanity from the Grigori, the sons of fallen angels who could ravage the world. A chance meeting in Istanbul will change both Ava and Malachi's destinies forever. Their attraction should be impossible, but it could also be the only thing that will keep them alive.

THE SCRIBE is the first book in the Irin Chronicles, a contemporary fantasy series by Elizabeth Hunter, seven-time USA Today bestselling author of the Elemental Legacy.

> Loved this book! It had great intrigue and romance. It was sexy, well-written and suspenseful. ...I was gripped from the very beginning, enticed by adventures in faraway places.
>
> — VILMA IRIS BOOK BLOG

PRAISE FOR ELIZABETH HUNTER

Hunter weaves a magical tale of love and myth, set against culturally and historically rich backdrop.

— ZEMFIRKA BLOGS

Sexy, well-written, and suspenseful.

— VILMA'S BOOK BLOG

I travelled through Istanbul. I visited the markets, tasted the roasted almonds and smelled the spices. ...And I did all of that from the comfort of my sofa through another amazing and fabulous book by Elizabeth Hunter.

— PAULA, GOODREADS

An enticing and addictive epic.

— WICKED SCRIBES

Five "oh-my-romance" stars.

— JAQUELINE'S READS

The bottom line: if you're not reading Elizabeth Hunter's novels, you should be!

— A TALE OF MANY BOOK REVIEWS

THE SCRIBE

IRIN CHRONICLES BOOK ONE

ELIZABETH HUNTER

To the Telerant-Faith clan

For making me feel so very much at home,
even thousands of miles away.

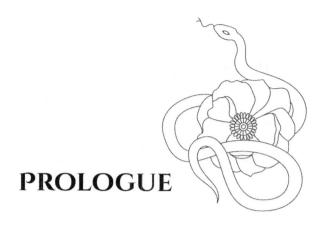

PROLOGUE

Tel Aviv, Israel

"You're going to think I'm crazy."

"Are you?"

"No. Though I suppose most crazy people think they're sane. So it doesn't matter what I say."

There was a pause as the doctor studied the young woman. The listless mouth and relaxed demeanor were belied by the fierce expression in her gold eyes. Barely suppressed anger and... resignation. An odd combination for one so young.

"Why do you assume I will think you're mentally unstable? You're a professional woman. Obviously intelligent based on our previous conversation. University educated. Successful in a highly competitive field—"

"They all think I'm crazy, Doctor Asner." She shifted in her seat, letting her gaze drift out the window to the tree-lined street as a mother with two laughing children passed. A flicker of sadness in her eyes, then nothing again. "It's okay. I'm used to it."

"You hear voices?"

"No question mark on the end."

He blinked and looked up from his pad of paper. "Excuse me?"

The look she gave him was almost amused. The woman's dark curls fell over her shoulder as she angled herself toward him and crossed her arms. "No question mark. I hear voices. Your intonation held a slight lift at the end of that statement, indicating you questioned what you were saying. There is no question. I hear voices. I told you before. I've heard them for as long as I can remember. You can believe me, or you can think I'm insane. But it's not a question."

"You've studied linguistics."

"Linguistics. Phonetics. Ancient languages. Modern languages. I have a very generous stepfather who likes it when I'm not home. Getting several degrees seemed like a good way to pass the time."

"But you became a photojournalist."

"I'm a travel photographer. You don't have to make it sound more important than it is."

He shrugged. "Your work has appeared in major magazines. You make your living with what you do. Are you embarrassed by your work?"

"Not at all."

"Then why qualify?"

"I don't believe in putting on false fronts. Dishonesty irritates me. I am not a photojournalist. Remember the generous stepfather? He also gives me a very generous allowance in order to keep me out of his hair and out of the country. I can afford to travel lots of places that make for pretty pictures. Magazines like to buy them. I'm not saving the world or exposing the horrors of war. What I do is fun, not meaningful."

"Would you like to do something more meaningful?"

A rueful laugh was her first reaction. "God, no."

"Why not? The... voices?"

"There's that unspoken question again. Yes, the voices."

"Is that why you've never had a serious relationship?"

"So my mom called you before the session, huh?"

Asner smiled. "She's concerned about you. That much was evident. Are you and your mother close?"

"I suppose so." The young woman shrugged. "She's the reason I'm not locked up, so I can't really complain about her."

Her eyes drifted to the window again.

"Miss Matheson?"

"Ava."

"Excuse me?"

Ava blinked and turned her eyes back to the doctor. "Call me Ava. Matheson is my stepfather's name."

"But he raised you? Your stepfather and your mother raised you, didn't they?"

"Yes."

"And you only recently met your biological father."

Her eyes narrowed. "Is that why Mom and Carl insisted on this appointment? Because of my father?"

"He's a new presence in your life."

"Not really. I've been a fan for years."

He gave her blank look.

Ava sighed. "Yes, he's a new presence."

"He's a musician?"

"Please don't pretend you don't know who my father is. It's irritating. I knew him as an old friend of my mother's—that's it. When I found out he was my actual father, it wasn't a big deal. I've known since I was little that Carl adopted me."

"But you had no idea the man was your real father."

"No."

"Did he know you were his?"

"Yes, but he agreed to let my mom raise me. He's not the most… together person. He knows that."

Asner paused thoughtfully. "Do you think your voices have anything to do with your father? A shared… creativity, perhaps?"

She curled her lip. "My father—as messed up as he is—is a

brilliant composer. He hears music in his head and writes it down and makes lots of money. I hear garbled voices I don't understand. Not really the same thing. You don't get locked up for being a brilliant composer."

"Do you fear being institutionalized?"

The fierce expression returned. "Why would I? As you said, I'm a successful photojournalist. Plus, thanks to my surprise dad, I'm rich enough to be eccentric instead of crazy."

He couldn't stop his own smile. "Tell me more about your voices. What do they say?"

She shifted again, and her eyes drifted back to the window. "I don't know."

"What do you mean?"

"I mean exactly what I said."

"So you *don't* hear language. You don't hear other people's thoughts?"

"I don't know what I hear." Her eyes swung back and narrowed on him. "But I know you believe me more than the others. I wonder why that is."

"I'm an open-minded individual."

"Maybe."

"Tell me more. How do you know I believe you? Can you hear me?"

"Yes."

"What am I thinking?"

"I can't tell you that. That's not the way it works."

"Do you sense my feelings?"

"It's all in the tone of your voice. The voice I hear, anyway."

"And what voice is that?"

"The one everyone has."

"Everyone?"

She took a deep breath and he saw the hints of resignation again. "Every country and every age. Different voices speaking the same language. That's what I hear."

He leaned forward. "Every voice sounds the same?"

"Of course not. Everyone has a different voice. They just all speak the same language."

"Everywhere in the world?"

"Everywhere I've traveled so far. So... a lot of it."

"What language is it?"

"I don't know."

"What are they saying?"

Frustration flashed. "I don't know."

"So how do you—"

"It's a language, doctor. There are rises and falls in the rhythm. There are common words and phrases I hear again and again. I hear the same things from the minds of people all over the world. I just don't know what they're saying."

He had to pause to contain his reaction. It didn't matter.

She cocked her head. "That's exciting to you."

He smiled. "It's very interesting, Ava."

"Interesting is one word for it."

He heard the irritation in her voice. "Though I'm sure it is frustrating, as well. I imagine it can be quite distracting."

The corner of her mouth turned up. "It's enough to drive you crazy."

Asner laughed a little, and Ava relaxed a bit. "How do you sleep?"

"Probably the same way you do. A bed is usually involved, but I'm pretty comfortable on trains, too. Planes are harder. Buses, practically impossible."

"What a clever and humorous deflection of my question." He stretched his legs in front of him, almost spanning the small office. "When you sleep, do you dream?"

"Vividly. Always have."

"And these voices... do you hear them in your dreams?"

She frowned, and Asner wondered if he was the first mental health professional to ask that question. Ava Matheson had seen more than her share.

"No. No, I don't hear them in my dreams."

He smiled. "That must be a relief."

"Yes, it is."

"Is that part of the reason you prefer to work alone? No voices?"

"Yes."

"And happy, relaxed places. Vacation spots instead of conflict areas."

"It's all falling into place, isn't it, Doc?"

"Have you tried medications?"

"All sorts of them." She reached out and grabbed the arms of the chair she sat in. "Most of them make me sleepy. Kill my appetite. That's about it."

He nodded, jotting down more notes as she examined him. "Do the voices… are they always the same volume? Are some louder than others?"

"Everyone is different. Some people are clearer than others. Yours right now is very quiet, but… urgent. You want to get this information as quickly as possible, but you're trying to remain calm."

He stopped and looked up at her. "That's very disconcerting, Ava."

She gave him an innocent smile. "Imagine what it must be like for me. What do you want, Doctor? You want something."

He paused, trying to decide how to answer. "I'd like to refer you to a colleague. He's someone I think might be able to help you."

"Why?"

"I remember him speaking once about a patient with similar symptoms. Do you mind traveling to see him?"

She waved at the distant ocean. "I was in Cyprus when my mom called and told me to go to a doctor in Israel for my yearly 'what's-the-matter-with-Ava' appointment. What do you think?"

"Excellent."

"I might not go, though." She shrugged. "Carl and Mom

get pushy about once a year, but mostly, they leave me alone. Especially now that I have Jasper's money."

"Jasper is your father?"

"Yeah." A hint of a smile crept across her face. "I guess you could call him that."

"I don't want to take up too much of your time. I know we've gone over the hour—no charge, of course—but..." Asner scribbled down a name and telephone number from memory. "I do hope you'll see my colleague. He's in Istanbul. Have you been before?"

Ava's eyebrows furrowed together. "No, but I've been told it's beautiful, even though it's crowded."

"And you don't like crowds because of the voices?"

"That and the lack of deodorant on hot days. I might check it out." She shrugged. "Like I said, no guarantees. If I happen to be in Istanbul, I'll look him up."

He smiled politely and rose to his feet as she stood to gather her things: a large messenger bag, a battered camera case, a light scarf thrown around her neck to keep the dust of the city away. She grabbed the paper from Doctor Asner's hand and had started toward the door before he spoke.

"May I ask...?"

The young woman turned, tucking a curl behind her ear before she put her sunglasses on. "You can ask whatever you want. If I don't want to answer, I won't."

He frowned. "Your name—Ava—means 'voice' in Persian. Did you know that?"

The sunglasses hid her eyes. "Yes."

"Who gave you your name?"

She paused. "My father did. It was the one thing he asked for. To name me Ava."

"Do you know why?"

"No."

"And you never asked?"

She shrugged. "Does it matter? It's a nice name. Maybe he just liked the actress, you know?"

"Names are important."

She smiled a little. "Good-bye, Doctor Asner. Fun chatting with you. I probably won't see you around."

MIKHAIL ASNER WATCHED HER THROUGH THE WINDOW AS SHE wound through the narrow streets of Neve Tzedek and wandered north toward the city center. The slight woman with curly black hair melded into the city landscape effortlessly, a seasoned traveler accustomed to blending with her surroundings. He watched for a few more minutes, then picked up the phone, dialing a number from memory.

"You haven't called me in some time," said the voice on the other end.

"I found someone of interest."

"Did you give her my number?"

"Yes."

"Her name?"

"Ava Matheson. American."

A notable pause followed Asner's declaration.

The voice asked, "Will she come?"

"I honestly don't know."

"Did you tell her I could help her?"

"Of course."

"Then she'll come."

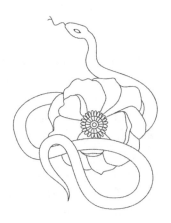

CHAPTER
ONE

Istanbul, Turkey

Malachi spotted the Grigori foot soldier at the edge of the bazaar. The man walked slowly through the spice market, stopping occasionally to examine wares he wouldn't buy, scanning the crowd for…

Her.

Dark curling hair shielded her face, but her figure was slight and quick. The human woman radiated energy, even as she strolled through the cacophony of sounds, sights, and smells that careened through the market in the heart of Old Istanbul. Vendors yelled out their wares as tourists sampled the variety of spices, dried fruits, and nuts the market held, and deft boys dodged the traffic, delivering trays of dark tea.

The woman seemed to exist in her own space, blending into the colorful mosaic of the bazaar, though she spoke to no one.

Malachi's gaze drifted away from her, back to the Grigori soldier. In his mind's eye, he approached the man quietly, stalking him to a deserted corner before he grabbed him silently and stabbed a sharp blade into the base of his skull, killing the murderous creature and releasing its soul to face judgment.

Then he melted into the crowd, another passing traveler at the crossroads of the world.

You're reckless. Looking for trouble instead of using your head.

The voice of his last watcher mocked him, so Malachi did none of those things that morning. Instead, he fought back the instinctual rage and watched the man carefully.

The Grigori was hunting.

Casually adjusting the silver knives he wore under his shirt, Malachi tossed a few lire toward a vendor, then grabbed a small bag of roasted almonds, just another nameless tourist in the market that morning. Though he was one of the taller men in the crowd, hundreds of years had taught Malachi the art of blending into his surroundings. He followed the Grigori as the creature followed the woman. Hunting him, hunting her. The soldier kept his distance but never let the woman stray too far ahead. There was no sense of urgency as was usually seen when a Grigori was tracking his prey. The man almost looked relaxed if one didn't notice the dark eyes that never left the figure as she wound her way toward the courtyard that separated the bazaar from the mosque.

The man was nondescript, as the best soldiers were. Local, if he had to guess, though he'd never seen him before. But Malachi had returned to the country of his birth after hundreds of years away. It was possible one of his brothers was familiar with the soldier who was tracking the woman with such restraint.

Who was she?

Her face still obscured by her thick hair, she could have been Turkish or foreign, local or tourist. Her clothes were unremarkable, a loose pair of linen pants and a long-sleeved T-shirt. Modest, but not religious. The only feature that struck him as notable was the messenger bag she carried. It was expensive. Worn. A man's bag. Once belonging to a father? A brother? It was a decidedly masculine accessory for the delicate female.

She stopped at the exit of the L-shaped building, turning

back to take a picture with a small black camera, just another tourist taking in the sights. As her face lifted to the sun, he saw her features. European... with a distinct hint of something else. A common enough look in a city like Istanbul. The breeze lifted her curling hair as she raised the device and held it away from her body as she framed the entrance to the building. The Grigori stopped near a small mountain of hazelnuts and tried to ignore the eager vendor who shouted at him about a sale.

The woman paused, and with his shoulder turned away, the Grigori missed the quick glance she gave him as well as the slight shift in angle as the woman captured his image with her camera. Malachi had to smile. The clever female had spotted the tail, and she'd captured her pursuer before he could duck away. But she didn't give Malachi notice before she turned and sped out into the sunlight just as the call to prayer began to echo through the heavy summer air.

Who was she?

The Grigori finally shook off the hazelnut vendor and turned, picking up his pursuit. Malachi continued to follow at a distance, watching him, watching her. The woman ignored the müezzin who called the faithful, stepping lightly along the crowded streets as she made her way back toward the train station. She turned right near Gülhane Park and followed the tram line up the hill, walking a few blocks before she stopped near the lobby of one of the larger hotels.

Then she stepped into the glass-fronted building and out of sight. The Grigori stopped a block away, watching for a few moments before he pulled out a mobile phone, called a number, and spoke animatedly to whoever was on the other end. After a quick conversation, the man took one last look at the hotel, then walked away, back toward the train station.

But Malachi waited. The Grigori didn't know he had been spotted, but Malachi had seen the quick recognition on the woman's face. She hadn't recognized the man, but she'd known she was being watched. Perhaps, like him, she could sense it.

She was more perceptive than the average human; Malachi would have to be careful. He sat down at an outdoor café to wait, ordering a tea and continuing to munch on the roasted almonds as he scanned the streets from behind black-shaded glasses and pretended to read a newspaper someone had left on the table.

A full forty-five minutes later, the woman emerged. She lingered at the entrance for a few minutes, holding a map in front of her as she scanned the streets from behind her glasses. Satisfied her follower had left, she started back up the hill.

She crossed the street, heading toward the hippodrome. The hairs on Malachi's neck rose as he walked. The walls whispered, centuries of secrets held in the cobbled brick and marble of Byzantium. As he strolled, ancient graffiti flickered black and grey in the corner of his eye. He saw the woman pause and take a picture of an old graveyard before she kept moving. As Malachi passed, he saw a lazy cat stretching in the sun.

Who was she? And why had she attracted the attention of the Grigori that morning? More, why had the soldier not hunted her in the common way? Grigori didn't show restraint when seducing a target. Their wicked charm was relentless. If the woman survived the encounter, she was discarded. To follow a woman so discreetly indicated some other, more enigmatic, motivation.

She walked the length of the hippodrome, past the obvious tourist traps, then turned right near a small café. Climbing up a side street, she dodged a car coming out of a parking lot as she put her map away. It looked as if she was walking into a dead-end street before she took a sudden left and disappeared. Malachi followed cautiously, hoping to not appear too conspicuous as he approached a building tented for renovation. He stopped to read a sign detailing the improvements to the structure, which housed a museum. Then he watched from the corner of his eye as the woman approached what looked like an old Ottoman house but was probably one of the many boutique hotels that had sprung up in the last few years. A discreet doorman stepped outside, opened the door, and spotted him. Without a pause, Malachi walked away.

He turned back to the hippodrome, pausing to take note of the glowing red lanterns in front of the Chinese restaurant near her hotel before he began the trek back to Galata. The woman, whoever she was, was staying at the small hotel. He'd find her again if he wanted to. As for the Grigori's odd behavior…

He'd have to ask Damien if he'd seen anything like it before. His watcher had centuries more experience than Malachi. He might be prone to recklessness, but he knew how to use the resources he was given.

Stuffing the almonds back in his pocket, Malachi's thoughts turned to decidedly more practical matters. With the heat of the day rising and too many salted almonds in his belly, he needed a drink. Throwing one last glance toward the wood-fronted house, he started back toward home.

He slammed the door shut on the small refrigerator.

"Doesn't anyone buy beer besides me?" he yelled to the empty kitchen. "If you don't buy it, you shouldn't drink it!"

From upstairs, a faint voice came. "You spent too much time in Hamburg. You're back in Istanbul, Mal; we drink raki." It was Maxim, no doubt lying in bed, waiting for the city to cool before he emerged.

"Or tea," another voice added in the same thick Russian accent. If Maxim was upstairs, so was his cousin, Leo. "Gallons of tea."

"Oceans of it."

"If only the Bosphorus flowed with vodka."

"We should get the brothers in Odessa working on that…"

Damien walked into the kitchen, glancing upward as the

cousins continued to rib each other. "Drink water. You're not used to the heat yet."

Malachi grimaced. "I'll be fine. I was born here."

The watcher pulled a bottle of water from a cupboard and threw it toward him, the tattoos on his bare arms rippling as he threw the plastic bottle. "But you haven't lived here for hundreds of years. The city has grown, and that makes it hotter."

"Anthropogenic heat," said Rhys, walking into the kitchen from the library and holding his hand out to Damien for another bottle of water. The pale man had been sweating nonstop for three days—not surprising considering the air conditioner had broken around that time. His dark brown hair was plastered to his forehead, and his normally pale skin was flushed. "Human activity produces heat. More humans. More heat. Not to mention climate change. Bloody humans and their automobiles will kill us all."

Damien and Malachi exchanged amused glances. The cranky British scholar was constantly nostalgic for preindustrial times.

"Heat can't kill us, Rhys!" Leo called from above.

"But your whining is doing a fairly good job of torture," Maxim added. "Is whining a violation of the Geneva Convention?"

"Does the Geneva Convention apply to us?"

"Ask Rhys. He knows everything."

The scholar's face only grew redder. "Maybe if I wasn't the only one working—"

"Stop." One quiet word from Damien was all it took. The three men fell silent, even the ones on the second floor, who could hear their watcher's voice from a distance.

Damien was of average height and weight. His face could make humans stop and stare, or he could blend into a crowd, based solely on his demeanor. The only remarkable thing about him was the intricate tattoos he had inked all over his arms. Malachi knew the work covered most of the man's legs as well, though he kept them carefully covered. Malachi glanced down at his own markings. Four hundred years of scribing himself still hadn't left him half as covered as Damien. Who knew how old the man was?

Damien continued in a low voice, "Leo, did you call the man to repair the air conditioner?"

A thundering set of footsteps came down the stairs and the hall. The man they belonged to stopped in the door, filling it with his massive frame. "They said they will come tomorrow. Beginning of the summer means lots of work. They're busy." Sweat dotted a pale forehead topped by a thatch of sandy-blond hair. Maxim followed Leo, a mirror of his cousin. The two were inseparable, cousins being as rare as siblings in their race. Their mothers had been twin sisters, and the men looked like twins themselves. Even their tattoos were almost identical, though their personalities couldn't have been more opposite.

"So no air-conditioning until tomorrow?" Rhys asked.

Damien shrugged. "Sleep on the roof. There are beds up there and the breeze will be better when the sun goes down."

For some reason, Malachi's thoughts flicked to the woman slipping into the wooden house near Aya Sofia. The house had a plain street view, a classic Ottoman; it was probably cool and shaded in the interior. There might have been a courtyard. And air-conditioning.

"I should have kept following the woman," he muttered.

Damien's ears caught it. "What woman? Why were you following her? You know you're not allowed to—"

"Do I look like a foolish boy?" He glared at the man. "There was a woman at the spice market. She'd caught the attention of a Grigori soldier. I was watching him, and he was watching her."

All amusement fled the group. Each man knew the danger of a Grigori attack.

Maxim asked, "Did you kill him before he got to her?"

Rhys offered a bloodthirsty smile, forgetting his misery in the contemplation of Grigori death. "Set his soul free to be judged, brother? I wish I could have helped."

"I didn't. I'm being cautious, remember?" He aimed a pointed look at Damien. "Besides, his behavior was… odd. I wanted to ask you about it."

Damien narrowed his eyes. "Odd how?"

"He was hunting her, but he wasn't. He never approached her. Never tried to charm her. He was actually trying to remain unnoticed."

Leo shook his head. "No, that's not how they work. They seduce. They—"

"We all know what the Grigori do, Leo." Damien was staring at Malachi. "What happened?"

"He followed her back to a hotel, and…"

Maxim said, "And what?"

"Nothing. He just watched her, called someone on the phone, then left."

Damien was silent. The others were silent. It was, just as Malachi had suspected, unusual behavior for the Grigori of Istanbul. He had hoped Damien would have some clue, but the man's face registered nothing. Not shock, not recognition. Nothing.

The watcher finally said, "So you know where this woman is staying?"

He smiled. "I do, but the Grigori doesn't."

"I thought you said—"

"She spotted him at the market. Took his picture when he was looking away. She went into the lobby of one of the hotels near the palace, waited for forty minutes until he'd left, then went to her real hotel. The Grigori never saw where she's actually staying."

Damien nodded, seemingly impressed with the resourcefulness of the human. "Clever."

Leo nodded and grinned. "I like the clever ones. Was she pretty, too?"

Maxim elbowed his cousin. "That's not important." Then he turned to Malachi and narrowed his eyes. "But was she?"

"She was... interesting." She had been pretty, Malachi realized. He'd been concentrating so hard on the chase that he hadn't really noticed until he remembered her fine features, the slope of her eyes. "Yes, she was pretty." Not that it mattered to him, but the cousins were still young enough to find human women attractive. They had never known true beauty like the older men had.

"I want you to go back to her hotel tomorrow," Damien said. "Find out more. And you're sure she wasn't...?" There was a slight, hopeful rise in his voice.

"I don't think so," Malachi said quietly. "She would have heard me if she was. And the Grigori wouldn't have shown any restraint."

"Of course." Damien looked away. All the men found things to look at, other than each other. "Go back tomorrow," Damien said. "Find out more. We need to know why she's attracted their attention this way. This is different."

Malachi took a deep breath, alternately concerned and excited about the chase. It might be his most interesting day in the Old City yet.

THE WOMAN TOOK A LOT OF PICTURES. AND FROM THE LOOK OF her equipment, she was a professional. She took picture after picture of the Sultanahmet's mosques and streets. The alleys and corner gardens. Odd angles a tourist wouldn't think of. Glimpses of old women selling lace and children selling toys. She even lay down on the dirty sidewalk at times. She ate corn and chestnuts from the carts in front of Aya Sofia and watched the tourists feed the pigeons. She captured it all, from the grand to the gritty.

No one was with her, and the Grigori hadn't found her again. Malachi watched her for hours the next morning as she made her way through the old city. Every now and then, she would duck into a quiet alley or deserted shop, hold her head in her hands, and rub her temples.

Was she dehydrated? She'd been sipping water all morning but looked to be suffering from a terrible headache. Still, she didn't return to her hotel. Her face, now that he was looking at it, was a picture of well-concealed tension. Crowds seemed to make her particularly nervous, and she avoided the swarms of tourists that came off the cruise ships at regular intervals.

Was she afraid of them? Was that why she took shelter in the quieter corners when she could? Malachi didn't think so. She looked, more than anything, exhausted, though every now and then a child or group of children would pass and her face would light up. She liked children. So did Malachi. The thought made him smile.

Despite her exhaustion, she continued taking pictures all morning, checking her phone every now and then. He would guess she was a regular traveler. The way she navigated the city, the way she talked to people, there was something about her manner that told him she was very comfortable with new places. If she was a professional photographer, it would make sense. What didn't make sense was why the Grigori soldier had been following the human woman yesterday, but not hunting her.

She worked her way through the Sultanahmet and toward the Galata Bridge, closer to the neighborhood where he and his brothers made their home. She picked up the tail just before the tram stop.

There were two this time, still watching. Still hanging back far enough that Malachi could keep them in sight while watching the woman. She paused near the train station, then turned back and turned left to an emptier side street. What was she doing? Was she headed for the park? The police station? No, she turned right again. She was headed back up the hill.

Malachi tried to get closer, only to see her turn to look over her shoulder at the two Grigori following her.

She'd spotted them.

He could tell she was trying to lose the tail, ducking into crowds when she could and darting across the street, coming far too close to cars for his liking. She walked quickly, but the soldiers were good. Just before the street opened up, she made a quick left into an alley and Malachi's heart leapt.

Bad move, woman. Why were humans so stupid at times?

He sped up. They wouldn't attack her in the open during the day, but Grigori would have no qualms about disappearing with her. If they caught up to her, she was history. No government in the world would find a trace. The soldiers turned left and followed her into the alley.

Malachi started running, no longer worried about attracting attention. He had to get to her. Had to keep them from—

"And that is why you don't fuck with someone with pepper spray, asshole! What? Did you think because I'm a tourist I wouldn't be able to protect myself?" She kicked one in the kidneys, standing over both men and holding a small can. Malachi turned his head away as the breeze drifted toward him. Both Grigori soldiers were on the ground, writhing and clutching their faces, holding preternaturally sensitive eyes and noses that were, no doubt, in agony from the pungent concoction she'd sprayed from the can.

Malachi was gaping. How had she caught them by surprise? Their race could move almost silently. No human should have been able to fend off—

"And you!" The woman was pointing at him now, aiming the can in his direction. He brought his right thumb to his left wrist and began tracing, silently rousing the spells that would protect his senses should she choose to attack. He felt it, the warm glow of magic spreading up his arm, suffusing his body with power, activating the tapestry of magic that protected him. In seconds, Malachi would be covered with an armor even the fiercest warrior could not penetrate. "Why the hell have you been following me?" she demanded.

"I haven't been following you."

"Don't lie to me."

"I saw these men follow you into the alley." He lifted his hands, no longer worried about the pepper spray. He could feel the ancient power swirling over his skin. "I'm just trying to help."

"I said don't lie to me!" Her energy was high, her adrenaline staining the air as she walked toward him. Malachi backed away, drawing her out of the alley and into the safer street. "You were following me yesterday. You've been following me all morning. Why?"

How had she known?

"I haven't been following you," he lied. "Do you need some help? Is there someone I can call for you?" She was attracting enough attention just by her raised voice. He didn't want to attract the police. That was the last thing either of them needed. "Put the pepper spray down. I'm not going to hurt you."

"I might. If you tell me why you were following me all morning."

"For the last time, I have not been—"

Her temper burst. "I heard you, you lying asshole! Do I look stupid? Why were you following me?"

The ground beneath him shifted. The spells on his arms pulsed.

I heard you.

Malachi blinked as his vision scattered, and then he focused on the fearless woman in front of him.

"What did you say?"

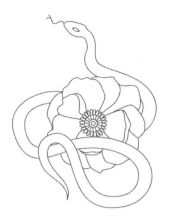

CHAPTER
TWO

I heard you.

Time stopped as the words left her mouth of their own volition, launching into the air between Ava and the stranger who stood at the mouth of the alley. A thousand whispers surrounded her, and the voices of the city washed over her mind. The words flew, cutting through the cacophony that followed her. Three words that never should have left her mouth.

The man halted immediately, eyes widening as they reached him.

"What did you say?"

He knew.

"Nothing. Leave me alone." Forget her questions, she had to leave. Ava stepped over the prone bodies of the strange men who were still writhing on the ground. Instinct told her the man whose voice she'd heard following her since the day before was far more dangerous than the thugs who'd caught up with her near the bridge. She'd been lulled by it; something about the tone and pitch of this man's inner voice was more resonant than most. She'd allowed the voice to follow her, soothed by its tone.

It had been the one pure sound in the redolent, clashing air of Istanbul.

"What did you mean, 'I heard you?'" he called.

He was following her out of the alley, abandoning the wounded men to their own moans and the growing crowd of concerned citizens and tourists. Ava slipped through them, never gladder to have perfected the art of weaving through crowds with as little contact as possible.

The stranger's whispers followed her, alive with excitement. Curiosity. Hope? She walked faster, trying to leave his voice and the memories it brought behind.

He wasn't completely unique. Ava had come across the strange resonance before in India. Another time back in Los Angeles. Once, outside a lonely house in Ireland. The resonance of his inner voice was different, though no more understandable, than the rest. Most of her waking hours were filled with the whispers of anyone and everyone she passed, but Ava had no clue what they were saying. It was as if she stood in a crowded room where everyone was whispering. Crowds blended into an off-key hum she'd battled to control for as long as she could remember.

What do your whispers mean, Mommy?

What whispers?

Everyone has whispers.

The strange looks, then the voices others could hear, too.

Crazy.

Troubled.

Dangerous?

Ava's eyes caught the corner of a leg sticking out of a blanket. A homeless man sat up from a bench near the entrance of the park, eyes wild and body swaying. Their gazes locked for a moment and Ava fought back the pang of sympathy and kept moving. If not for her mother, she might have been him.

She crossed the road at the entrance to the park, headed back to the hippodrome and the relative safety of the heavily touristed areas. Her camera banged against her hip as she walked. Normally, it would be out. She wouldn't pass up a chance to capture the smiling couple or the woman rolling out bread in a window. She would have captured the small dog watching the young woman tying a carpet in a store window. The two boys ducking behind a display in a shop. Snatches of life in the city. Family and friends going about their lives.

It was a bittersweet triumph, to capture moments she would never have.

The stranger's voice still followed, the lone bright thread running through the tapestry of the Sultanahmet. It was as if a single voice whispered to her, not off-key, but in a melodious timbre that stroked her mind. It wrapped around her as it had the day before. She had known it followed her, but she felt no instinct to run. The voice called to her, tempting her to turn and follow it. Urging her to abandon caution and seek it out.

The tone of the stranger's voice revealed his mood, though the meaning was still a mystery. Disbelief, frustration, and hope, all wrapped together. Ava ignored the urge to turn, stubbornly focusing on navigating the streets, dodging traffic, and avoiding the frightening swarms of tourists trailing mechanically behind the cruise ship guides.

Despite the crowds, she couldn't stop the thrill and awe as she passed Aya Sofia and the Blue Mosque. She loved it here, which had been a surprise. Ava hadn't loved a city in a long time. But this city was seductive. Layer upon layer of history. East meeting West. Modern colliding with ancient. Istanbul had been a revelation of the senses.

The stranger's voice was still following her when Ava turned the corner near her hotel, almost jogging up and down the completely unnecessary hill the house sat on. If you didn't look closely, it might have been no more than a very gracious residence in the heart of the city. In reality, it was an exclusive hotel that catered to travelers looking for luxury, safety, and privacy. Made of wood in the Ottoman style, it was almost plain from the front. But as she approached, a guard opened a door, letting her into the cool interior of the refuge, searching behind her when he saw the hint of panic still evident on Ava's features.

"Ms. Matheson?" he asked in lilting English. "Is there a problem?"

She shook her head. "I'm fine, thanks. I thought... It was just my imagination, I'm sure. Is the roof garden open?"

The guard's eye widened. "Right now? It is open, but the day is very hot, miss. Perhaps when the sun goes down—"

"It's fine." She shot him a tense smile. "I just need some privacy."

"Of course." He nodded and lifted a hand toward the elevators, but Ava didn't want to chance that someone might join her. Voices always grew more agitated in confined spaces, and the elevators in the hotel were small. She walked toward the stairs instead. Her phone was already out and she was dialing her mother's number when she pushed the door to the terrace open. Sunlight flooded over her, baking the tile that covered the roof. Ava took shelter under one of the generous shade covers that marked a quiet corner. As she suspected, the terrace was deserted. Keeping away from any windows or open doors, she let the phone ring across the world in Los Angeles.

"Hello?" Lena Matheson answered in a groggy voice. "Ava, what's wrong?"

It was just past midnight in L.A.

"Did you and Carl hire someone local?"

"What?" She heard Carl's voice in the background, a quiet growl that her mother shushed. "What are you talking about?"

"Did you hire someone, Mother?"

There was a quiet huff. "Well, really, Ava, what did you expect? You asked Carl to have pepper spray delivered to your hotel. He—"

"That's precautionary, Mom! I do that anywhere I've never been before when I'm traveling alone." A tight, nervous part of her stomach relaxed. It wasn't a stranger after all. Despite the unusual voice, the man following her was just another guard hired by her overprotective mother and stepfather. Nothing she couldn't handle.

"Just go about your business and ignore him. He has a job to do, and you know Carl won't fire him."

No, but he might hire more if he got wind of the incident in the alley today. "This is Istanbul. It's very safe as long as you're smart. I'd probably be in more danger traveling in New Jersey. You really don't need to—"

"Have you forgotten Cassie Traver? She was in Paris and she was kidnapped. Let's not take any chances, Ava. You know how he worries."

You mean how his accountant worries. The only reason her stepfather had started up with the guards again was because of the enormous amount of money the Travers had been forced to pay to Cassie's kidnappers. Ava had no illusions of paternal concern.

"Just tell him to keep his distance. I know you won't fire him, but I don't want to see him anywhere near me."

"Do you want to talk to Carl?"

"What do you think?"

There was a heavy pause on the line. "Okay. Are you... having fun?"

She heard Carl growl again. Her mother covered the phone with her hand.

"It's late, Mom." Ava swallowed the lump in her throat. "I'll call you back another time."

"No, it's fine. I'll just—"

"I gotta go. There's someone I need to meet with. For work."

"Call me back tomorrow?"

"I don't know—"

"Later, then. Just call me later."

"Sure." Ava collapsed in one of the luxurious chairs under the shade and ran her fingers along the frond of a potted palm. "I'll call you later."

"I love you."

"Love you, too. Bye." Ava hung up before Lena could say anything more, then stared over the rooftops of Istanbul, far above the crowds.

Silence. At last, silence.

AVA STARTED EARLY THE NEXT DAY. SHE'D BEEN TO TOPKAPI Palace before but had woken when the first prayer calls floated over the city and couldn't get back to sleep. She lay in bed for a few hours, loading and editing work on her laptop, then decided to beat the crowds and some of the heat. She headed toward the opulent palace in the center of the old city, walked past the first gate, and started working.

Photography had been her escape for years. There was something about the intense visual focus that helped Ava block out the voices around her. She could get lost behind the lens. An observer instead of an outsider. She snapped pictures of the stunning architecture, trying to capture it from unique angles in the morning light. But more and more, she found herself drawn to the people who began crowding the various courtyards.

Whispers of excitement.

Routine hums.

The clear, pure thoughts of the youngest children, uncluttered by the static of their parents and guardians.

And each and every one completely unintelligible to her. She recognized common words and phrases. She could probably quote things from memory, though she had no idea what she would be saying. People's inner voices didn't work the way their spoken voices did. They thought in slips and starts. Their minds drifted from one emotion to another, often so quickly it made her ill.

"Excuse me," she said, working her way through a tour

group and toward an empty corner where she could watch the growing crowds.

Workers. Tourists. Families on holiday and the odd wanderer like herself. Ava turned her camera on them, capturing their fleeting expressions and sudden smiles. People were nice... from a distance. She'd avoided cities for years, preferring the peace of wilderness destinations and hidden enclaves where the voices of the locals weren't quite so over-whelming. She was still in shock that she'd agreed to come to Istanbul. Couldn't explain why, exactly, but she'd felt drawn to it. Maybe it was the promise of help. She couldn't allow herself to believe this doctor—Doctor J. Sadik—could actually help her. But perhaps she *could* allow herself to be curious.

She wandered the edges of the palace, looking out over stunning views of the sea and snapping pictures for hours. Every now and then, she'd catch a glimpse of him at the edge of her frame.

Hello, stranger. Ava snapped another picture of him, pushing a button on her camera to examine him more closely.

At least they'd hired an attractive one this time.

He looked Turkish. Taller than average. Most professional bodyguards were far from the romantic notions portrayed in movies or books, even farther from the giant thugs who followed musicians around. The best were men and women who could blend into any crowd. They were overlooked until they became necessary, and they rarely garnered an admiring stare.

But this man was... not handsome. Compelling. Something about him made her eyes want to linger. Lean muscle covered his frame, and despite the heat, he was clothed from head to toe, though his suit appeared to be made of linen and not some hotter material. His collar lay open, exposing the edge of an intricate tattoo. That was unusual. His hair was dark and straight, falling onto his forehead and almost into his eyes. He could use a haircut, which meant he was probably not married. She glanced at the three college-age girls who checked him out as he pretended to read a book at the café. He didn't even give them a glance. Focused. He blended into the crowd admirably for someone as physically imposing as he was, but there was still something about him that drew Ava's camera over and over again.

Or maybe it was just his voice.

She'd caught it almost as soon as she'd left the hotel. Thankfully, the bodyguard was keeping his distance. Carl must have clarified his instructions. The man followed, but not too closely. Occasionally, Ava would turn and deliberately snap his picture, letting him know she'd seen him. He looked away every time she did, a slightly irritated expression crossing his face.

She caught him at the edge of another frame just as he was pulling out a mobile phone. Probably calling Carl to complain about her.

"Won't do any good," she sang under her breath.

Her stepfather had tried for years to understand how Ava could pick up on any security he assigned to her. He knew she could hear them—her mother had never hidden her secret from Carl—he just chose not to believe. He wasn't a bad guy, really. Carl adored her mother, and he was honest to a fault. The fact that he'd been saddled with a stepdaughter who was slightly crazy was just the cost of capturing Lena Russell's heart. Ava couldn't fault his indifference as she'd never made an effort with him, either.

The stranger was still talking, so Ava grabbed a coffee and perched on a bench, lifting her camera to capture a boy who was laughing at something his mother had said. They teased and giggled with each other as Ava clicked. A common moment between mother and child set in the grandeur of the old Ottoman court. It was exactly the kind of photograph she loved.

A young man brushed a little too close, causing her to tense, to grip her cup as her coffee spilled hot over her fingers. Her bodyguard started toward the man, but Ava gave a small shake of her head.

Not a threat. The unspoken message seemed to reach him, because he stopped, looking between the retreating man and Ava.

She closed her eyes and breathed deeply, trying to rid the angry sound of the young man from her mind.

Sharp, piercing tones. His thoughts were shot through with a deep thread of pain. Most people's inner voices were like tiny orchestras in the moments before a concert. An odd cacophony of emotion and tone only occasionally smoothing out into a discernible voice. The young man who had just passed her was angry, but also in pain. It was all there in his voice.

Ava took a few more deep breaths and looked up to find her bodyguard staring at her. His voice, in contrast, was the smooth, clear note the moment before the orchestra played. Perfectly in tune. She didn't know quite what to make of it.

Time to say hello.

If she wanted him to cooperate and leave her be without reporting every flinch to her mother and Carl, she'd have to play nice. Tossing her coffee in a nearby trash can, she stood and walked over. He didn't run. Didn't look away. He stared at her from behind shaded lenses as she tucked her camera in her bag and held out her hand.

"Hi, I'm Ava. I imagine you know that already."

The bodyguard just blinked at her, staring at her hand as if it might bite. Finally, she dropped it. She had surprised him. His silent voice whispered in circles so rapid she felt as if she was in the middle of a minor storm. But he didn't speak to her, not out loud.

"I know I heard you speak English the other day. It might not be your first language, but I'm sorry, I don't speak any Turki—"

"English is fine."

His spoken voice was deeper than his silent one, but it held the same odd resonance that had drawn her since she first heard it. Ava tried not to lean closer, even though the urge was there.

"Okay." She nodded. "I just wanted to introduce myself."

"Hello."

What about his one-word greeting did Ava find amusing? She didn't know why she smiled, but she did. "That back there? With the guy... I get headaches—it's a medical thing that's not a big deal—so don't panic if you see me looking like I might pass out. I've never passed out in my life. And I have no idea why Carl hired you, but since I can't get him to fire you, we might as well be friendly."

He just shifted in his seat, clearly uncomfortable with the conversation.

"I know you're going to be following me, so please don't feel like you have to hide. If you could just keep your distance and stay as unobtrusive as possible, that'd be great. I've had guards before, but I'm pretty independent. I'm honestly not sure why Carl felt like he had to do this, but since there never seems to be any reasoning with him, let's just go with it, okay?"

The big man was still blinking at her silently. Ava tried not to sigh. His eyes had seemed intelligent enough, but maybe they hadn't hired the guy for his intellect.

"What I'm trying to say is... The incident you saw in the alley doesn't need to be reported to my stepfather. I took care of it, and we really don't need more people at this little party, do we?"

Complete and utter silence. It was almost inhuman. She caught him taking a breath when the collar of his shirt moved, revealing more of the tattoo work around his collar. They were letters, she thought, but nothing like she'd ever seen before. Other than that one breath, he could have been one of the statues on display.

"Do you have a name?" she asked.

He frowned. "You want my name?"

"Well, it would feel rude to refer to you as 'the big, silent guy' in my internal monologue, so yeah, a name would be nice."

He was still silent. Ava frowned. "Is that not part of your job or—?"

"Malachi."

She smiled. "Malachi?"

"My name is Malachi."

"Nice name."

"I like yours."

She shrugged off the internal pleasure. "It's… easy to spell. Anyway, I have an appointment this afternoon, so I'll be heading back to my hotel now. I'll be trying to take a nap for approximately forty-five minutes, but will realize it's too hot, so I'll then take a shower and read a book. Maybe dump my pictures on the computer. All of this will be happening *in* my hotel, which has very good security, but please feel free to lurk around the entrance so you can shadow me to my appointment later."

Malachi stared at her, still silent. Finally, he put down the book and crossed his arms over his chest, leaning back in his chair and looking at her as if he was trying to solve a puzzle.

"Nothing to add? Any questions? I'm not sure how much Mom and Carl told you. I'm just here in the city for a while. Taking pictures… for my job. With a magazine."

More silence.

Ava shook her head and stood. "Fine. Whatever. I'll see you around, Malachi."

She turned to go, but he said her name in that low voice and she turned back.

"Ava."

"Yes?"

He stood and walked toward her. He didn't hold out his hand, didn't touch her in any way, but she still felt surrounded. Her breath caught as his inner voice took on an urgent tone.

"I will protect you."

She could feel her face heat. There was something intimate about the words, despite knowing he was only doing his job.

"I know. And I want you to know that I appreciate—"

"If there is any threat to you, I will protect you." He took another step closer, and Ava tried not to shrink back. "I promise."

She felt short of breath. Not from panic, but... "Wow, you take your job pretty seriously, huh?"

The first hint of humor crossed his face, and she saw the corner of his mouth inch up. "I do."

"Okay." She stepped back, no longer able to sustain his presence. There was something magnetic about the man, and she didn't want to know more. "I'm going back now. Don't forget, appointment later."

"After not-napping."

She forced a smile. "Exactly. See? You're an expert at my schedule already."

He said nothing more, but his quiet amusement followed Ava all the way back to her room.

HE PICKED HER UP AGAIN ON THE CORNER NEAR THE HOTEL BUT stayed a polite distance back and didn't try to approach. She walked to the tram station and hopped on board, Malachi shadowing her. Then she stood, swaying with the movement of the car as the tram followed the tracks, down the hill and across the bridge to the New City. Instead of marble and brick, she was met with concrete and glass when she got off. Soaring buildings that would have been at home in any metropolitan area of Europe or Asia.

Malachi came a little closer as she walked toward the modern building that housed the doctor's office. Ava noticed several names and office signs that seemed to indicate it was an office building for different medical or mental health professionals. She took the elevator up to the third floor, ignoring her shadow, who seemed thankfully content to linger in the lobby.

"Ms. Matheson?" A receptionist greeted her in the small waiting room.

"Ava, please."

"Dr. Sadik will be just a few moments."

"Of course."

A few minutes later, a nurse peered into the waiting room and smiled before escorting her back to an utterly common office. There was a desk in one corner and a grouping of comfortable chairs in another. A chaise as well.

Ava had to smile. Apparently, Dr. Sadik was a traditionalist. She hadn't seen a chaise in a psychologist's office since she'd been a kid.

Green plants filled a small corner solarium, lending a verdant energy to the room, and Ava settled into a chair to wait.

She knew very little about Dr. J. Sadik other than the recommendation of the psychiatrist in Tel Aviv. Still, the shrink in Israel was supposed to be one of the best in his field, so Ava was willing to give his recommendation a chance. There wasn't much online about him, but maybe that was common for Turkish doctors. She had enough experience with mental health professionals to spot a quack from a mile away. So far, everything about the office and the staff seemed exactly like what she would expect.

"Ava?" She heard her name from the back of the room. Odd, she hadn't sensed the man before he entered. She must have been more distracted than she realized.

A thin man wearing glasses approached, holding out his hand for Ava to shake. He looked like he was in his early forties, younger than she was expecting. A pair of green eyes peeked out from behind simple gold rims. His English was slightly accented; Ava would guess Dr. Sadik had studied in England.

"You must be Dr. Sadik." She smiled, trying to be polite. She could be polite. He was probably a perfectly nice man, even though he wouldn't be able to help her. He took her hand in his and grasped it warmly.

As soon as he did, an unprecedented sense of peace filled her. It was as if the tension fled the room. Ava felt... clear. Unburdened. She cocked her head and smiled at him.

"What on earth..."

"I hear you have had trouble with voices, Ava. I'd like to help. From what little Dr. Asner has shared, I think I have had other patients with the same affliction."

"You have?" Nothing about this made sense, but not a single alarm bell was going off in her mind.

"I believe so. I hope my treatments might help you as they've helped others. My other patients have learned how to manage their condition, allowing them to live more serene lives. I believe I could do the same for you, if you'd be willing to meet with me. I'd very much like to help you."

The peace stole up her arm and through her shoulders, loosening them as Dr. Sadik still grasped her hand.

"That sounds..."

"Yes?"

"Wonderful. It sounds wonderful. But I'm not going to lie—"

"You have doubts." He cast an understanding smile toward her. "Of course you do. You're an intelligent woman. But let us sit." He motioned toward the chairs. "And talk more. Ask me whatever you like, Ms.—"

"Ava," she interrupted. "Just call me Ava."

"Very well, Ava." Dr. Sadik smiled and settled into his own chair. "What would you like to know?"

CHAPTER

THREE

A cruise on the Bosphorus was hardly how Malachi would have chosen to spend a ninety-degree day, but that didn't matter. He was still following Ava, which meant he did what she did. And currently, that meant sitting through an uneventful narration of the history of Istanbul while on the water. Ava perched on the port side of the cruise ship, snapping pictures. She was evenly split between amusement and boredom if he had to guess from her expression. He'd become reluctantly familiar with the human woman in the days he'd been guarding her.

There, the privately bemused smile.

There, the bored lift of her right eyebrow.

There, the slight pinch of her mouth when someone passed too close.

Malachi might have had his suspicions, but he questioned whether they were mere figments of his own hopeful imagination. He hadn't spotted a Grigori in days—not surprising since the two who had approached her in the alley had seen Malachi, as well. No Grigori would willingly take on a trained Irin scribe alone, or even with a partner. But could Ava be what he suspected without attracting their attention? None of it added up.

Malachi heard his phone ring.

"*Allo?*"

"It's Damien. Anything new?"

"You're missing out. It's a beautiful, hot day on the water. Lots of tourists. Sadly, no beer."

His watcher ignored him. "No one is following her?"

"Other than me? No."

There was a pause.

"If there has been no other threat to her——"

"They saw me." He stood and moved to a more secluded part of the deck near the back, where the wind would carry his voice out over the water. He still kept an eye on Ava. "I imagine they're being cautious. And since she thinks I'm some personal bodyguard her family hired to protect her, I don't even have to hide. She sees me and says nothing. It's the perfect cover to find out more about her."

"Malachi, Rhys and I have been looking into her family history. There is no evidence——"

"That she's Irina? I told you what she said."

"She said, 'I heard you.' One statement that could mean any number of things, and then she ran away. If she was Irina, even if she didn't know it, she'd be drawn to you. It's part of who we are. And how could she be unaware?"

"If she was born after the Rending——"

"She was born Ava Russell, to Lena Russell, a single mother, in 1985. Born in Los Angeles, raised in Santa Monica. The scribe house there has no record of her or her mother. There is no father listed. What Irin would leave a child without giving her a name, Malachi? What Irina would raise her child outside the safety of a retreat?"

He had nothing to say. Damien was right. The number of Irin children born after the Rending could be counted on a few hands. They were never unguarded, particularly the young

Irina. They were hidden away and treasured by their mothers, most of whom were in hiding. His people hadn't been whole for two hundred years.

"I still think there is something different about her." His voice was irritatingly hoarse. "How else would you explain the Grigori watching her like that?"

It was Damien who paused then.

"Jaron is…" His voice was halting. "Not as some others are. Since he has moved West, his people have not been as aggressive."

A derisive snort was the only answer Malachi gave him.

Damien said, "It's in their nature to be predators, yes. But there haven't been as many deaths in Istanbul as you'd expect in the past twenty years. And yes, preying on women in the middle of the day like that is unusual. It's possible that whoever was following her has been taken care of. He's very controlling. That's why this area has experienced the relative calm that it has."

"You're acting as if there is some kind of truce between you and him."

"There isn't. There can't be; you know that. His nature has not changed, nor has ours. But he keeps a lower profile than what you were used to in Germany. Jaron is not Volund. He doesn't like attention, and his Grigori are more subtle in their pursuits."

Their pursuits. Malachi sneered. What a polite name for the Grigori practice of aggressively seducing and bedding human women, often leaving them half-dead or impregnated with children that could kill them simply by being born. Malachi had been tracking and killing Grigori soldiers for over four hundred years. It was his burning purpose in life. He had yet to see any soldier exhibit restraint.

"Nevertheless, I am going to stay with her."

"And when she leaves? Rhys said she's scheduled to leave Istanbul in another two weeks."

"Then we'll see what happens in two weeks."

"You're not following her out of the city, Malachi. I won't allow it."

Malachi bristled instinctively at the command. "Damien—"

"I am your superior," his watcher reminded him coldly. "I will not allow it. Leave the human woman to whatever fate the Creator has for her."

Malachi struggled to put into words the compulsion he felt. Ava Matheson needed to be protected. He knew she couldn't be one of his kind, but there was still something...

"I sense something in her, Damien. Something different. I feel—"

"You feel hope, my friend." The watcher's voice softened slightly. "Something most of us haven't felt for a very long time. But this hope... it's your own desire. Nothing more. You're not thinking clearly. She's not Irina. She can't be."

"I know that."

"Do you?"

Did he? His eyes returned to her. Ava was sitting next to a group of children, her eyes easy, her expression relaxed. Everything Damien had said about Ava made sense. There was no logical way she could be one of their kind. None. But something about her—her reactions, her energy—screamed that she was more than human. She was other. Different. Even the way she held herself away from the crowd while trying to blend in was familiar.

"I'll follow her while she's in the city. After that..."

"You'll return to your duties, Malachi. You have a job to do. Leo and Maxim are already covering your shifts."

A smile touched the corner of his mouth. "But I thought Jaron's Grigori were the civilized ones."

"A civilized Grigori is still a threat and an abomination. Some things will never change, including our mission."

Malachi was tired of Damien's constant discipline. Tired of the endless nights of stalking and waiting and violence. Perhaps someday he would join the more peaceful of their brethren in a rural scribe house like Rhys was always talking of doing. He would cloak his armor and spend his days copying sacred texts and his nights watching the stars, perhaps even some day counter the spells that prolonged his life so he could fade into the heavens as so many Irin had after their mates were torn from them.

Malachi had no mate. Only a handful of scribes did. And it was because of the cursed Grigori that he and all his kind were fated to spend their long lives alone.

He was kidding himself. He'd never retire from a warrior's life. Malachi would fight them as long as he lived.

"You have a job to do, Malachi." Damien was still talking. "And that job is not following a human woman who happens to catch your eye."

"Yes, Watcher."

"Keep me informed of your movements. I want to know where you are."

"Have Rhys enable the tracker on my phone. He can do that now, you know. You can watch me move on the map, if you want."

Damien paused. "He can do that?"

Malachi chuckled. "Welcome to the twenty-first century, old friend."

THE TOUR BOAT HAD REACHED THE END OF THE GOLDEN HORN and had turned back toward the Galata Bridge when Ava approached him. He'd been playing a game on his phone, some mind-numbing activity Leo was addicted to that involved shooting birds at pigs. It was oddly satisfying; the pigs exploded in a puff not unlike the Grigori when you put a knife in the right place. He glanced up when he saw her move, then watched silently as she approached the bench in the corner where he had positioned himself. Her camera bag bumped against her thigh as she walked, an unwieldy cargo he'd never seen her without.

She paused in front of him, then sank onto the wooden bench opposite as Malachi hid his phone.

"I'm incredibly bored."

He shrugged. "So why did you take the tour?"

"You're supposed to take a tour of Istanbul from the sea. Didn't you know that?"

He smiled. "Do you always do what you're supposed to?"

"Hardly ever, but this is work."

"What do you do?" He already knew. Rhys had given him a full profile on her the day after he'd discovered her name.

"I take pictures for travel magazines."

Ava Matheson was considered one of the top travel photo-journalists in her field, distinguishing herself by her willingness to go to the most remote location and capture it for the hungry print and online world. In fact, the more remote the location, the more attractive the job seemed to be for her. She'd climbed mountains in Peru and Nepal, traversed the Gobi Desert, and boated the Orinoco. The burgeoning ecotourism industry loved her. Ava specialized in finding the luxurious in the most remote places in the world. She seemed to avoid cities unless there was a specific assignment calling her to one. Malachi had no idea what she was doing in Istanbul, as Rhys could find no record of a commission from any of her usual clients.

"Which magazine do you work for?"

"Lots of them." Her gaze drifted off for a moment until it snapped back to his face. "I don't want to talk about work. Isn't that boring? I bet you hate to talk about bodyguard gigs. You probably have some great stories you can't tell anyone though, huh?"

You have no idea. He lifted an eyebrow. "So what do you want to talk about?"

He hoped she wasn't thinking about coming on to him. That

was destined to end badly, then she'd call her parents—or whoever she thought had hired him—and start asking inconvenient questions.

"Are you Turkish? You don't have the same accent as most of the people I've met."

He could actually be honest about that one. "I am, but I've traveled a lot. Lived in a lot of other places. I imagine that's influenced the accent. You?"

"All-American girl."

"They write songs about your kind, you know."

She laughed. "*My* kind? That's a good one. I can pretty much promise they don't write songs about *my* kind. Not good ones, anyway. Have you been to the States?"

"I lived in Chicago for a time, but that was years ago."

Ava leaned forward, resting her chin in the palm of her hand as the breeze pulled dark hair into her eyes. "And what did you do in Chicago?"

I helped kill the upper echelon of Grigori soldiers belonging to a fallen angel who preys on the women of the Upper Midwest. And his pack of dogs. He was pissed about the dogs.

"The same thing I do here."

"Exciting."

"It has its moments."

"Did you ever guard Oprah?"

"I don't think so." He frowned. "Not directly."

"So, Malachi…" She shifted again, leaning back and lifting her face to the sun. It poured over her, warming her pale skin and lighting the red in her hair. She tilted her head back, closing her eyes behind her sunglasses. "Are you an independent contractor, or do you work for one of Carl's usual companies?"

She was subtly digging for information, but he couldn't figure out why. He decided to play along for now. It would be less suspicious.

"I'm somewhat independent, but I work with a larger

company. The headquarters is in Vienna. I imagine Mr. Matheson was referred from there."

"Probably. He's doing a lot of work in Eastern Europe lately. Low production costs."

Her stepfather was a film producer, but Ava seemed unimpressed. In fact, everything about her spoke of boredom. Jaded expression. Cynical quirk to her mouth. Malachi sensed something else, though.

Lonely. The woman was desperately lonely.

"Do you like to travel alone?"

She seemed surprised that he'd asked a question. Her head tilted forward and she looked at him. "What?"

"Am I not allowed to ask you questions?"

"It's unusual."

"Call me unusual, then."

She smiled then, a genuine smile untouched by cynicism. "Yeah, I like it. I'm not the most social person in the world."

"I've noticed."

"Wow. That bad, huh?"

He shrugged. "You just seem to like your own space. I don't see you chatting with many strangers like a lot of the tourists do."

"My own space?" Her smile hinted at some inside joke. "You could call it that. I don't travel much in cities. They're very…"

He waited, but she seemed to expect him to interrupt. He didn't.

Finally, she said, "They're crowded. Noisy. Too many smells and sounds and sights all crashing together. I don't like them, usually."

"Not even Constantinople?"

"You mean Istanbul?"

He grinned. "Are we going there?"

"We better not." She laughed again. "I'll have that song

stuck in my head for days. But to answer your question, despite the noise and the people and the heat—"

"The heat is something else, isn't it?"

"No worse than L.A. most summers. Despite all that..." Her eyes drifted toward the water. "I like it here. There's something about it, isn't there? It's..." Her eyes sought his. "Seductive."

Malachi could feel the tattoos covering his chest pulse. *No... Not going there, either.*

He straightened and cleared his throat. "It's a fascinating place. Very complicated history."

"I can tell." Her golden-brown eyes seemed to mock him. "Just by looking at it."

Silence fell between them as she held his stare. The wind picked up, teasing the fine hair at the back of his neck. He saw her glance down at the tattoo work along his collar, but she said nothing. Asked nothing.

"Why are you here?" he asked. "Really?"

"Headaches." The mask fell over her face. She had answered without thinking. He was betting she didn't do that often.

"Headaches?"

"The condition I mentioned the other day." She waved a careless hand. "There's a doctor here who specializes in it. The appointment last week, remember? I was referred to him. And you don't need to report that to Carl or my mom."

"I don't report on your activities to anyone unless I think there is some aspect of your safety in jeopardy. I'm not a stalker; I'm a guard."

"Good."

"Is he helping?"

"The doctor?"

"Yes."

Her head bobbed back and forth, considering the question. "Maybe. I try not to get my hopes up, you know? I've lived with the headaches my whole life."

Malachi knew all about not getting his hopes up. So why was he having a hard time believing Damien?

"And there is no cure for them?"

"Not that anyone has found. It's not a tumor or anything. They're a bit of a mystery."

As are you, woman. It wasn't headaches. At least, that wasn't all of it. He didn't know exactly what was going on with the interesting American woman, but he was determined to find out.

Malachi said, "It's better to be cautious, even with doctors. If there is any background information you'd like on this doctor, let me know. I know many people in Istanbul. Maybe some of my friends or associates have gone to him."

From her expression, she didn't like that idea. "I'll keep it in mind. I'm fine for right now."

"I just wanted to offer."

"Noted." She forced a smile. "But not necessary. I'm fine."

You are anything but fine.

The tour boat was pulling into the dock, and passengers rose to their feet. Ava joined them without a word, leaving Malachi behind to watch her walk down the gangway. Wordlessly, he stood, then followed her at a comfortable distance as she grabbed a fish sandwich from one of the floating restaurants and walked back toward her hotel, lonely and silent in the afternoon crowd.

MALACHI STRODE INTO THE HOUSE AND STRAIGHT TO THE library, not even stopping to rib Maxim about the bottle of beer the younger man was drinking in the kitchen. He'd left Ava exhausted. He was fairly sure she was done for the day, but the tiny tracker he'd slipped in her bag would alert him if she left the perimeter he'd set up around the grounds of the hotel. And if she was done for the day, then he had some questions for Rhys.

"Sadik," he said when he spied the shorter scribe sitting at his computer. "He's the doctor she's seeing. I saw it on the directory at the building we visited. J. Sadik. I need to know everything about him."

Rhys turned and frowned. "Had a great day, thanks. The air conditioner is fixed, and the activity logs have been updated and sent to Vienna. And I covered your patrol last night. How was the dinner cruise? Was there a show?"

"No dinner. No show. It was hot but informative." He paused and tried to slow his brain. "Thank you for covering my shift."

"Well, since you're on babysitting duty for the mysterious human, we're all *more* than happy to pitch in." Not even Rhys's polite accent could hide the sarcasm. Malachi knew the others thought he was following a rabbit trail, but he didn't care.

"Dr. J. Sa—"

"Sadik." Rhys turned back to the computer. "I heard you the first time. I'm just trying to force you into social niceties you seem to have forgotten living among the barbarians." Rhys's fingers began typing rapidly. The three-hundred-year- old scribe had taken to modern information technology like a duck to water. Not all Irin did. Damien still considered anything more advanced than a telegraph suspicious.

"Thank you, Rhys."

"Don't mention it. Really. What kind of doctor?"

"I don't know. She says she has headaches."

"Headaches?" he muttered. "That could by physical, psychological... You have no idea what kind of headaches?"

"She wasn't exactly forthcoming. She said he was a specialist she was referred to."

Rhys gave him a quiet " hmph" and kept typing.

"Where?"

"He's in the city. Just a few miles from here. She saw him last week after the attack in the alley."

More typing.

"Sadik? You're sure of it?"

"Who is he? Yes, I'm sure." Malachi leaned in, looking over the other man's shoulder, but nothing on the screen made sense.

"There are a number of Sadiks, but none of them are specialists in anything to do with headaches." More typing. More muttering. Rhys shook his head. "Nothing in the government system... nothing in private. Here's one who is a pediatrician. An oncologist?"

"It didn't sound like cancer."

"That one is a woman, anyway. She said it was a male?"

"Ava referred to 'him.'"

More typing. "I'm not finding anything that would match. Not in this part of the city."

Alarm bells started to go off. "What do you mean? There has to be a record. Maybe he moved his office."

"I'm not finding anything..." Rhys started typing again. "If he's practicing anywhere in Turkey, I should be able to find him. He's not in initial searches. I suppose I can keep looking..."

"Yes," he said. Then quickly added, "Please."

"See? You *can* be taught."

J. Sadik, who are you?

He patted Rhys's shoulder. "Thanks for checking. I may have to look in other directions."

Rhys was still frowning, and Malachi knew the scribe was irritated that he hadn't been able to find the answers his friend was looking for. "She was in Israel before she came here. Maybe the referral came from a doctor there. I'm going to search her medical records. I'll see what I can find online."

For some reason, the idea of Rhys digging into Ava's background irked him. "Is that necessary?"

"Do you want to find out who this doctor is and why she's seeing him?"

"Yes."

"Then why do you care?"

The other man went back to furious typing while Malachi drifted back toward the kitchen. It was a good question.

Why *did* he care?

CHAPTER

FOUR

Ava looked up from her tea when she heard the clanging streetcar moving down İstiklal Avenue. She leaned back and watched it. Pedestrians in the crowded Beyoğlu neighborhood moved around the car. Tourists. Locals. Merchants. She was in the heart of Istanbul, but for the first time in her life, the city was... peaceful. The hum of voices had become quieter, easier to ignore. The manic energy that seemed to envelope her most days was absent. Ava felt grounded.

She took a deep breath and had to admit that, for the first time in her life, a doctor's treatment seemed to be working.

Dr. Sadik's methods were unusual, to say the least. Holistic in practice, the psychologist had prescribed her a diet of mostly Mediterranean foods and was using a kind of pressure-point massage in addition to talk therapy. She'd been skeptical. But one of his nurses assisted with the massage, and when she'd left the office after the first treatment, Ava had to admit the voices were slightly muffled. She'd felt more focused and relaxed. After a few days, the effects had worn off, but the next appointment showed even more relief. She was going in every three days and was starting to wonder whether she'd ever be able to leave.

Glancing over her shoulder at the man sitting a few tables

away, she wondered what her mother would do if she decided to stay. Would she and Carl continue to pay her shadow? Malachi had started following her more closely since the cruise but still kept his distance. He was both the least and the most annoying bodyguard she'd ever had. He was more than discreet and carried himself with a quiet confidence that put her at ease. At the same time, Ava sensed he wanted to come closer—to talk to her, to know her more—but he didn't. She supposed that was her own fault. It wasn't his job to keep her company.

Still...

She glanced over her shoulder again. He was sipping tea two tables away from her, lounging in a low chair and pretending to read a paper. Behind his sunglasses, she could see him scanning the street, still vigilant despite the peaceful morning.

Keeping her eyes on him, she spoke in a low voice. "Malachi."

His eyes zipped immediately to her.

"Yes?"

"You have good hearing."

"Among other talents."

She grinned. "Why are you sitting two tables away in an empty café?"

One dark eyebrow lifted. "I believe I was told to keep my distance by a certain prickly photographer."

"Well, that was before we got to be friends."

"We're friends?" There was an amused smile on his lips, and Ava saw the hint of a dimple on his slightly stubbled cheek. He had thick dark hair and would likely have a full beard within days if he didn't keep clean-shaven. Handsome? Not classically. But the man had definite appeal.

"Of course we're friends. Do you think I habitually strike up conversations with random men in foreign countries?"

"I wouldn't even try to guess the answer to that." He had set the newspaper down and leaned back in the plush chair, bringing the glass of tea to his full lips as she watched him, watching her.

"I don't. Strike up random conversations, I mean."

"Is there something you want, Ava?"

She let her eyes wander over him, not caring that he noticed her perusal. "You said you're from Turkey?"

"Yes."

"So why don't you stop following me and just show me around?" She surprised herself with the question. Usually she never asked for company. Prolonged contact of any kind could become maddening. But the treatments had calmed her mind, making the soothing resonance he exuded even more appealing. For the first time in her life, the thought of spending the day with a man was attractive, not overwhelming. "I'm bored by myself."

He put down his glass of tea, almost scowling. "I'm not paid to be your tour guide."

The disappointment was quick and sharp. "Fine."

She spun around and turned her back to him, resisting the urge to get up and flee. It would be humiliating for him to see how his rejection had affected her. Besides, he'd just follow her anyway. She picked up her tea with tense fingers and sipped, grabbing a book out of her bag. She briefly debated taking out her small camera and capturing pedestrian traffic, but she'd been trying to take a day off from work and enjoy her newfound calm.

After a few minutes, Ava heard him rise and approach. She gritted her teeth and kept her eyes on her guidebook.

Damn, damn, damn. He'd rebuffed her. The least he could do was pretend to ignore her existence.

No, instead he was sitting down across from her, all six feet and something; his long legs slid under the table, unavoidably brushing against her own. She refused to move.

"Ava."

"What?"

"My apologies. That was rude."

"Yes, it was."

She was still staring at her book. He continued to sit across from her silently. His inner voice took on an amused tone that made her scowl.

"Ava?"

"I'm reading."

"That's impressive."

She rolled her eyes and finally looked up. "What? Reading?"

He tried to control the smile, but the dimple gave him away. "Reading upside down. I can do it as well, but it took many years of study."

Her cheeks burning, she set down the book. "What do you want?"

Malachi was still wearing sunglasses, but she caught the quick glance he gave her. It wasn't clinical.

So, not indifferent, after all.

Feeling slightly smug, she said, "Well?"

"You asked me to show you around the city. I would be happy to do that."

"Maybe I should just hire someone."

Oh, he didn't like that. She could tell by the tightening in his jaw and the way his voice changed. "You could. But, as you pointed out, I am local, and I know the city well. I am already guarding you. It would make the job more…"

"Friendly?"

The dimple was back. "Yes."

"Fine." She picked up her book, flipping it right side up. "I guess so."

"You guess so?" His eyebrows furrowed together. "That's not very *friendly*. Didn't you just say we were friends?"

"Well, that was before you pissed me off, Mal."

"Mal?" He sneered. "My name is not Mal."

Ava cheered internally, pleased to have found something so convenient to annoy him with. "Oh, it can be."

"When I piss you off?"

"Mmhmm."

"Are you always like this? I think I should be warned ahead of time if we're going to be... friends."

"Like what?"

"Irritable and moody."

She looked up in mock indignation. "This is me in a good mood, Mal."

He closed his eyes and shook his head, but the telltale dimple gave away his amusement, and his inner voice was practically laughing.

"Fine. Put down the guidebook. You don't need it anymore."

"It's a good one, though. And I like learning about the history of the places I visit."

"Trust me, I know the history." She looked up, skeptical, but his voice was confident, bordering on smug.

"So you're a historian as well as a bodyguard?"

"Something like that."

The way his lip curled made her want to bite it. He must have caught her look, because the corner of his mouth turned up even more.

"Trust me, Ava." He leaned forward, resting his elbows on the table. "With me, no guidebook is necessary. I'll tell you everything you need to know."

IT WAS COOL AND QUIET; THE ECHOES OF PEOPLE IN THE CISTERN melded together with the whispering voices, creating a mesh of quiet noise Ava glided on in the darkness. Beneath the bustle of the streets above, the Basilica Cistern stretched hundreds of yards into the black underground. Held up by endless marble pillars and dotted by gold lights, the shallow water rested, and

Ava watched shadow fish dart over the flash of coins visitors had thrown in its depths.

Malachi followed her, letting her take in the grandeur of the vast room before he spoke in a quiet voice.

"Some people call it the Underground Palace. It's the largest of the ancient cisterns in Constantinople, originally built by Constantine, then rebuilt by the Emperor Justinian in the sixth century. There are hundreds of cisterns beneath the city, but this one…" His voice held a note of awe. "It is the largest. It fed the palace itself."

Ava was at a loss. "It's…"

Stunning.

Eerie.

Otherworldly.

"It's beautiful," she finally said.

"It is that," Malachi said softly. "The city cisterns were fed from aqueducts the Romans built. Some still lead back to their water source or have tunnels leading between them. During its use, the water would have been far higher. Over our heads." They strolled along the raised platform, damp with water dripping from the domed ceiling above. "Modern Istanbul holds pieces of Greece, Rome, the Byzantines, the Ottomans. New conquerors, new rulers, new buildings. Still the same city, just with a different face. The bones remain the same."

"Archaeologists must have a field day here."

He nodded. "There's much to discover still. Istanbul is a puzzle, and I doubt all her secrets will ever be revealed."

"I don't think I want them to be," she whispered. "I like the mystery. I love this place, this Underground Palace."

Malachi's eyes took on a distant stare. "It's set apart. Another world, almost." He walked to the edge of the platform, looking out over the dark water. "There are many places like this in the city. Places where the present and the past seem to coexist at once. As if they live next to each other, only a ripple away."

She watched him as he turned back to her, eyes still scanning the darkness. Who was this man?

He caught her glance. "What?"

"Who are you?" she asked. "You don't sound like any body-guard I've ever had."

Malachi smiled. "I'm not so unusual. Perhaps you keep too much distance."

"It's necessary."

"Why?"

Was it the darkness? In the quiet underworld, she felt as if she was talking to a shadow. "I just can't be around many people. They make me uncomfortable. It's exhausting."

"Why?"

Ava turned away. "Find a new question, Mal."

Silence fell between them, filled with the echoes of voices in the dark. Ava could feel him—actually feel him—approach from behind. She tried not to tense.

"You have been more at ease than when we first met." He kept the question light. "Is your doctor helping?"

"Yes, he is."

"That's good."

She forced herself to turn and smiled. "I'm optimistic. Istanbul might just become my favorite city."

"Because of the doctor?"

They kept walking, strolling farther through the cisterns. Ava paused at the edge of a tour group, but the guide was speaking German.

"Partly. But I think the attraction was here even before I met him. There's just something about this place, you know?"

"I don't know, I—"

She interrupted him with a laugh. "You're from here, so you probably don't really get that. I mean, I know people love L.A. Love Hollywood, but it never seemed all that special to me because I grew up there. Istanbul is probably that way for you."

"No."

He had stopped behind her. Ava turned to him. "No?"

"I understand. It's part of the reason I came back. This city... It feeds the soul."

A strange fluttering started in her chest. "I didn't know my soul was hungry."

"Didn't you?" He smiled. "Hmm."

"Oh, Malachi..." Ava turned and pretended to read a sign. "The things you say in a single 'hmm.'"

She felt him step closer. Could feel her body react. His lips were sealed, but his voice whispered to her. Taunting, teasing whispers that begged her to come closer. She turned her head, and her heart raced as his eyes dropped to her mouth. He leaned down, parting his lips as if to speak, but before he could say anything, a child bumped into Ava from behind, giggling as she sent Ava stumbling into Malachi's chest.

He caught her elbows, and she heard him suck in a breath.

There was a flash of awareness. A sense and a silence. In that second, his pure voice was the only thing she heard, and the sense of harmony threatened to overwhelm her. Ava gasped.

She needed.

Wanted.

Needed.

Utter and complete peace enveloped her for a brief moment, then it was gone when Malachi dropped his hands. Eyes blinking, he backed away, and she let out the breath she held. Once again, the voices wrapped around her, muffled—like a distant chorus they circled and taunted her.

For a second, they had been gone. Completely gone.

And his voice was the only thing she'd heard.

"Malachi?"

"Hmm?" His face was an impenetrable mask, half-cloaked in darkness.

"I..." What was she going to say?

Touch me.

Hold my hand.

Can you make them go away?

"I… don't feel very well," she breathed out. "I'd like to go back to my hotel now."

"Of course," he said quickly, immediately ushering her toward the exit.

Did he know? Could he feel it, too? Ava shook her head to try to shake some sense into it. Of *course* he hadn't felt it. He wasn't nuts. The odd feeling was probably a result of the strange mood in the underground cistern combined with dehydration and an unexpected—and entirely impractical—attraction to the man.

It had snuck up on her, but she was honest enough to acknowledge it, even as she recognized the futility of the attraction.

What man would want a relationship with her? Her lovers were fleeting. They had to be. Prolonged contact only made her condition worse. Her longest relationship had been during college. It was only three months before he'd been overwhelmed by her, and she by him. She'd flooded him with her energy, her moods, her manic bursts of activity.

"I can't keep up with you."

"You're exhausting."

"Too much, Ava. You're just… too much."

Too much.

It was all too much. She and Malachi walked through a tour group coming down the stairs. Dozens of people brushed past her, almost causing her to stumble. For a second, tears welled in her eyes. She saw Malachi reach for her hand instinctively, then he stopped, drawing his fingers back like a child not allowed to touch. She stayed close behind him, letting his broad shoulders clear a path through the crowd. When they finally reached the outdoors, the sound of traffic overwhelmed the wash of voices. The honks and shouts of the drivers were an unexpected relief.

Ava slipped on her sunglasses and, without waiting for her shadow, started back to the hotel.

HER APPOINTMENT WITH DR. SADIK COULDN'T COME EARLY enough the next day. She left Malachi drinking tea at a café across the street and walked up to the office, opening the door on the third floor landing before she made her way down the hall and into the office. The pleasant receptionist greeted her with a smile.

"May I get you some tea, Ms. Matheson? You are a few minutes early. Dr. Sadik should be ready for you shortly." She rose before Ava even answered, moving to the corner where a pot of the tea sat in a clear carafe. Taking one of the modern armchairs, Ava held out her hand when the young woman brought her the drink.

"Thank you. And please, call me Ava."

"Such a beautiful name," the receptionist said with a smile. "Please let me know if there is anything else I can get you, Ava."

"Thanks." She settled in, sipping the tea and listening to the quiet hum of the woman's mind drift over the meditative music that filled the room. In a few minutes, she heard the door on the other side of Dr. Sadik's office close, signaling that his other client had left. A few moments later, his smiling face poked through the door.

"Ava! How are you this morning?"

Immediately put at ease by his presence, she rose. "Doing fine, thank you."

The look in his eyes told Ava that he knew there was more to the story, but he didn't prod in front of the receptionist. She walked to the office and quickly took a seat on the chaise. "Is Rana here yet?"

The nurse who helped with the massage was usually there when Ava came in the office.

"She is running just a bit behind today. I apologize. Why don't we talk for a few moments?"

She took a deep breath. "Sure."

"How have the voices been?" He cut straight to the chase.

"Um... good." She smiled tentatively. "Well, better."

Dr. Sadik nodded, his gold-rimmed glasses flashing in the light from the window. He was sneaking up on middle age, but something about his expression and manner seemed far older. It was probably just a cultural difference.

The doctor said, "I believe I told you to expect that, did I not? We are not attempting to *cure* you of anything, because it is my belief, and yours as well, that there is no mental illness to cure. What we are doing is learning to manage the unique circumstances—an unusual perception, shall we say—under which your mind works."

"Yes." She let out a breath and tried to relax. "I like it. I feel better. And I'm glad you don't think I'm crazy. You're probably the first person to treat me who doesn't think so."

He smiled. "I told you, you are not my first patient with this condition. And the others saw relief with the treatments, as well."

She glanced at the clock on the wall. "Did Rana say how long she'd be?"

"Just ten minutes or so."

Most of the pressure-point massage happened in the head, neck and shoulders, but Dr. Sadik seemed to be very cautious about contact with Ava unless his nurse was present. He'd insisted on it from the beginning, which had put her at ease. Ava was eager to end the small talk and get on with her appointment.

"How are you enjoying Istanbul?" he asked. "You are traveling alone, am I correct?"

"I am. But everyone here is so friendly, I almost feel like I've been here before and they recognize me."

He smiled. "Turks take hospitality very seriously. It is a wonderful part of their culture."

Their culture? She frowned. Ava had assumed the doctor was

Turkish. "Yes, well... I'm enjoying it. I'll definitely come back. Someone I met told me that Istanbul feeds the soul. I think he may be right."

She caught a flash in his eyes, as if he recognized the saying. Was it a common proverb in Turkey? The expression fled, and polite interest took its place again.

"Istanbul has been important to many world religions, particularly Islam and Christianity. But even before that, it has always been rich with enlightenment and culture. One could definitely say it is good for the soul."

"Maybe that's why the voices aren't as loud," she joked. "My soul isn't as hungry here."

"Perhaps." He didn't seem to take it as a joke. "There are many beliefs about the soul. Ancient Persians were one of the first to classify the soul as something distinct and eternal. They believed the soul survived death, as do Jews, Christians, and Muslims. The Egyptians believed the soul existed with five distinct parts, one of which was the heart." He smiled and patted his chest. "Others believe the soul is what gives a person their personality and creativity, though we know those are functions of the brain, of course."

"Of course." Why was he on this tangent? And when was the nurse going to get there? She didn't have all day.

Well, actually she did.

"But the mind is where *my* interest lies, of course." Dr. Sadik was still talking. "The mind... such a complicated, wonderful organ. So many mysteries to solve. Perhaps the mind is the seat of the soul. After all, it is the seat of creativity, which many world religions consider a reflection of the divine."

"What is? The mind?"

"Creativity," he said, his eyes gleaming. "Surely, as an artist, you have experienced this. The flash of insight that seems to come from outside yourself. Some would say creativity is the voice of the soul."

His inner voice was muffled, but she could still sense his

excitement. "I'm… I'm just a photographer, Dr. Sadik. I don't really create like that. I'm not a painter or anything."

"Ah." He leaned back in his chair. "Perhaps that is not where your true creativity lies."

At that moment, Ava heard the door open and Rana walked in.

"Dr. Sadik, I am so sorry! Ms. Matheson, forgive me. My father is unwell, and—"

"Not to worry, my dear." Dr. Sadik rose from his chair. "Ava and I have just been chatting. But we should begin." He turned to her and held out a hand. "Ava, are you ready?"

She heaved a sigh of relief that the odd philosophical conversation was over. "Absolutely."

CHAPTER
FIVE

I t was close to dawn when Malachi heard his watcher stir. Damien paced outside the locked ritual room the scribes used to write *talesm* as Malachi worked. Candles flickered against walls inscribed with their own unique magic, old protective charms the Irin who built the house had carved into the limestone walls. No electric light was allowed in the room. No windows pierced the web of incantations. A meditation fire burned constantly, tended by the watcher of the house. It was probably why Damien was pacing.

Let him wait.

Malachi didn't look up from his skin. He was working on a new spell for his right arm, a particularly intricate *talesm* to guard against temptation and provide focus. The ivory needle pierced his skin at lightning speed, the sacred ink luminescing with a faint silver glow as the spell worked itself into his body. He could feel it pulse and grow, the new magic twining with the ancient symbols that surrounded it. Malachi, like all Irin scribes, had become inured to the physical pain the tattoo produced. He only stopped to dip the needle into the ink made from the ash of the ritual fire. Within minutes, the characters of the Old

Language took shape, twisting and joining the existing pattern of spells.

When he finished, Malachi took a deep breath and focused on the flames. He gave silent thanks to the Creator. To his mother who bore him, and his father who trained him. To his teachers. The council of the Elders. He closed his eyes and let the magic take hold. Then slowly, he opened them and looked down.

On a human, the skin around the tattoo would still be red and weeping, but Malachi wasn't entirely human. The *talesm* was already sealed, a thin layer of ink dried over the old letters; by morning, the scab would be gone. The silver glow surrounding the tattoo would fade until activated by his *talesm prim*, the circular spell inscribed on his left wrist.

As if sensing the waning magic, a soft knock came at the door.

"Malachi?"

"You can come in, Damien. I'm finished."

The door cracked open and Damien entered, clad only in the ceremonial wrap all watchers wore when attending to the sacred fire of their scribe house. The wrap covered his hips and upper legs, allowing the rest of Damien's *talesm* to warn anyone watching of his years and skill with magic.

Malachi, still flush with new power, sat back in the wide chair and let out a long breath. He could feel the magic working within, connecting and bonding with the older characters that marked his body.

"Good morning," Damien said, "You're up early."

"I slept little."

Damien grunted and rubbed his eyes. "You have finished your new *talesm*?"

"I have."

The watcher glanced over at Malachi's bicep, and his eyebrow lifted. "Self-control?"

"And focus."

There was a thoughtful pause before he asked, "Have you given thanks?"

"I have, Watcher."

Damien nodded.

Malachi took another deep breath as the other man kneeled before the fire, lifting his left wrist and tracing the letters of his own *talesm prim*. As the magic rose, Malachi could see the faint silver glow travel over Damien's body, from the newest spells on the man's legs to the family tattoos marking his shoulders and back. Malachi had similar tattoos, the only ones he had not written himself. He'd received the first from his father at the age of thirteen. The first taste of the ancient strength he would spend centuries perfecting.

As a boy, his mother's power had protected him, but at thirteen, Malachi was no longer considered a boy. His eyes were drawn to the first halting letters on his left wrist. The old spells hadn't faded, but the clumsy, boyish work still made him smile. The characters slowly grew more sophisticated as they traveled up his arm, trailing over his shoulder and collarbone before they started their centuries-long journey down his right arm. Wrapped and stacked around each other, each was unique, an expression of the scribe who wrote it.

Spells of protection on his forearm.

Long life over his wrist.

Strength.

Speed.

Keener vision. Steadier reflexes. Immunity to poisons and drugs. An Irin scribe as old as Malachi was practically immortal in battle unless he willingly gave his magic to another. But as Malachi had no mate…

His eyes flickered to the marks below Damien's left shoulder, directly over his heart. The scribe was rising from his knees, finished with his morning prayers, and collecting the ash from the brazier to make more ink.

Malachi asked, "Have you heard from Sari lately?"

Damien shot him a dark look. "Why?"

"Just curious."

"None of your business."

Silence. Malachi should have known better, but the urge to rankle his superior and the flush of magic made him brave.

Finally, Damien muttered, "No."

"I'm sorry."

The watcher shrugged. "I know she's safe. That's the most important thing. I can see her in our dream-walks; she just chooses to ignore me."

The light-headed feeling of new magic finally passed, so Malachi rose to his feet and dropped the tattoo needle in a basin to clean it. Then he gathered the linen cloths marked with ink and blood and tossed them in the fire. He stood, watching the pieces burn as Damien swept up the remains of the ash.

"I am drawn to her," Malachi confessed in a low voice.

"Since I'm going to assume you haven't lost your mind and aren't referring to my mate, I must assume you mean the human woman."

"Ava."

"Ava," Damien said thoughtfully. "It is a good name."

It was an Irina name. Malachi had wondered, but he knew humans used it too. It meant nothing.

"I touched her."

The brush clattered to the table and Damien grabbed him by the shoulder, spinning him around. The watcher's eyes were frigid pools of blue.

Malachi was quick to continue. "It was only a second. An accident caused by an unruly child in the crowd."

"She was not harmed?"

"No. It was only a few moments. No."

The grip on his shoulder relaxed slightly. "You're sure?"

Malachi lifted his hands. "She was tired afterward and asked to go back to her hotel, but I sensed it was the crowd bothering her more than anything. It had become busy at the cistern, and her head was aching again." And he'd reached out to relieve her as if she'd been Irina, Malachi realized later. Luckily, he'd drawn his hand back before their skin could connect. "She had a doctor's appointment the next day. She seemed completely healthy."

"Good." Damien took a deep breath and turned back to his tasks. "Has Rhys made any progress finding information about this doctor?"

"He's found her doctor in Tel Aviv, but there's no record of that man referring any patients to a Dr. Sadik in Turkey. Or any doctor in Turkey, for that matter."

Damien grunted again. "You two trust your computers too much. You think just because it isn't written in some electronic cloud, it cannot exist? Not everything is written, you know. Especially if this does have something to do with the Grigori. They would know better than to leave a record."

"Her doctor is not Grigori. I've seen him. And all his staff are women."

Damien nodded. Both men finished their tasks and walked out of the ritual room, which remained unlocked and open unless a scribe sealed it to mark *talesm*.

"I want you to patrol tonight," the watcher said. "I'll put Leo to watch the girl."

"Leo?" Malachi instantly felt mutinous. "Leo is too young."

"He's over two hundred years old, brother." Damien smirked. "How old do you think he needs to be to watch a tourist sleep in a hotel and go out to dinner? She won't even see him; make sure you're ready to fight tonight. I don't like any of us to go too long without battle."

Malachi wanted to object but knew it was useless. Damien ran the scribe house; his word was final when it came to matters of safety or strategy. Though he deferred to Malachi or Rhys on occasion because of their age, he didn't have to.

"Fine." He walked to his room, wishing he'd gotten better rest the night before.

Damien called out, "She's human. How much trouble could she attract in one night?"

MALACHI WATCHED THE EDGE OF THE WATER WHERE THE WAVES crashed up against the embankment as a giant freighter glided through the narrowest part of the Bosphorus. It was a normal sunny day along the water, so why was his mood so dark?

"What's with you today?" Ava nudged her foot against his knee. She was relaxed again. The change in her temperament would last for a few days after each appointment before the agitation would start again. It was a curious cycle, but one he couldn't question more without arousing suspicion. He caught the tip of her shoe in his hand, pinching her toe under the leather before he released it. Another curious thing. He found himself finding ways to touch her without contact with her skin. A brush of arms as they passed each other. A hand on the small of her back as they walked through a crowd. It was fleeting and probably unwise, but he couldn't resist.

He didn't really want to.

He frowned when he realized he'd never answered her question. "I'm fine."

"You're being all broody, Mal."

He muttered, "I really wish you'd stop calling me that."

Ava picked up her glass of tea and sipped before she answered. "It's good to want things... Mal."

He couldn't help it; she made him smile. He shook his head, relieved that she hadn't wanted to do anything more strenuous than stroll along the waterfront and shop a bit. She'd bought an embroidered purse for her mother, earrings and a scarf for herself. The earrings were so long they almost brushed her bare shoulders, and the scarf held her hair back, its colors vivid against her dark curls. He felt it again, the pull to put his hands on her. To stroke the skin where the jewelry touched. To pull the scarf from her hair.

They'd retired to a café, one of Malachi's favorites, to drink tea and grab a quick bite to eat. Bread and cold salads covered the table, a mezze platter of eggplant and yogurt and the spicy tomato salad she loved. Black olives and oil-soaked cheese. Ava tore off a piece of bread and dipped it, still tapping her foot against his.

"Have you always fidgeted?" he asked.

"Yes. My mom says it's the reason I'm so thin. Couldn't keep still if my life depended on it."

"Even though you eat constantly."

"Hey, you burn through a lot of energy when you contain this much awesome." She winked, but the smile on her lips held a trace of bitterness.

He fell silent again, thinking about going out on patrol that night. He wondered why Damien was insisting on it. The watcher hardly needed to worry about Malachi being battle-ready. He'd done almost nothing but fight for over two hundred years. First in Germany, where his parents had been killed, then in Rome for a time. Buenos Aires. Chicago. Johannesburg. Atlanta. He'd traveled the world, killing the Grigori who had slaughtered his family, then others—any others—he could find. He'd become known for his quick, brutal killing style and relentless drive. He was focused and disciplined in battle, though reckless regarding his own safety. Nothing and no one came between Malachi and his target once his sights were set.

Her foot just kept tapping…

Hot tea spilled on his pants.

"Oops!" Ava laughed. "Sorry about that."

"It's fine." He picked up a napkin, dabbing at the tea as he watched her from the corner of his eye.

She was jiggling her foot, tapping it to the rhythm of the street musician playing on the corner. The woman burst with life, more than any human woman he'd ever met. When

Malachi looked at her sometimes, he wondered how her skin could even contain her personality. Her eyes might have held pain and exhaustion at times, but her body was in constant motion.

For a moment, he reveled in the fantasy that she had enough energy even for his touch.

Fingers linked. Arms wrapping around her slight frame. Drawing her to his chest as his mouth descended to her skin. Laying his rough cheek to the satin of hers. Pressing his lips to her neck. The curve of her jaw. Her lips. Feeling the pulse of life seep into his skin. Her fingers digging into his neck. Gripping his hair at the nape. The touch of her mouth to his.

The touch…

He banished the rebellious thoughts, disgusted with himself. He was no better than a Grigori.

"Hey," she whispered, her own cheeks flushed as if she shared his thoughts. "Malachi, where did you just go?"

He blinked and looked up. Nothing had distracted him in two hundred years.

Who was he kidding?

He swiped a quick hand over his face and shook his head to clear it. "Sorry. Didn't sleep well last night."

"And then I dragged you out."

"It's fine, Ava." He grabbed an orange from a dish on the table, letting the bitter spray from the peel wake him. "I'm just a little tired."

"We could head back," she said. "And don't you have some kind of backup? I mean, not that I don't prefer your company, but surely you have someone who can… fill in for you, or something. If you're sick?"

It was the perfect opportunity. Leo was scheduled to take over for him tonight. Damien was confident Ava wouldn't even notice the younger scribe watching her, but Malachi wasn't convinced. After all, the woman had spotted a Grigori stalking her through a crowded market; he doubted a six-foot behemoth with a mane of blond hair would be hard to pluck out of the crowd. "I... uh... I do have someone, as a matter of fact. His name is Leo. He's very reliable. Maybe I'll call him."

She reached out to pat his hand, but Malachi tensed before she paused and drew back. "That's a good idea. I'm wearing you out."

"You're fine, Ava. I don't mind."

"No, I do it to everyone." Her face had fallen back into its polite mask. He could practically feel her withdrawing. "It's... fine. You should call your friend. Take a break from me."

He didn't want to take a break from her. Leaving her with Leo seemed like an even worse idea than it had only a minute before. Her mask was an open wound to him. The confident, energetic woman was gone, replaced by a cool, carefully contained stranger.

"Ava." He waited until she finally looked at him again. "I enjoy spending time with you. It's no chore. You're intelligent. Funny. I like that you're so curious about everything. And it's my privilege to show you around Istanbul." He allowed himself to smile. "Besides, it makes my job easier when I can keep you within grabbing distance."

Not that I could actually grab you without hurting you.

The sadness behind her eyes still didn't flee, but her mouth turned up at the corner. "You, too. Well, not the grabbing-distance thing. You probably don't want that."

You have no idea.

He cleared his throat. "Better keep it professional, Ms. Matheson."

She took another bite of bread. "Absolutely... Mal."

THE NARROW STREET STUNK OF URINE AND ROTTEN MEAT. Malachi and Rhys stalked the edges of the city where the Grigori preyed. Here, a missing girl would go unnoticed. Her family might worry, or they might not. But either way, these were the people the authorities ignored. Missing girls from this neighborhood were quickly forgotten. Girls who appeared mysteriously pregnant were hidden or sent away, even killed by family members convinced the girl had brought dishonor on herself. Foolish humans.

The Grigori didn't care.

Damien had heard police reports of girls going missing in this neighborhood. It was possible the monsters had found a new hunting ground.

Malachi saw Rhys's shoulders angle toward a dark alley.

"Hmm?" They spoke as little as possible on patrol.

A nod was his only answer. Malachi saw Rhys trace the characters along his wrist, calling on his magic. Malachi copied the action. Within seconds, he felt the power creep up his arm, crawl over his shoulders, then down his back. In the time it took him to draw a silver dagger, his vision sharpened; the black became grey. His arms flexed with new strength. His skin pulsed with a web of incantations that made him impervious to human weapons.

Malachi followed Rhys into the alley, alert to his surroundings as his brother focused on a point in the darkness. He heard the scribe utter a soft oath in the Old Language, then he ran and fell to his knees, pulling on gloves before he lifted the broken figure on the ground, making sure his skin didn't brush hers for fear of further harm.

"Too late," Rhys muttered as he stood and started walking. "It's Grigori, and from her condition, he hasn't been gone long. Do you sense anything?"

"No smell. Not even a hint." A seductive smell of sandalwood usually followed Grigori attacks. Malachi followed the other scribe as he rushed back toward the street. "Is she alive?"

"Barely."

As they approached the street lights, Malachi got a better look at the victim. She appeared to be no more than sixteen or seventeen. Her skin was pale and her breathing shallow. The young woman's torn clothing was traditional but new. He saw Rhys's gloved thumb brush her cheek.

"A child." The raw fury bubbled under the surface of the quiet man's voice. "She's a little girl, Malachi."

"They don't care."

Grigori soldiers seduced mercilessly, using their otherworldly charm and beauty to convince a human woman to give them the soul-energy they craved. The women went willingly, joyfully, never aware of the magic that drew them. And when the monsters were finished, they left, the female but a forgotten moment of sexual gratification in their centuries-long lives.

Dead. Unconscious. Drained of their most vital energy, most humans didn't survive an encounter with a Grigori. The rare one who did was often impregnated by the monster. If the survivor was lucky, she would live to bear a very gifted child, one who bore an echo of his or her otherworldly parentage. It was a cruel twist that had resulted in some of history's geniuses. Diluted Grigori blood was laced through the human population, like a black thread through a colorful tapestry.

"Call Maxim," Rhys said. "See if his friend's clinic is open tonight."

Malachi pulled out his phone as Rhys walked back toward the Range Rover they'd parked under the brightest light on the main road. A few curtains flickered, but at two in the morning, not even the nosiest Turk would ask what the two imposing men were doing with the woman they carried. Malachi opened the back door and Rhys slid the unconscious girl inside.

They couldn't take her to a hospital. The human doctors would have no idea how to help her, and her family might be contacted. There wasn't much that could be done except rest, fluids, and oxygen. If the young woman survived, she wouldn't even realize she'd been attacked. Most Grigori survivors went searching for their attackers, convinced they had experienced an act of the purest love imaginable. Often, they became obsessed.

The phone kept ringing with no answer. Eventually, Maxim's voicemail picked up.

"Max, we have a girl here," he said softly. "Grigori attack. She's alive. Young. Call us. We need to take her to your friend's clinic."

Only a few humans in Istanbul knew of the existence of the scribes. Maxim's doctor friend was one. He was discreet, and he and his wife did their best to help any girls who survived Grigori attacks. As they crept slowly through the neighborhood, Malachi rolled his window down. The summer night was cooler, and a breeze blew off the water. Turning a corner, he caught a whiff of the telltale incense.

"Rhys!"

"I smell it." He slowed the car at the corner, glancing between Malachi and the girl in the back. "We've got to get her to the hospital. She's dehydrated. Her breathing is shallow, and—"

"You go." Malachi wrenched the door open. "I'll go after the bastard."

"Be careful," Rhys yelled, but he didn't try to stop him. It would take more than a single Grigori to worry any of their kind. Even a small group of them was considered no more than an annoyance. Their greater numbers were all that made them a threat. Still, Malachi was careful. It was miscalculation of Grigori strength and cunning that had led to the horror of the Rending.

He paused on a deserted corner, closing his eyes to take a breath and trace a few more temporary spells on his forearm. Magic not inscribed on the body would fade in time, but it was enough to give him a quick burst of strength. Just as he finished one set, he caught the scent again, but stronger. The Grigori was coming toward him.

Malachi grinned and ducked behind the corner of the building, a small café that was struggling to remain respectable in the crumbling neighborhood. He could see the graffiti that had been painted over, layers of it, rising to his eyes as the magic flowed through him.

Curses and political slogans. There was an advertisement for Coca-Cola that had been painted over many, many times. Still, the words drifted up, as if reaching for him through the years. In a city like Istanbul, every building held ghostly writing only an Irin scribe would see. Words through the ages, ever and always visible to his kind.

Their gift. Their curse.

The smell of sandalwood and a seductive laugh.

"I will get in trouble," the girl protested weakly. "I don't... No, it's fine. I...I don't care."

"Of course you don't." The monster had his arm thrown around the young woman, who looked up at the handsome man adoringly. He was European; sandy-blond hair gleamed under the streetlights. His accent sounded German.

"Your voice," the woman whispered. "It's so beautiful."

"I know." He gave her a wicked smile. "Do you love me?"

"Yes," she breathed out. "Say my name."

"I don't know your name," Malachi heard the man say as he led her to an alley just as filthy as the one they'd rescued the last girl from. He watched them, waiting to see if the Grigori was alone. Often, they would hunt in pairs or even small packs. This one appeared to be alone.

"Is this all right?"

"Yes. Touch me. Please... kiss me again."

Unwilling to wait another moment, Malachi sprang from behind the building, his dagger ready. He rushed into the alley and grabbed the man's shoulder. Spun him around, only to be met with a silver dagger gleaming in the grey light.

With a grunt, the scribe fell back.

It was a trap.

"You must be the one they call Malachi," the Grigori said with a leer. "We haven't met."

"No need to introduce yourself," Malachi said softly as the

two men began to circle each other. "I'll be killing you soon." If the Grigori had been carrying an ordinary weapon, Malachi wouldn't have hesitated. His *talesm* were a living, pulsing armor around his body. But something told him that the Grigori's blade wasn't an average dagger. It shone with a dark metallic gleam.

"I'm sure that would usually be true," the other man said. "I could barely sense you. Your concealment charms must be older than me."

The Grigori *was* old. Malachi hadn't examined the man when he'd been walking down the street, but on closer inspection, Malachi sensed his opponent's age. His scent was deep, not like the lighter scent of a young soldier. His green eyes were calculating. And now that he had drawn Malachi in, he had no interest in the woman, even kicking her away when she tried to cling to the man's legs, desperate for his touch.

"Please," she begged. "I beg—" She cried out when the Grigori flung her into the wall.

He was stronger than the young ones. If Malachi had to guess, he'd say the Grigori was almost as old as Rhys.

Which meant he had taken part in the Rending.

Malachi snarled, curling his lip as the realization struck. As if reading his mind, the other man grinned, watching Malachi with taunting eyes.

"I have killed your kind, Scribe. But please feel free to underestimate me for a while longer. That will suit my plans perfectly."

He was speaking in puzzles. Malachi lunged to the right, taking the man off-balance as he tossed the dagger to his left hand and reached around, trying to pierce the base of the Grigori's skull.

His opponent ducked and countered. The blade slashed along Malachi's stomach, sizzling as it hit the protective spells. Malachi's skin held... then split open with a hiss.

It was no ordinary blade. The Grigori carried an angelic weapon.

His mocking laugh echoed off the walls. "I do love that look of surprise! When was the last time you saw one of these out of Irin hands?"

Malachi grunted as he sucked in the pain, weaving it into the fabric of his armor as he shifted and hooked his ankle around the other man's knee, sweeping his foot out from under him and causing the man to stumble back. The blade clattered away.

The smirk fell from the Grigori's face. He dropped into the fall, rolling over and away from Malachi, reaching for the dagger where it had fallen. Malachi saw his eyes dart into the night sky a second before the footsteps landed behind him. Three Grigori soldiers had joined their friend.

The Grigori with the angelic blade muttered, "Too soon."

Malachi grinned as he spun around. Taking stock of his new opponents, he realized that all of them had human weapons. He kicked out, catching one in the solar plexus as his right arm extended toward the other. In one smooth movement, he had twisted the Grigori's head around and plunged the knife deep into the base of his skull.

The human woman screamed, then passed out as the body Malachi held began to disintegrate. Within seconds, there was only a fine gold dust, drifting up in a column, reaching toward the heavens.

He looked over his shoulder, but the blond Grigori had fled, leaving him with the other two. One was just getting to his feet, and the other one looked like he wanted to run after his friend but was too frightened.

Malachi strode to the Grigori he'd kicked, curious whether the other would take the opportunity to run.

He didn't.

Malachi ignored the glancing blow the gasping man swung

toward his shoulder. The dagger hit the scribe's *talesm* and bounced off, no more dangerous than a child's toy. Malachi twisted the man's neck around and ended him, too. Then he waved the second cloud of dust away and frowned at the last Grigori.

The young man was ethereally beautiful, like all his kind. He had curling dark hair and porcelain skin. His eyes were a light hazel green; his scent was designed to entice his prey.

And he was scared to death.

"Why didn't you run?" Malachi asked, stalking toward him. "I'm going to kill you now."

The Grigori couldn't have been very old. His scent was bright and panicked. "I… I know. But I have to stay here. With you."

Malachi halted.

"*…please feel free to underestimate me for a while longer. That will suit my plans perfectly.*"

The second trap snapped shut.

"What does he want?" He lunged at the man, lifting him in a chokehold and pushing him against the wall. "Why are you still here?"

Malachi knew the answer before the man's lips moved.

"The woman," the young soldier gasped. "He's… after the human woman. Had to… keep you distracted. All of you."

"All of us…?"

They had plans for Leo, too.

Malachi twisted the man's neck around, striking quickly, and then he began to run. Behind him, a faint cloud of dust rose to the stars.

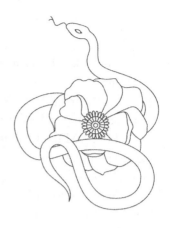

CHAPTER
SIX

L eo flipped through channels on the television as he ate
   another massive sandwich Ava had ordered from room
   service. His accent sounded Russian, but he reminded
Ava of a giant happy Labrador with his gold hair and cheerful
disposition. They sat in the hotel's library, which doubled as a
lounge. Books lined the walls and a television sat in one corner,
streaming international shows from all over the globe. Ava was
processing images on her laptop, so Leo had turned on the
television.

She'd met her new bodyguard that afternoon after Malachi
had called him to meet her in the hotel lobby.

"Who's this?"

"This is Leo. He'll be guarding you tonight if you need to go
anywhere." He'd handed over a small slip of paper. "This is his
number. You already have mine."

Ava had turned to Leo. "Hi."

The blond giant gave her a boyish smile. "Hello, Ms. Matheson."

Malachi said, "She likes to be called 'Ava.' Don't leave her unguarded; you have my number."

Then Malachi had turned and walked away without a glance back.

Asshole.

Ava turned to Leo. "Care to come inside? I was just about to order room service because I don't feel like going out. I'll buy you dinner since you're on babysitting duty tonight."

She saw Malachi pause at the door. She'd never once invited him into the hotel. They always met in the lobby.

"Sure," Leo said. "Thanks!"

Malachi half-turned, then stopped, meeting her eyes over his shoulder before his narrowed and he spun around again.

"Night, Mal!"

Now she was wishing her silent shadow would return. There was nothing wrong with Leo; he was friendly as a pup, but he exuded energy, not calm, the way Malachi did. His internal voice bounced and jumped, almost always cheerfully, but much louder than Malachi's did. And though his voice held the same odd resonance, it felt slightly out of tune. All in all, his presence was distracting.

A voice from the television caught her attention.

"What was that?" she asked.

Leo lifted an eyebrow. "What?"

"The TV."

He'd already flipped past the channel. The one he'd stopped on looked like a soap opera set in Topkapi Palace.

"Turn it back."

"Turn it back to what?"

Ava stood and grabbed the remote.

"Hey!"

Not that. Not that. Not that... There.

"Him." She pointed at the TV. It was a news program, and an old man was being interviewed on the screen. "That man. What language is he speaking?"

Leo frowned. "That's Farsi. It's a Persian program; I'm surprised they even have it at this——"

"No." Ava shook her head. "I've heard Farsi. I've been to Iran. That doesn't sound like Farsi."

The bodyguard shrugged. "Well, it is. His accent is odd. Let me..." Leo's voice trailed off as he listened intently. After a few minutes, he said, "He's Assyrian; that's why it sounds different. He's speaking Farsi with an Assyrian accent. They're interviewing him for a cultural program. It's just a different part of Iran. The accent is different."

Her heart sank. "Oh."

"Why did you want to know?"

"I didn't... It just reminded me of a language I heard once. That's all." Ava watched the old man for a few more moments, memorizing the rise and fall of his voice before she handed the remote control back to Leo. It had to be a coincidence, but for a brief second, the man had sounded like he was speaking the silent tongue of the voices she'd heard her whole life. Ava had studied languages. She'd traveled the globe, listening to accents and intonation. The peculiar rhythm of foreign lands. She'd spent years searching for the language that haunted her.

She was never successful.

Leo was still watching her, clearly suspicious of her excitement over the news program. She concentrated on the computer screen, ignoring him, but his silent voice was colored with curiosity.

Ava tried to change the subject. "So how many languages do you speak?"

"I…" He hadn't been expecting the question. "I've never counted, to be honest."

"That many?"

Leo shrugged. "I'm not fluent in all of them, but I speak many. It helps when you travel."

"Have you worked for Malachi long?"

"We, uh, we work for the same company. He's more senior than I am, but we've both worked for the company a long time."

"Oh?" She continued fiddling with the color balance on one file. "You're not from Istanbul, I'm guessing."

"Outside Moscow, originally. But I've traveled a lot."

Ava snorted a little. He couldn't have been older than his late twenties. Of course, she knew firsthand you could cover a lot of ground when you wanted to avoid home.

Leo asked, "How about you?"

"Malachi didn't tell you?"

"No." His answer caused Ava to look up. He'd finished his sandwich and was wiping his mouth. "He wouldn't. He hardly talks at all except to yell at me and my cousin if we drink his beer and don't replace it. He's known for being very focused when he's on a job."

For some reason, Ava found that endearing. It sounded like her shadow was a cranky old man to more than just her.

"I'm from L.A."

"Really?"

"Yep. And I hate it."

Leo laughed, a deep chuckle that filled the lounge and made her smile.

"So that's why you travel all the time? Because you don't like home?"

"Among other reasons." She couldn't concentrate on her work. Leo's silent voice was alive with excitement, like a little kid just begging to play. She finally snapped her laptop case shut. "Why don't we go for a drink? There's a café on the corner. I feel like getting out of here."

"I don't know…"

She could tell he was uncomfortable with the idea, but Ava knew drowning out Leo's presence would be easier in a crowd. Hopefully, he could blend in with the group of people and create a white noise affect that wouldn't pierce her temple.

"Okay," she said, standing. "How's this? I'm going to go for a drink because you're not, in fact, my babysitter. Then you can follow me, like I know Malachi told you to do. You can either sit with me or lurk suspiciously on the edge of the room. It's up to you, but I'm going." She packed her laptop in the case and walked down the hall to her room. Within moments, she was back in the lobby, and Leo was waiting, glancing at his phone like he was expecting a message.

Ava nodded at it. "You already tell on me?"

"It's just… Malachi said you usually stay in at night."

"That's when I've been walking all day. I'm not tired. I want a drink." She brushed past him and opened the door, nodding at the burly doorman on the way out. "See you."

She was barely at the curb when Leo caught up with her.

"Are you always so stubborn?" he asked.

"Yes."

The man was looking around as if he expected commandos to come pouring out of the fashionable doorways of the Sultanahmet. Ava shook her head.

"Seriously, Leo, relax. You're too young to worry this much."

"Haha."

"You're not even going to drink, are you?"

"Not if I want to remain living."

AVA WAS HALFWAY THROUGH A BOTTLE OF VERY MEDIOCRE RED wine when she noticed it. First one had drifted in. Then another.

"Whoa."

"What?" Leo looked up from his phone. He'd been madly texting someone for the last ten minutes. Ava was guessing Malachi was busy. Too busy to worry about her, anyway. Poor Leo. He was tense, poised on the edge of his seat like a dog waiting for a command. He hadn't drunk anything, not even the tea the waiter had set in front of him at the café that looked down to the water. Ava had visited before, but not at night. It was a decidedly different crowd. A football match was playing on the television, and young people of every nationality hung on the score. It was definitely a tourist place, but a friendly one. And that night, it had more than its share of very pleasant scenery.

"You probably haven't noticed unless you're into guys, but this bar has suddenly become hot guy central." She looked around in wonder. It couldn't just be her imagination. Every woman in the place seemed to be under a spell. The whole place was full of wildly handsome men. "Is there some kind of... modeling conference in town? Fashion week or something?"

"I don't know," Leo said tersely, still typing madly on his phone.

"This is so weird. I mean, I'm not complaining—"

"Whatever you do," Leo interrupted as he stood. "Do *not* leave this spot. I need to make a call, and I need to be able to see you through the window."

She sneered automatically. "Hey, buddy—"

"I'm serious, Ava." He did look serious. "Don't leave. And avoid talking to anyone if you can. I'll be right outside."

Her eyes narrowed as she watched him walk away. Leo glared at one of the handsome men who sat in the corner with two women draped over his arms. The man turned and locked eyes with Ava; she glanced away, looking for Leo, but he was already outside. What was with him? Was one of these guys with his ex-girlfriend, or something?

There was the one Leo had passed, sitting by the door with two women. He looked like someone she'd seen in an underwear ad. There were two other men sharing a table on the opposite side of the bar. They might have been brothers with their stunning blue eyes and dark brown hair. They were currently the focus of at least five fawning women. There was a blond by the hallway leading toward the restrooms, and still another sitting directly across from her, giving her sultry dark eyes that did absolutely nothing but make her think of a self-absorbed actor she'd dated once in college.

"Whatever," she muttered and refilled her glass. She was starting to get a perfectly nice buzz that was helping to drown out the voices. The last thing she needed was bossy men ordering her around or coming on to her. She was tempted to leave the place, just for spite. But... She wasn't going to waste a perfectly good—well, adequate—bottle of wine.

One of the men across from the bar winked at her, then the one who'd been standing by the hallway came up and sat in the chair Leo had occupied.

"What's your name?" he asked.

"None of your business." He looked shocked, but the whole situation was giving Ava goose bumps. What was the game here? She didn't get it. There was something going on, but the wine had muffled the voices, making it harder for her to read the intentions of the man sitting next to her. She looked around the place. She was in a pair of old jeans and a T-shirt, hadn't even attempted to dress up. Why was this guy talking to her? She had no illusions about her own beauty. Ava knew she was moderately attractive, but she wasn't the kind of woman who turned heads. Certainly not heads that looked like they belonged in fashion magazines.

"I'm just curious. You're a beautiful woman, and you're all alone."

"Yes. Happily alone."

Keep telling yourself that, Ava.

Stupid wine.

"But you weren't alone earlier."

"Your point, Einstein?"

"Did your boyfriend leave you here?"

"None of your business."

"So he *is* your boyfriend? Do you know what he is?"

What? Ava took another drink. This guy wasn't making any sense. Maybe it was a language thing.

"You know," she said in a low voice, sliding closer. "I'd really like you to…"

He leaned in. "What?"

"Leave."

Hottie's eyes narrowed. "I don't think you know just who your boyfriend is, do you?"

Irritated, Ava blurted out, "He's not my boyfriend! But he will take care of you if you don't leave me alone. Now."

Well, that made him happy.

"So he's not your boyfriend! May I join you?"

She squinted. Yep, buzz definitely getting spoiled. "Are you deaf? No! Are all Turkish men this forward? Do I look like I want company?"

He said something she really didn't listen to. The noise from the television seemed louder. Had the bartender turned it up? Hot Guy was still talking.

Was it some kind of game? A bet? She looked around, but none of the other men were looking at them. In fact, even Mister Wink Wink across the bar was looking away. Ava was starting to get nervous, and she really wished Leo would come back. She pulled out her phone and saw that he had just texted her.

Meet me by the door I left through.

Normally, she'd ignore him. After all, he worked for her—or her stepfather. Whatever. She didn't have to do what he said. She finished the glass of wine and narrowed her eyes at the handsome man who still looked like he expected Ava to fall into his bed. He was watching her like she was the most fascinating thing in the world.

"What are you?" he whispered with barely contained excitement.

"I'm an American photographer. It's really not all that exciting."

"I don't think that's what you really are."

Weirdo. He might have been handsome, but the guy did nothing for her. She was about to pour another glass of wine when she heard her phone buzz again. She looked down. It was Malachi's number.

Ava, go to Leo. Now.

"Ugh." Her head fell back and she groaned. "Bossy men. Damn *bossy* men. Who the hell do they think they are?" She'd tell them off in person.

Ava stood and picked up her purse. As soon as she did, she felt a hand on her arm. It was Hot Guy, who had morphed into Mr. Intrusive.

Okay, not cool.

"Hey!" Feeling bold with wine, Ava rounded on him as she yanked her arm away. "Do *not* touch me, do you understand? Did I give you permission to do that? Did I indicate in any way that I wanted your attention, mister?"

The man's green eyes widened in shock.

"You pulled away from me."

"For heaven's sake, do you really think you're God's gift? Get over yourself, buddy!"

She was starting to draw attention. Luckily three-quarters of a bottle of wine meant she didn't really care all that much. She was only a block from her hotel, after all. And there was always—

"Leo!" She grinned, her annoyance forgotten. She turned to the pushy stranger. "Now this guy? He's a catch. For one thing, he's handsome without looking like he's been airbrushed, because really?" She waved a hand in front of the guy's face. "Are you wearing makeup? I mean, whatever, if that's your thing, but see, Leo here—"

Leo cleared his throat. "We should go, Ava." He was trying to steer her toward the door with a hand on her shoulder, but Ava ignored him, still talking to Hot Guy.

"See, Leo's got the confident-without-being-arrogant thing. You need to learn that. Because girls don't usually go for... a guy who looks in the mirror more than they do." Ava giggled as she looked around the place. "Well, obviously not some of these ladies, but where I come from... that's probably a bad example. Still—"

"Ava." His low voice sounded across the bar. She turned, stilling immediately when she heard it. Heard *him*. Their eyes met.

There you are.

Even slightly inebriated, she was shocked by how the realization hit her.

He was here. And he belonged with her.

Malachi strode into the room, looking rough and angry. His shirt was torn at the collar and there was a bandage across his ribs. He was still the best thing she'd laid eyes on in... ever.

"You're here," she murmured, letting his voice wash into her mind. Relieved. He was relieved, but worried. She reached out for his hand. She knew if she could just hold it—

He dodged her at the last minute, slipping around Leo's back and standing between the stranger and Ava, pressing a warm hand to the small of her back. She could feel it through her shirt. The heat. The calm. She wanted to surround herself until she lost her mind in his.

"Let's go," he said, pushing her toward the door.

As soon as her feet started moving, she came out of her daze. "Hey, I'm not—"

"You're done. We're going back to the hotel. I'll explain more there."

"You'd better. And I don't appreciate—"

She broke off when the man with two women, who was sitting by the door, leaned toward her as she walked by. There was a snarl, then before she could blink, Leo had shoved her behind his back, and Malachi had the gorgeous man pinned against the wall of the bar, his hand around the man's throat. The girls at the table started shrieking and calling for the owner.

Ava peeked from around Leo's back, and she heard Malachi whisper, "If you want to survive to see the dawn, come no closer. My dagger hungers for your neck."

She gasped. "Holy *shit!*"

Leo spun and almost shoved her past Malachi and the other man, dragging her onto the sidewalk outside the bar.

"What the hell was that?" she yelled.

"Ava, let's get going."

She shook off the hand that had reached for her shoulder. "You people are maniacs! Get away from me!"

Ava was practically running toward the hotel. She could see the doorman sitting outside the door, smoking one of the sweet cigarettes he always carried. She could smell the waft of tobacco reach her nose a second before a hand grabbed her shoulder. Malachi spun her around, then immediately raised his hands in surrender.

"Let me explain, Ava."

"Explain what? How you threatened to stab some guy because he was making a pass at me?" She backed away from him, inching closer to the doorman with every step. "He wasn't even making a pass at me. He *leaned* in my direction, and you—"

"There was a girl almost killed tonight."

"That's horrible." She kept backing away. "But what the hell does that have to do with me?"

"Those men are..." She saw him give Leo a panicked glance. "They're... in a gang."

Liar. She shook her head. He was lying; she could hear it.

"And that gang is the one responsible for this girl's attack. They specialize in... human trafficking, and they're targeting foreign women traveling alone."

He was just making things up as he went along, but his voice... His inner voice was still panicked. Worried. He was lying, but it was out of fear. Something had frightened the big, bad bodyguard, and it had to do with her safety. That reason alone caused her to take a deep breath and stop backing away from him. Logic, even the fuzzy logic she had to work with from all the wine, told Ava that if Malachi wanted to harm her, he'd had plenty of opportunities in the week and a half they'd already known each other. He'd had her alone many times. So obviously something else was going on.

She asked, "What does this have to do with me?"

"There were four of them in that bar, Ava. One attacked me earlier as an associate and I were rescuing a girl they had kidnapped and almost killed. We have a standing assignment from our bosses in Vienna about this organization. They're active all over the world, and for some reason, they're targeting you. We don't know why."

For the first time, his words had the ring of truth. Ava took a deep breath. She still felt like there was something she wasn't seeing, but at least some of what he said made sense.

"Carl," she muttered.

"What?"

"My stepfather, Carl Matheson. He's rich as Midas. Richer, maybe. In addition to being a film producer, he also has all this family money. Shipping. Oil. He's loaded. If it's human trafficking, they probably want me for ransom. It wouldn't be the first time someone has tried."

Or succeeded. She tried not to think about the awful week when she was eight. Routine, they had called it. The monsters who had taken her in Brazil had laughed and called it a routine kidnapping when they teased her. One girl for one million dollars. A respectable week's work. She hadn't slept through the night for a year afterward.

Malachi said, "That must be it. They've become bolder, and I don't know why." He stepped closer cautiously. "I'd like to stay at the hotel. I called already and booked the room next to yours."

And just like that, she was pissed off again. "Didn't ask me, did you? Did you ask Carl? Is anyone going to even pretend to keep me informed?" She spun around and walked toward the doorman. He frowned for a moment before he said something to Malachi in Turkish. Malachi barked back, then the doorman shrugged and opened the door to their group.

"Some security you are," Ava muttered. "I was told this hotel had the best security in the city. I stayed here for that reason. I don't need handlers. I don't want someone watching me eat breakfast and following me to the bathroom, Malachi."

A wave of embarrassment washed over her as she walked to her room. For a few days, she'd almost felt normal. The voices were quieter. She was going out and touring a city she was growing to love. She'd forgotten Malachi had been hired to look out for her. She'd felt like she had a friend who enjoyed her company. Enjoyed spending time with her. Maybe even…

She was foolish to have forgotten. Other people got those things. Not her.

"Ava." His voice was softer, pleading. She refused to turn around. "I'm trying to keep you safe."

"By getting a room in my hotel without even asking me?" she asked in a hoarse voice. She had to get away from him. She was seconds away from crying. "By ordering me around like I'm a child?"

"Please—"

"I'm going to bed now. I don't want to talk to you. I'm tired, and we'll talk more about this in the morning."

He fell silent. She could feel the warmth of his hand inches from the nape of her neck. His breath stirred her hair, then he drew away. "Fine. I'll be in the room next door."

"I don't want to know that," she said. "I'm pretending…"

That you'll meet me tomorrow for breakfast, just because you want to see me.

That we'll tour the city, and you'll joke with me, and the voices will be a little easier to bear.

I'm pretending… that you're my friend.

"I'm pretending you don't exist, Malachi. Stay away from me tonight."

She slid her card in the lock, then quickly walked in and shut the door. She turned the dead bolt and the sliding lock, then she walked to her window and checked the locks there, too. When she was sure her room was secure, she sat down on the bed and waited to hear him leave the hallway. After a few minutes, Malachi moved toward the lobby, talking to Leo in Turkish.

Seconds later, she pushed back the tears that wanted to surface, and her phone was in her hand.

"Mom?"

"Ava!" Her mother's voice was brimming with excitement. "Isn't it late there? I'm so glad you called! How are you liking—"

"These guys Carl hired, Mom. They're out of control." Her voice was shaking with anger. "He needs to dial them back, or I'm ditching them completely. You know I can."

"But Ava—"

"They practically shoved me out of a bar tonight because some guy was making a pass at me. You know me. I can take care of myself, and they went way overboard. I'm surprised no one called the police. Is that the kind of publicity that Carl wants?"

"Who—"

"*And* one of them is staying at my hotel now! He says there's some kind of threat against my life! Has there been a threat and you haven't told me? I mean, I know shit happens, but you've always told me if there has ever been any specific——"

"*Ava, shut up!*"

Her mother never raised her voice. She shut up immediately.

"I want you to listen to me very carefully." Her mother's voice sent chills down her neck. "Are you alone?"

"Yes."

"The man Carl hired quit over a week ago. There was some sort of scheduling conflict, and I convinced him you were perfectly safe since you were staying in the city. Ava... he didn't hire anyone else."

She sat on the edge of her bed, breath coming in small panicked bursts. "Mom..."

"Whoever these people are who *say* they are guarding you, Ava, they were not hired by us. Do you understand?"

She nodded, but no words left her mouth.

"Ava, are you still there?" Her mother's voice was panicked. "Carl!"

"I'm here, Mom."

Lies. Lies. Lies.

It was all a lie. Ava had never felt more vulnerable in her life. The chill at her neck spread. She heard her mother and Carl muttering in the background, then her stepfather picked up the phone.

"Ava?"

"Yeah?"

"This man, he's been following you for a week?"

"Yes. We've... been friendly. He seemed nice. Very professional."

"Does he have any idea you suspect him? Did you tell him you were calling home?"

"No."

There was a pause. "I'm calling my contacts in Istanbul as

soon as we get off the phone. In the morning, there will be a package waiting for you at the front desk. I want you to find out who these people are." Ava heard her mother protesting in the background, but Carl's voice was cold and clear. "If you're threatened, if you're in danger at all, use it. I know you know how. We can take care of any fallout after you're safe."

Ava took a deep breath. "I understand."

CHAPTER
SEVEN

" And you're sure she has no idea?"

"With this woman?" Malachi looked around the open-air patio where the hotel served breakfast. He could see Ava's door from where he sat, so he kept his voice low. "I'm not sure of anything with her."

"Leo said she didn't react normally to the Grigori."

"No. She seemed completely immune to them."

There was nothing but silence. What could Damien say? All human women had the same reaction to the Grigori. All women, except Ava. It was inexplicable.

Finally, Damien said, "Rhys is doing things on the computer. Max is out hunting his sources right now. Whatever this is, it's now a priority. Leo stays with you."

"Who was the blond in the alley?"

"It sounds like Brage. I've met him before. He's skilled. I didn't know he was in Istanbul. This is a new development."

"What do you know?"

"He's Scandinavian, but I'm not sure from where. Not one of Jaron's. Older. About four hundred or so."

"One of Volund's?"

"Perhaps. I don't know."

"But he's in Jaron's territory with an angelic blade."

"Yes, I noted that in your report. And I've passed it along to Vienna."

Obviously Damien didn't know any more than Malachi. He heaved a sigh and noticed movement in Ava's room. All the rooms in the hotel opened onto the beautifully tended central courtyard. Tiled fountains and lush potted plants created tiny oases within the scattered tables. A few early morning travelers were already up and packed for day trips. They were eating breakfast while Malachi drank his tea. He'd slept only a few hours; luckily, he didn't need much to be alert. He'd woken with the first prayer call at dawn. The curtains in Ava's room moved.

"Damien, I should go. I'll text you later."

"As long as you don't expect me to text back."

Malachi smiled. "I don't. Have Rhys keep me updated if he finds anything."

"What are you going to do today?"

"Whatever she wants, I suppose. I'm still supposed to be her bodyguard."

"And how long is that going to last?"

"As long as I can manage. I was half expecting the police to storm my room last night, but it didn't happen. So I'm guessing she was too angry to call home."

"Just be prepared for anything. If they make a move——"

"The only one I'm worried about is Brage with that dagger, but since Leo's with me, I doubt he'll show his face. He won't take on two of us at the same time. I think the show last night didn't go as planned. They were supposed to keep me occupied longer."

"Don't underestimate them."

"I won't."

He hung up the phone when he saw her door open. He wondered if she would sit with him. He wondered if she'd speak to him at all, or if they were back to how they'd started. Her pretending he didn't exist and Malachi pretending she was just another anonymous human he'd taken a vow to protect.

She stepped into the morning sun, gold touching her hair and making her skin glow. Her fierce eyes met his and froze.

Malachi decided he was done pretending.

"Good morning," he said as she approached.

Ava sat down, but she didn't speak. A smiling waiter brought her tea and set down a plate of fruit between them. Figs drizzled with honey and fresh green grapes. She pulled at one of the grapes and popped it in her mouth before she spoke.

"You were injured last night. How are you feeling?"

"Fine." She couldn't have sounded more disinterested, but he supposed he couldn't blame her. The woman wasn't stupid; she wasn't buying the story he'd told her the night before, so he'd have to be more convincing this morning.

"All right. Convince me why I shouldn't call my stepfather and have you and Leo both fired for being so high-handed."

A fraction of the tension fled. She hadn't called home.

"I apologize for how we handled things at the bar last night. I was worried, and I overreacted. I'd just come from a confrontation with one of this gang, and I saw one talking to you, obviously trying to trick you into going somewhere with him—"

"Did you also see me telling him off in my somewhat inebriated state? He wasn't really all that appealing."

"I'm glad." He paused to watch her bite into a fig. "But I'd just watched my friend take a half-dead girl to the hospital. I wasn't entirely rational at the thought of the same thing happening to you."

She paused with the fig at her lips, met his eyes for a moment, then looked away, leaning back in her chair and looking around the courtyard as she nibbled on the fruit. Malachi was practically growling in frustration. How could this human woman be so impossible to read? Her calculating stare and disinterested posture ate at him.

Malachi continued to sip his tea as casually as he could as Ava ate breakfast. He had expected a torrent of questions. Anger. Doubt. Instead, there was… nothing. It was maddening. Finally, she put down her fork and looked at him.

"I think I'd like to get out of the city today. It feels like it's going to be hot and the traffic… Are there any places we could go that are close? Day hikes? Maybe some trees? Somewhere with not so many people?"

What was her game? Whatever it was, he could play along. "We could go the islands. They're just off the coast. It's a day trip if you take the ferry. One of the islands has a nice hike up to an old monastery. Very beautiful. There are no cars allowed. On foot or horses only. Some carriages if you don't feel like walking."

"No. Walking sounds perfect. I could use a good stretch."

"Okay." He looked at the clock on his phone. "If you're ready, we could catch the ferry in about an hour. Wear good shoes."

"Sure thing. Meet you in the lobby? I have a couple things to do in my room. I need to clean up. Make myself presentable, even if we're hiking."

She looked fine to him—she looked beautiful, if he was forced to admit it—but Malachi wasn't about to question her.

"I'll see you in a bit."

She stood and turned toward the lobby, heading for the front desk. Malachi followed her. She picked up a small box the concierge slid across the desk, then tucked it under her arm. Malachi intercepted her before she made it back to her room.

"Ava, if that was delivered last night, I might need to check—"

"You really want to go through the feminine-hygiene products my mom sends me, Mal?" She gave him a rueful smile. "I mean, it's possible someone snuck a bomb in with the tampons, but I'm kind of doubting it."

He cleared his throat and stepped back. "If it's from your mother, I'm sure it's fine."

"That's what I thought."

She turned and walked to her room, Malachi's eyes following her every step.

THE RIDE ACROSS THE SEA OF MARMARA WAS SMOOTH, BUT AVA didn't sleep as Malachi thought she might. She remained quiet and watchful, clutching her bag as they rode the waves out to the Ottoman-style ferry terminal on Büyükada, the largest of the Prince Islands. Once the favored spot for exiled royalty, the islands had become an even more-favored vacation spot for Istanbul's wealthier citizens. Shops and cafés dotted the street leading to the central square, which was dominated by a clock tower. Instead of stopping for lunch in the square, Ava picked a few snacks from one of the shops catering to the summer tourists.

"Okay, which way?" She packed the snacks in her small knapsack and threw it over one shoulder.

Malachi pointed toward the carriages by the clock tower. "Are you sure you don't want to hire someone?"

"Definitely. I could use the walk."

"This way, then."

It was early summer and the middle of the week. There were a number of tourists, but most seemed to head toward the beach or the restaurants. Only a few stopped to hire a phaeton to take them up the mountain, and even fewer looked ready for the steep climb through the town and up to the Monastery of St. George. As Ava and Malachi started out, they were alone. Leo stayed near the terminal, watching for any visitors, per Malachi's request.

"Are you ready?" he asked as they headed up the hill. "It's not a short hike."

Ava took a deep breath as they stepped away from the crowds. "Trust me, this is just what I had in mind."

Her expression began to clear the farther they got away from other people. They walked through a neighborhood filled with luxurious mansions on their way toward Luna Park.

"Your house in L.A.?" He nodded toward one mansion. "Is it grand like this?"

"My mom's house?" She shrugged. "It's bigger. Carl likes people to know how much money he has."

"You don't have your own home?"

"No."

They kept walking. Malachi wondered what it would feel like to live in a grand home. The retreat where his parents raised him in Germany was simple, and scribe houses were more like monasteries. The most well-appointed rooms were reserved for the books, scrolls, and tablets, not the scribes who copied or preserved them. He knew some Irin lived with more wealth, those in cities who worked in human businesses. After all, the retreats and scribe houses had to be supported financially, but Malachi had never had the head for human business. His life had been protecting the accumulation of knowledge until it had been about avenging his parents' deaths. He didn't know anything else.

"Tell me more about this organization you're after, Mal."

He wasn't prepared for the question. Luckily, he'd rehearsed an answer that morning while he was waiting for her to wake. "They're an organized, international criminal enterprise that specializes in human trafficking. They're very secretive; you won't find much about them online. Officially, they don't exist."

"Really?" Her voice had that distant, skeptical tone again. "No international task forces? Interpol? United Nations?"

"Governments don't want to acknowledge things they don't know how to combat. It makes them feel helpless."

She raised an eyebrow behind her sunglasses. "So why are you guys after them? I'm assuming your company is being paid."

Curious woman. Curious, *bothersome* woman. The surge of reluctant admiration annoyed him. "Let's put it this way— they've hurt some very powerful people in the past. Those people want to make sure it doesn't happen again, and they're willing to put their resources behind our company to take care of them."

"You mean kill them?"

"Ava, I don't—"

"'My dagger hungers for your neck.'" She mimicked his voice from the night before. "Who talks like that? I'm assuming you were threatening his life."

They were past the houses now, on the edge of the park. Pine trees lined the road along with fluttering scraps of ribbon and cloth, markers left by the pilgrims who'd traveled the road before them. Ava didn't look at him, but he knew she was waiting for his response.

"Yes, I was threatening him. According to the law, he is not a criminal, but he kills and kidnaps with impunity. What should our response be if one of them threatens an innocent person?"

The color on her cheeks was high, and she was starting to breathe more heavily the longer they climbed.

"But you're not police. You're not military. Basically, you're out for revenge on these guys."

"We're keeping them from hurting more women and children. Is there something wrong with that?"

"Well, when you put it that way…" Her fingers trailed along the brush, twisting around one particularly long ribbon that was tied to a low branch of pine. "What are these? What are they for?"

"They're prayers. Pilgrims tie them as they walk up to the monastery. Most of them are from women who want children. The monastery is associated with fertility."

He saw her pause, her fingers twisting around a ribbon, clutching it for a moment before she released it and continued walking.

Malachi saw the quick crease between her eyebrows, and his fingers ached to smooth it.

"Do you want children, Ava?"

She glanced at him, surprised. "None of your business."

"You're right." He swallowed back a frustrated curse and kept walking. "It is none of my business. I apologize."

"It doesn't matter. I won't have them." Her voice was soft, but he caught the words muttered under her breath anyway.

He stopped, turned. "Is it because of your health? Your... headaches?"

"We're not talking about my headaches," she said with a glare before she marched off the path and into a stand of trees.

Malachi watched her, confused for a second before he followed. "Ava, where are you going?"

She was still walking, ducking under low branches as they walked over the forest floor covered with pine needles. He could barely hear her steps as she headed even farther off the path, toward a rocky outcropping that overlooked a desolate beach.

"Ava!"

She stopped. Turned. And pointed a gun at his chest.

"Why don't you stop lying now, Malachi?" she asked softly, her voice chilling him to the bone. "And start telling me the truth about your 'organization' and who really hired you?"

Slowly, he brought his hands together in front of his body, subtly tracing the *talesm prim* on his wrist. The old spells took hold, covering him with magic. "I can explain."

"Good. Start talking."

"Please put the gun down." He was more concerned about her injuring herself or some random hiker than he was himself. "Ava, please put the gun—"

"You are not ordering me around, Malachi." Her hands didn't tremble on the weapon. She stood in a ready stance, obviously well-acquainted with the weapon. "You're not being honest with me. I can tell when you're lying."

"Really?" he stepped closer. "And how do you know that, Ava?"

"I just do." Her eyes were cold. Nothing remained of the teasing, friendly woman he'd come to know.

"Ava, please," he repeated her name again softly. "Put the gun down. Do you really think I would hurt you?"

For the first time all day, he saw her expression crack. "I don't know what to think."

"I have been with you for over two weeks. If I wanted to hurt you—"

"Who hired you, Malachi?"

"—I could have done it. But I won't, because I don't want that."

"Just tell me who you're working for."

He took another step closer, holding his hands out. "You don't understand."

"No, I don't!" Her voice rose. "Why don't you take this opportunity to explain it to me? That seems like a good idea when I have a gun pointed at your chest!"

"Please, Ava—"

"Stop saying my name like that!" Tears gathered at the corner of her eyes. "You're a liar. And I trusted you."

He shook his head. "I would *never* hurt you."

"You already have!"

"Ava, put the gun down."

"Just tell me what is going on!"

"Don't you understand I can't!" he shouted, then muttered a frustrated curse under his breath.

As soon as the words left him, her mouth dropped open. Ava froze. The hand holding the gun sank and the weapon fell with a soft thud on the pine needles. Malachi dove for it, grabbing it to put the safety on, only to realize it had been on safety the whole time.

"Ava, what on earth——?"

"What did you just say?" she whispered.

"I said *what on earth*——"

"Before." She was taking rapid breaths. He looked up from the gun. Her eyes were panicked; she was reaching for him. He had to back away. "What did you say before, Malachi?"

He shook his head. "What?"

"Before!" she shouted with a choked sob. "What was it? Please!"

She looked ready to collapse. She was trembling, tears rolling down her face, and he didn't know what to do.

"Ava, I don't understand what you're asking."

"Please." Her face crumbled. "Just tell me what language it was. I heard you. Just... just tell me I'm not crazy."

Malachi wanted to grab her. Calm her, but he couldn't. She was wearing nothing but a tank top. She'd taken off her long-sleeved shirt halfway up the mountain. And his touch would hurt her. No matter how much he wanted, he would never ——*could* never...

He finally registered what she'd said.

Tell me what language it was.

He'd cursed in the Old Language. Most people never even noticed.

Her eyes pleaded with him, and her shoulders shook. "Tell me I'm not crazy, Malachi."

"Ava, did you..." He drew in a quick breath as the pieces began to fall into place.

The headaches. Her nervousness in crowds. His instincts had warned him, but everyone said it wasn't possible.

'I heard you...'

Malachi shook his head.

Defeat washed across her face. "Please... I've heard it for so long." She fell to her knees. "I just need to know——"

"What language are you talking about, Ava?" He knelt

cautiously next to her, still stunned. Ava shook her head, eyes glassy and dazed.

"My whole life…" She wrapped her arms around herself. "They called me crazy. And now I'm imagining it out loud. I *am*—"

"This language?" he asked softly, whispering in the ancient tongue of the angels. "Ava, is this the language you're talking about?"

She gasped and clutched the front of his shirt. "Malachi?"

He continued in soft words he knew she couldn't understand. "Where have you heard this, beautiful one?" Malachi lifted trembling fingers to a curl of her hair, then he asked in English again. "Where have you heard this, Ava?"

She clutched his shirt tighter. "Everywhere," she choked out. "I hear it everywhere!"

He shook his head, disbelieving. "It can't be."

"Every person. All over the world. I hear them, Malachi. In my head. The same language, over and over." Her tears kept falling, and she wouldn't let go of his shirt, almost as if she was afraid he would run. "I'm crazy. I know it. I told myself if I could just figure out what they were saying, it would make sense, but—"

"You're not crazy." Malachi lifted a tentative hand to her cheek. *He had to know.* "You're not crazy, Ava, you're—"

He broke off when she leaned her face into his hand, resting her cheek against his frozen palm.

Ava whispered, "You make the voices go away." Then she closed her eyes, let out a soft breath, and Malachi *felt* her.

The rush of energy filled him, lifted him. His heart raced as the force of it elevated him. Malachi lifted his other hand to her neck, tracing the ancient letters over her skin, watching as the faint golden glow illuminated in the shadow of the pines. A choked laugh bubbled up in his throat and Ava's eyes flickered open. His hand traced lower, brushing over her bare shoulder, down her arm, and everywhere his hand went, her skin gave off a faint, shimmering gold.

"You're not crazy." He couldn't tear his eyes away from his fingers touching—actually touching—her. "You're not crazy, Ava. You're… a miracle."

"I don't know what's happening," she whispered.

"I don't know, either." The contact was intoxicating. Malachi trailed his hand up her arm again, finally cupping her face in both hands.

"Malachi?" The frown was back, but this time, he let his finger smooth away the line between her eyebrows.

"*Irina,*" he breathed out, then his lips lowered to hers. The first brush of his kiss was soft and testing. Reverent. But Ava didn't faint. She leaned closer, and Malachi was lost.

His hand slid around to the nape of her neck to hold her as he let himself linger at her mouth. His other hand slid down her arm and around her waist, pressing her closer as he deepened the kiss. Her mouth moved against his, searching. Then he felt her hands.

He pulled away, groaning, "*Yes.*"

Her hands came around his neck, fingers lacing together as she held him against her. Malachi's mouth fell to her neck, pressing kisses against the soft skin there as she laid her cheek against his and held him close.

"Closer," he murmured. "More."

She left one hand at his neck and brought the other to his cheek, stroking the rough skin there. "Malachi?"

"Touch me, Ava." He kissed up her neck and over her jaw, searching for her mouth. "*Please.* It's been so long."

His rough hand stroked the small of her back, over her shirt, then he let a finger slide under the edge. She didn't faint. Didn't grow weak. Instead, the energy he felt from her seemed to surge wherever their skin touched. He slid his hand under her shirt, pressing it full against the small of her back as Ava let out a breathy moan.

"So good…"

He captured her mouth again, his tongue tracing along her lips until she opened to him. He slid closer. Tongues and lips. Her teeth scraped against his lower lip.

More.

More.

Her mouth was as eager as his when she pressed closer, gripping the hair at the nape of his neck as they knelt under the trees. Her knees buckled and he laid her down on the soft bed of needles, rolling on his side and bringing her with him, never breaking her glorious hold.

"Ava, Ava, Ava," he whispered against her lips. He let one hand trail down her arm, tracing along her skin, feeling the rush of magic that followed. "You're a miracle."

"I don't know what you're talking about, but don't stop."

"I can't stop. I don't want to ever stop."

Her hands were brushing over his cheeks again, her fingernails scraping against the stubble. He'd forgotten to shave that morning. Usually he never thought about it, but he did now. He wanted nothing between her skin and his. He let the hand at the small of her back rise, fingers trailing up her spine as she pulled away and arched her back with a moan. He kissed her neck. Her shoulder. The delicate skin over her collarbone.

"Ava, wait…" He groaned. "We have to stop. I don't want to, but——"

"No." She was trembling in his arms. "More."

"This is——"

Just then, she let out a shudder that racked her whole body. Malachi felt her heave a great sigh, then she stilled, going limp in his arms. He pulled away, panicked for a moment until he saw the deep breaths she was taking. He put his ear to her chest; her heart was strong and steady. There was a peaceful smile on her face. He gently laid her back on the bed of pine needles and pulled off his shirt, tucking it under her head. Then he lay on his side and stared at her.

Malachi brushed tentative fingers over her arm, still disbelieving what he saw with his own eyes. The gold glow was there, if anything, brighter than it had been at first. He scrolled letters over her, brushing spells across her skin to aid in rest and health. To give her peace of mind and sweet dreams. The breeze swept over them both as they rested in the dappled shade that overlooked the sea.

Ava rested, and Malachi watched.

A miracle.

A mystery.

Malachi hadn't seen one in over two hundred years.

Irina.

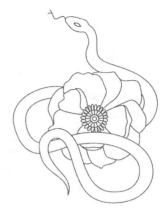

CHAPTER
EIGHT

A va woke slowly. Her eyes were stiff and heavy with exhaustion like she'd never known before. She stretched her legs, moving languidly in the cool sheets that smelled of lemon and... Malachi?

She forced her eyes open, blinking as she looked around. Early morning sun spilled across the sheets, crisscrossed by shadows from the wooden blinds. She was alone in the room, but it wasn't hers. A thousand mornings waking in foreign rooms had trained her. Her bag would be in one corner. Her phone by the bed. Shoes set by the door.

This room was not hers.

It was dominated by a wall of bookcases. On the bookcases were volumes of paperbacks, hardcovers, and more. Intricate, leather-bound tomes. Books in boxes. Even a few scrolls. And the walls that didn't have books had art. It was a small room, narrow and long, but packed with traces of its owner.

It was Malachi's room. It had his smell. Even more, there was a certain odd balance and masculinity to it that reminded her of him. Simple and bold at the same time. At the foot of the bed, Ava noticed some books had been pulled out. She crawled that direction, unwinding the sheet that covered her.

How had she gotten here?

She searched her memories, but they were fuzzy. Her whole head was fuzzy, an odd feeling for her, though not entirely unpleasant. Usually, Ava woke restless. She rose with the feeling that she was already behind in… something. Some task had escaped her. Some memory forgotten. If she was in a hotel, early morning voices whispered to her, almost always in a hurry.

Rush rush rush.

Mornings for Ava were manic.

But this morning…

She took a deep breath and leaned against the wall where the large bed had been pushed and looked around again. The room almost reminded her of a dorm room. A small desk was in one corner with a computer on top. Packing boxes were stacked in another. She saw a narrow door she suspected was a closet.

Or a bathroom.

She jumped up and ran to it, disappointed when she saw all the clothes. Luckily, another glance to the right revealed a narrow door open to a sliver of a sink. With a sigh of relief, Ava walked in and took care of her most urgent concern, looking around for a moment as she sat.

If this was Malachi's room—and she was almost certain it was—how did his shoulders fit through that door? Did he walk sideways into his own bathroom? And that shower was ridiculous. Did he crouch in it? His scent was stronger in the bathroom. As she was washing up, she picked up a bar of soap.

Yep, definitely Malachi.

"Think, Ava." Her voice was rasping and hoarse. She needed water. There'd been some in the backpack she took to the island…

"The island." She met her own surprised gaze in the mirror. "We were on the island."

The island. The mountain. The monastery.

The *gun.*

She groaned. Leave it to Carl to send her a .45. He knew

she was more accurate with a 9mm. Still, when one was sending contraband handguns to one's stepdaughter in Turkey, Ava supposed one couldn't be too picky. And leave it to Malachi to be more concerned than frightened when he saw it.

She walked back out to the bedroom, head still a little fuzzy.

What was she doing in Malachi's room? How had he gotten her there? The whole time between the hike and waking was a blur. They'd been hiking to the monastery. Ava had confronted Malachi with the gun.

And then…

The memory rang clear as the morning light.

Where have you heard this, Ava?

She almost ran into the door.

Malachi had spoken it! Her unknown language. Only a brief mutter at first, but her mind had latched on to it. Then more. He had spoken the words that haunted her. Not a whispered cadence. His voice had been real, and Ava had…

Well, she'd completely freaked out.

Where have you heard this, Ava?

He'd spoken it. Not in a whispered jumble. Not in a stutter or a whisper as she'd often tried. He'd spoken it like a native.

Malachi knew what her language was.

You're not crazy. You're a miracle.

A miracle of what? She closed her eyes and flushed at the memory of his kiss. More than a kiss. It had been *more*. Right and whole and real and true. Like the realization she'd had at the bar, it struck her soul-deep. Malachi was made to kiss her, and she was made to kiss him. He'd kissed her on the edge of that mountain like it was his purpose in life, and a small hopeful voice whispered to Ava that perhaps it was true.

She looked at the door, knowing that somewhere on the other side, she'd find him. She'd find Malachi, and he'd be able to answer her questions. Questions that had plagued her for twenty-eight years. And Ava had to admit the idea of finding answers was almost as frightening as the unknown. She sat down on the edge of the bed with trembling knees.

"Get a grip, Ava." She clenched her eyes shut and commanded her heart to stop racing. "Focus."

Irina, he'd whispered.

"Who is Irina?"

The sunlight flowed through the window, illuminating a book open at the end of the bed. There was a chest there with more books, but one was open, and Ava moved closer, drawn to the gold-trimmed page that glowed in the slanting light.

It was a manuscript. A very well-preserved one. The illuminations marked it as medieval, but the writing wasn't like any she'd seen before. Ava had studied enough foreign languages and religions to know it was probably Middle Eastern. Something about it reminded her of Hebrew, but it wasn't. It was older. Simpler. Not hieroglyphics. A simple alphabet that could be carved as easily as written, she was guessing. It had shades of both Hebrew and Arabic but was neither. Phoenician? And what was it doing combined with what looked like Medieval European illustrations?

The art next to the script was exquisite. It was a picture of a couple embracing. The man's upper body was covered in strange, silver tattoos, and his face was a picture of ecstasy. The woman held him, her body also covered in the same marks, but the artist had used gold to draw hers. They twined together, two halves of one whole. Everything about them spoke of completion.

She closed the book and looked at the binding. It was old, but well oiled. The book, whatever language it had been written in, was exquisitely preserved. There were marks in the corners of the vellum and a few pages had been torn at the corner. This was not a museum piece. It had been treasured but used. Finally, she opened it at the beginning.

The first thing she saw was an intricate page of illuminated letters in the unknown language. Text only. Then, there were pictures of men with glowing faces and white robes. Beautiful women embraced them. Ava continued to turn the pages, not understanding the writing, but looking for the story the pictures told. Children were born. The figures showed both joy and sorrow. Then the men with glowing faces left, the women's arms held out to them in supplication. There were more pictures of children. Pictures of young men building what looked like temples. Houses? More men copying books and building fires. Writing on walls. A room full of scrolls. A library?

There were pictures of women. Breathtakingly beautiful and detailed, the pictures of the women were wrought with infinite delicacy and vivid color. Women holding children. Women putting hands on the sick. Overseeing a building project. Tending and drying flowers. A woman standing in front of an assembly, who looked like she was singing. The faces of the audience, each rendered in detail, exhibited awe.

Ava paged through the book, questions flying through her mind until she got to the last page again. The page with the couple embracing. Tears had come to her eyes. Who were these people? And why had this been out for her to find?

From beyond the closed door, she heard voices. For a moment, it didn't register. She was so used to hearing it, Ava hardly noticed. But then, she did. She put the book down carefully and walked to the door.

There it was again. It was real. Low male voices spoke in the language she'd heard from her youth. Not whispers. Not murmurs. They were actually *speaking* it. Out loud.

"I'm not crazy," she whispered with a smile. "I'm really not."

Ava cracked the door open and peeked out. Malachi's bedroom was at the end of a dark hallway, and she could see stairs leading down. The room below glowed with morning light, and that was where the voices came from.

"Don't chicken out now, Ava." She patted her cheeks and

left the room, walking slowly toward the stairs. The voices began to rise, and she paused.

They were arguing.

She heard Malachi and another man arguing. Another, calmer voice occasionally chimed in, but mostly she heard Malachi.

Beautiful. Rise and fall. The cadence of his voice in the unknown language drew her closer. She reached the stairs and started down. No one halted the argument as she walked. When she reached the bottom, she realized she was in a large open living area with couches and tables. There was even a flat-screen television surrounded by chairs in one corner, but the voices were coming from a room off the main one, a room with a door half open.

Ava walked toward it. The arguing was getting even more intense, but she told herself to be brave. She had to know what was going on. Where the hell was she? Who did they work for? She was assuming she wasn't a hostage or prisoner, because she could see the front door from where she stood. No one guarded it. No alarms were going off. There was only intense arguing coming from unknown voices. She took a deep breath and walked in.

As soon as she stepped through the doorway, everything stopped. The arguing. Any and all movement. It was as if they had frozen.

She waited for someone to break the silence before she finally lifted a hand. "Hey."

There were five men. Five very large men. She recognized Leo in the corner as he lifted a hand and smiled. Ava smiled back, relieved that someone was acting friendly. There was another man next to him who looked like he could be his brother, but his mouth only gaped in shock. Ava's eyes swept the frozen room. Sitting at a desk, a tall, lanky man with black hair and very pale skin watched her with cautious green eyes. He didn't smile, but he didn't glare, either. And across the room, which appeared to be a library, Malachi stood with another man, braced for a fight.

The other man was even bigger than Malachi, almost a giant. His hair came down to his shoulders, but she could only see his back and bare arms, arms that were covered in the same intricate tattoos she'd seen in the book.

"Oh! The… the men. The ones in the manuscript? They have the same tattoos!"

Ava looked for Malachi, her eyes alight with curiosity, only to realize that—for the first time—his own arms were bare. He'd always worn long sleeves. Always. But he didn't now, and the intricate tattoo work that she knew started at his collar crawled down his arms, covering his forearms and biceps. The words were scrawled at odd angles, like they'd been added and crowded into every available inch of skin. She looked at Leo. To the black-haired man.

"Holy shit, you all have them. Just like the men in the book."

The giant threw up his arms and yelled, "I can't believe you showed her one of the books, too!"

Malachi said, "Damien, she has to know."

"Does secrecy mean nothing to you? Does the safety of our race—"

"She's part of it!"

"She can't be! We've searched the records. We know where she was born. We know who her mother is. There is no trace of—"

"Forget the records and look at her!" Malachi strode over to Ava, who stepped back. He slowed and held up his hands. "Please, Ava. I have to show them."

She gulped. "Show them what?"

"What are you doing?" The green-eyed man's voice was concerned. "Malachi, you mustn't—"

"Trust me," Malachi whispered, meeting her eyes. Ava felt instantly secure, warm and safe, despite the strangers surrounding her. Their inner voices, all alive since she'd walked into the room, were practically shouting now. "I won't hurt you."

"I know," she said. "I know you won't."

The green-eyed man rose to his feet as his hands reached out. "Malachi!"

Malachi stepped behind her, wrapping one arm around her waist as the giant named Damien yelled, "No!" He lunged toward Ava and Malachi, but before he could reach them, he halted, and his eyes went wide with shock.

She felt Malachi's finger trace along her collarbone and she shivered at the sensation. His finger moved up and down along her exposed skin. Was he writing? Her eyes were glued to the reactions of the men around her. Damien, who had been lunging toward them, fell to his knees, suddenly staring up at Ava with a wild expression of awe. The green-eyed man was just as shocked, his mouth frozen in an *O*. Leo and the other blond man grinned in the corner, expressions of sheer joy across both of their faces.

"You see?" Malachi pleaded. "It's true. She does not faint at my touch."

She might not faint, but swooning was a definite possibility if he kept drawing on her skin like that. It felt amazing and oddly intimate. She blushed furiously, aware of all the eyes on them as Malachi held her.

"Malachi, you have to…" She tried to push his arm away, but he wouldn't let go of her. He did, however, stop writing on her skin. She felt his mouth at her ear.

"I'm sorry. I didn't mean to embarrass you."

"It's fine," she whispered as his hand moved down her arm again. She glanced down to see his heavily marked forearm still around her waist, holding her up. His other arm lay against hers, and his finger was trailing… She blinked rapidly. "Holy shit, there are gold letters all over my arm."

Then everything went black.

WHEN SHE WOKE UP THIS TIME, AFTERNOON SUN SHONE ON THE red roofs outside the window, and Malachi sat on the edge of the bed, a cool washcloth pressed to her forehead. In the chair by the desk, Damien also sat, unabashedly staring. Ava pushed Malachi's hand away and sat up.

"What happened?"

"You fainted." Malachi smiled. "And Damien was convinced that I'd killed you until I picked you up and showed him how deeply you were breathing. Are you all right?"

"Why would you have killed me? And where am I?"

Damien spoke from the corner. "You are in the Irin scribe house of Istanbul, Ava Matheson. And my brother's touch would have eventually killed you... if you were human. But you're not entirely human, are you?"

She blinked and rubbed her eyes. "What are you talking about? Of course I'm human." She turned to Malachi. "And so are..."

You...?

She couldn't say it, because in that moment, Ava knew it wasn't true. Not entirely. The book. The strange tattoos. The language.

"Are you people aliens?" she whispered.

Malachi burst out laughing, and Damien rolled his eyes.

"What?" She was indignant. "What am I supposed to think?"

"Not aliens!"

"Well, I'm glad this is so funny to you, Mal. I'm just rolling with laughter here."

Damien said, "We are not aliens, Ms. Matheson."

"So, what are you?" She pulled her legs up and wrapped her arms around them.

Malachi smiled and put his hand on her bare foot. "We are the Irin. The heavenly race."

"What are you talking about?"

"Do you know history?" Damien asked. "Think about human myths and legends. Genesis. The Book of Enoch. The heroes of Greek myth. You have written about us; you just never knew the whole story. Haven't you heard the myths of those who fell from heaven? Of their offspring?"

"Fell from heaven?" she asked. "You're talking about... angels? Fallen *angels*?"

"Of course."

Her temper snapped. "Nothing is 'of course' about this situation!"

Damien said, "Please calm down, Ms. Matheson. We are trying to explain."

"But you're talking about *angels*."

"Yes."

"Actual angels. From heaven. Coming down and—and sleeping with human women?"

Malachi said, "Angels don't sleep. But if you're referring to sexual relations, yes. The Fallen took human women as mates."

She turned to him. "And you're telling me that you and your... whatever you all are would be their... what? Their sons? Is that what you're trying to get me to believe? That you're the sons of *angels*?"

"Not only the sons." Damien looked offended. "What would that have to do with you, then?"

She frowned. "What are you—?"

"Did you think the angels only had *sons*?"

All the air left her lungs. Ava's eyes were locked with Damien's, but she felt Malachi reach for her.

"Ava, we are the Irin people. We are the descendants of those first children. We are the sons... and *daughters* of angels."

"Daughters?" She looked back to Malachi as his thumb brushed her cheek. "Of angels? You must be—"

"Crazy?" he said quietly. "Is that what you think? Truly?"

"I don't know." She didn't know. Their words made no sense, and yet there was no hint of deception in them. No waver in their silent voices told her to guard from harm.

Malachi asked gently, "Did the humans call you crazy, Ava?"

"Of course they did."

She could tell the knowledge pained him, but he kept his hand on her foot. His fingers on her cheek. Gentle and constant, his touch soothed her.

Damien asked, "Malachi says you hear voices. Is that correct?"

She shrank back. "Yes."

"In the Old Language," Damien mused. "If this is true, then you hear as the Irina do."

"What does that mean?"

"The Irina hear the voice of the soul. It is one of their gifts."

Her chest was tight. She swallowed the lump in her throat. "I don't understand what that means. How can the soul have a voice?"

"How can it not?"

"I don't understand any of this." She was overwhelmed. Part of her wanted to keep firing questions, and the other part wanted to run away.

As if sensing her panic, Malachi grasped her hand in both of his. "We are all confused. None of us understands how this happened, Ava."

"I don't even know——"

"Know this: I believe you are one of us." His grey eyes met hers. They burned with passion. "I know it. We will find the answers. We will help you."

She nodded, keeping her eyes on his. Even if nothing else made sense, some instinctive part of her trusted Malachi. Through all of this, he had watched out for her. He grounded her with his utter and complete confidence. She allowed herself to take a deep breath.

"Okay?" he asked.

"Okay."

"Malachi speaks the truth as he believes it," Damien bit out. "I am not convinced. We know your mother is not one of us."

"My mom?" She looked between Malachi and Damien in confusion. "What about my mom? What do you know about my mom?"

"You look just like your mother," Damien said. "Almost exactly."

"Yeah, so?" She was starting to get irritated. "And how did you get pictures of my mom?"

Damien turned from her and spoke to Malachi. "Irina only come from Irina."

"That's what we've always been told."

Ava asked, "So why do you think I'm one of these Irina?"

Both men ignored her and continued to argue in low voices.

Malachi said, "She's reacting like the Irina. She hears the soul-voice. She can bear our touch. Judging from the color in her face, she even seems to thrive on it."

"It's not enough. We need to know how this could happen. Admittedly, she looks healthier than she did when she first came here, but—"

"What do you mean, 'when I first came here?' Who all was following me?" As irritated as she was, Ava had to admit she did feel great. Malachi was holding her hand and she felt calm. He was like the medication she'd tried once, but without the awful side effects. Holding his hand muffled Damien's inner voice, making it easier for her to concentrate. She felt centered and easy. Relaxed. Her head was clear, and she was starting to remember more about the day.

"She can't go back to the hotel," Damien said. "She has to stay here. Stay protected."

"Hello?" Her voice rose. "I am still in the room."

"The Grigori still followed her yesterday?"

"Leo and I lost them on the way back from the islands,

but—"

She squeezed Malachi's hand, trying to get his attention. "Who the hell are the Grigori, and why are they—" Her eyes widened. "Shit."

That one word was enough to silence the two irritating men. Damien asked, "What?"

"How long was I sleeping? After we..." She glanced at Malachi. "You know."

Malachi ignored her embarrassed flush. "I carried you back from the island yesterday afternoon. I thought you'd wake up after a while, but I think I underestimated your exhaustion."

"So I've been out of contact for over a day?" Ava pushed his hand away and scooted to the edge of the bed. "Where's my phone? I have to call my mom and let her know I'm not dead, or she and Carl will be sending out the commandos."

Malachi went to his desk and opened a drawer. "So you *did* call them the other night. Is that where you got the gun?"

"Carl sent it." Ava glanced at Damien, who was watching her like she was some curious animal at the zoo. "I..." She sighed. "I don't know what to tell her. Last I talked to them, I was convinced you guys were part of some international conspiracy to kidnap me."

Damien murmured, "You might not be far off."

"What does that mean? Does this have something to do with the Grigori guys you were talking about? What's a Grigori?"

Malachi handed her the phone. "There are others related to our kind who are after you. We're not sure why, but it cannot be good."

"Supernatural bad guys? Of course there are supernatural bad guys." She threw up her hands. "I mean, you don't get superheroes without supervillains, right?"

"I wouldn't call them super," Damien said with a frown. "But they do have an interest in you." He rose. "I need to call Vienna. Malachi, can I see you in the hall for a moment?"

Malachi glanced at Damien, then back to her. "I'll be right

back."

"And I'll call my mom." She waved her phone. "I guess I'll tell her... something."

By the time Malachi returned to the room, Ava had ended the call with her mother after spinning a very elaborate story about Malachi and the old bodyguard miscommunicating. About how, really, it had all been a huge misunderstanding, and Ava was fine, and it had all worked out for the best.

Because she and Malachi were now involved in a whirlwind romance.

If there was anything that could distract Lena Matheson, it was speculating about her daughter's love life. Plus, Ava figured that it would keep her mom from calling too often if she was daydreaming about the nonexistent grandchildren Ava might someday give her when she found "the right man."

She had the book open again, staring at the entwined couple, tracing the edges of the page and remembering the way that Malachi's touch had lit her skin from within.

"Ava?" His voice was soft and solemn.

"Hey."

"How is your mother?"

"Happy, actually. I convinced her that it was all a misunderstanding, and we're now involved in a torrid affair. That'll distract her." She kept her eyes on the book. Now that they were alone, she didn't know how to act around him. She craved his touch, but the craving put her on edge. Was it natural? Normal? If he was really part of some supernatural race, could he make her feel things she wouldn't otherwise feel? Her heart told her Malachi was trustworthy, but a lifetime of rejection warned her to be cautious.

Malachi said, "That would have distracted my mother, too."

There was a strange sort of sadness in his tone. A tone that told her, somehow, in the moments they'd been apart, something delicate had shifted. He stood a little farther back, and a shadow tinged his voice.

"Your mom..." She lifted the corner of the page and tried to pretend the shadow wasn't there. "She's..."

"She was Irina. Our women are called Irina."

"Ah. And you think I'm one of them." Her finger trailed lightly over the gold leaf on the woman's skin, illuminated just as hers had been when Malachi touched her.

"I think you have to be."

"You think I'm part... angel?"

"It's slightly more complicated than that, but yes." He brought a chair over and sat across from her.

"My stepdad would disagree strongly with that."

"It's not what humans think."

"But you think I'm like you." She pointed to the woman in the book. "Like her?"

"I do."

She paged through the book a bit more but kept coming back to the picture of the couple he'd left the book open to at first.

Malachi said, "You're taking this all rather well. No running and screaming. Part of me expected you to be on a plane back to Los Angeles by now."

"You have to remember"—she closed the book and let out a rueful laugh—"you're talking to a woman who's heard strange voices from people's heads her whole life, remember? I don't think you can classify me as a skeptic."

"I suppose that's true. So you believe us?"

"Sort of. Kind of. There's a lot I don't understand."

She heard him shift in his seat, but he didn't come closer. "Then we will help you find the answers."

"Is that why you kissed me?" she asked quietly. "Because you wanted to know if I was like them?"

He paused. "Partly."

"Of course." Ava nodded. "That makes sense."

Malachi said nothing, and Ava refused to look up. She just stared at the couple. A perfect balance of male and female. Perfect longing. Perfect love. She ached for something always out of reach. She'd thought she felt a hint of it with him, but maybe it was all an illusion. Malachi certainly wasn't making any grand declarations about his feelings. His arms were crossed over his chest; his eyes avoided hers. Ava itched to reach out and trace the intricate letters that were marked on his skin, taste the edge of his jaw the way she had when they kissed, but everything about his body language screamed stop, even as his silent voice coaxed her closer.

"Ava, there is a scribe house east of here, in Cappadocia. One of the oldest in existence. There are scribes there who are far older than me or even Damien. Scribes who might know how all this is happening. Understand why you have the magic you do, even though you weren't born Irina. I think there might be answers there."

"You want me to go with you."

"Yes."

"To Cappadocia?"

"Yes."

"To visit a bunch of old scribes."

He finally cracked a smile. "We're a bunch of old scribes, too. We just don't look it."

And suddenly, she was wondering just how old he was. "I'm almost afraid to ask. So, you really think there are answers there?"

"There's a greater chance of answers there than here. The library of Cappadocia has been preserved for hundreds of years. And it would also be for your safety. To get you out of the city. Damien will continue to investigate why the others are looking for you. But in the meantime, you'd be somewhere much safer."

"I don't know…"

"It's also very unusual." His tone was more coaxing. "You could visit the underground cities and churches. There is nowhere else like it on earth."

She narrowed her eyes, knowing that he was tempting her curiosity, but unable to argue against his reasoning. "I suppose… there'd be lots of time for pictures?"

"As much time as you want."

"So you and me—"

"It won't be just me," he said in a rush. "Rhys will go with us. He's our resident researcher and scholar. He's the one most familiar with our history."

"That's the black-haired guy by the computer, right?" The lanky one with the vivid green eyes.

"Rhys is also a very fierce warrior if he needs to be."

"So Rhys and you and me?"

"I know I'm asking you to trust me. Trust others you don't even know." He cleared his throat. "But I promise you have nothing to fear. You are… a miracle, Ava. Any one of us would guard you with our lives."

A memory of Malachi came to her. Rough and angry. Standing at the door of the bar with a bandage across his abdomen. Ava shivered, knowing there was far more to that story than she'd been told. "I don't want anyone hurt because of me. I'm not worth that."

"Of course you are," he said roughly. "You are Irina. We know how precious you are."

Ava took a deep breath. What were her options? Stay in Istanbul and continue seeing a psychologist for voices that never went away, or go to some place in the middle of Turkey with tattooed people she barely knew in order to research whether she was some obscure form of angel spawn.

Well, she couldn't call it a *boring* vacation.

"Okay. Why not?"

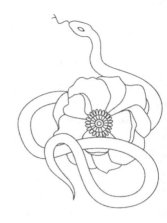

CHAPTER
NINE

Malachi was glad they had decided to drive but wished Rhys hadn't insisted Ava not be left alone in the back of the car. Because of that, he was forced to sit next to her, keeping his hands clenched tightly at his side to avoid touching her as Rhys drove. The old landscape whipped past, familiar and foreign at the same time. So much had changed since he was young.

Ava was napping across from him, and her leg slipped from her side of the Range Rover, stretching out to brush his as they bumped over the eastern roads.

His fingers itched to touch it. The memory of her skin throbbed in his mind, but so did the warning his watcher had given him.

"No, Malachi. Would you take advantage like a Grigori? She has no idea what it means to be an Irina. She has been thrown into this world."

"But—"

"We do not know what any of this means. And neither does she. Any Irina, deprived of an Irin family, would have reacted the same way."

The thought had floored him. Had he taken advantage? Were his feelings an illusion? Perhaps she would have reacted to any man's touch the same way. The memory of her lips haunted him. The memory of her skin underneath his hands was a silent torture.

"What's put you in such a bad mood?" Rhys asked from the front seat.

"Nothing."

"You're a bad liar." Rhys switched to the Old Language. "Tell me, what is wrong. Is it the woman?"

He didn't reply, because Ava shifted and her eyes fluttered open. A beautiful smile spread over her face.

"You guys have no idea how amazing that is."

"What?" Rhys asked from the front seat.

"Hearing it?" Malachi asked. "Out loud, instead of from our minds?"

She nodded, closing her eyes again as she turned her face to the sun.

"I've never understood how Irina handled that," Rhys said. "Hearing the soul of every person you meet? I'd think it would drive me mad."

Malachi smiled. "More mad than seeing the shadows of every word written on something?"

"That's different."

"Is that what you can do?" Ava asked. "You can see writing? Even if it's erased?"

"Erased. Painted over. Plastered over." Rhys glanced at Ava over his shoulder. "An Irin scribe can see beneath the layers to every word ever written. Like your gift, it's a blessing and a curse. We're graffiti experts, I tell you."

Malachi added, "It's also very useful when preserving and copying ancient documents, which is what most of us are trained for. All Irin magic is controlled and practiced through the written word."

"That's why you call yourself scribes?" she said with a smile. "I was wondering."

"Wonder no longer, my dear," Rhys said. "You may ask us anything."

"Really?" She glanced over at Malachi, but he only shrugged.

"Anything you'd like. If we don't want to answer, we won't."

"Oh, that's helpful." She sat up and brushed her hair back from her face. "Okay, my voices. You're telling me the voices I hear are actually souls."

"Yes," Rhys said. "What other explanation would you have for every person on earth speaking in the same language? Humans speak in many languages, but the soul…" Malachi saw his friend's eyes light up in the rearview mirror. "Our souls are the same. All of humanity, Irin, Irina. Even the Grigori have souls, though they're black as night."

"The Grigori are the bad guys, right? The ones who were following me before Malachi found me?"

"Yes, those are the Grigori."

"They sound scratchy."

Rhys laughed. "What? I've never heard that before."

"You Irin guys sound different than humans. Your voices are… bigger." She glanced at Malachi from the corner of her eye. "More layered, somehow. But you all—well, most of you—sound similar. And the Grigori voices sound the same, except scratchy. Like they're out of tune."

"I suppose that makes sense," Malachi said softly. "Every light casts a shadow. The Grigori are ours. We are the children of the Forgiven. They are the children of the Fallen. Our purpose is to protect humanity and preserve its knowledge. They are predators who have no purpose but to gain power for their masters and indulge their own perverse appetites."

Rhys said, "And reproduce, of course."

Ava paled. "What, really?"

"Grigori will procreate with human women, though it generally doesn't end well."

"And they were after me?" Her voice held a slight note of panic that infuriated Malachi.

"They won't get you," he said. "And they weren't acting normally with you. They were tracking you, but not attacking."

"And by attack, you mean…"

"Not rape the way you're thinking," Rhys said. "They don't have to be violent. Leo said you saw them in the bar. Is that right?"

"Yes."

"Handsome blokes, aren't they? Charming bastards, every one of them."

"They seemed a little full of themselves, if you ask me."

Rhys burst into laughter. "That's because you're not human. Grigori seduce. They don't have to attack humans. Women find them naturally appealing—well, *unnaturally* appealing, really. They go with them by choice. When a Grigori sets his sights on a human woman, she will go willingly."

"So…" Ava frowned. "I'm confused. I thought you said they attacked women. I mean, they sound like jerks, but that's not really an assault."

"It is when the women don't have a choice," Malachi said. "Human nature draws them to the Grigori, and the monsters take advantage. Is that any worse than drugging someone? To take away their free will? Take advantage of them?" He broke off when he caught Ava and Rhys's shocked stares. "It's wrong. That's all. The Grigori use women and leave them for dead most times. Most don't survive, and if they do, they become infatuated with the very thing that seduced and almost killed them."

"That's horrible!"

"Most humans legends of succubi are based on the Grigori," Rhys said with academic detachment. "If a human woman does bear a Grigori child—it happens occasionally—they're usually quite extraordinary. You can't discount angelic blood, after all."

"And are they… normal? The kids?"

"For the most part, yes. Usually very gifted in some way.

Mathematics. Music. Art. Many of the world's geniuses have Grigori blood."

"So I could have met a part-Grigori kid and not even known it?"

"Possibly," Malachi said. "The strongest magic is gone, but most would still have that inexplicable something that makes them stand out in human society. And the majority show no more evil tendencies than the average human."

Ava rolled her eyes. "Thanks so much."

Rhys said, "Hundreds, thousands of years they've been hunting in the world. Grigori blood is laced through human biology like a dark thread by now."

"I feel like I'm taking crazy pills," Ava muttered, and Malachi tried not to smile.

"You're processing all of this very well," he said quietly. "I can't imagine what you must be feeling."

Malachi saw her reach for his hand, then pull back. And he wanted—he *wanted* to grasp it. Wrap it in his own. He felt like a man starved, then given a single bite of bread. She was there. She needed his touch. If he could only—

"So if Grigori and Irin are basically the same with the bloodlines and stuff, why aren't the Irin men predators, too?"

Rhys curled his lip. "We have purpose, conscience, and discipline."

"Don't forget, Rhys." Malachi watched her. "We also have the Irina."

"The Irina," Ava said. "What you think I am?"

"Yes," Malachi said. "The Irina are our other halves. And they are stronger than human women."

Ava shrank back in her seat. "I don't have any super-strength, Mal. I think you guys are mixed up about what I am."

Rhys laughed. "Not like what you're thinking. And, for the record, the more time I spend with you, the more I agree with Malachi. You give off energy like a reactor."

"What do you mean?"

"Irina channel human energy; it's part of their own magic. And if you think about it, you've probably always had an excess. Humans would have called you nervous. Anxious. A bit jumpy and irritable."

"Maybe…"

Malachi knew from the tone of her voice that his brother had touched a nerve.

Rhys continued, "But what *humans* think is nerves or anxiety is normal for an Irina."

"You hear the souls of the world, Ava." Malachi tore his eyes from hers when she looked at him. "You absorb some of their energy. That's why crowds can be so overwhelming for you. It's inevitable."

"But *we* love it!" Rhys said. "We need it, really. Irin are only truly powerful when we're mated. Keeps us balanced. Healthy. Irin and Irina were created to work together."

They stopped at a small crossing to let a herd of sheep pass over the road. Rhys waved his hand out of the car window at the shepherd and continued driving. The terrain was slowly becoming hillier. They'd left the greener landscape near the coast and were heading inland, up the ancient Anatolian plain, not far from his own birthplace near the Sakarya River. The sun was hot, and the temperature was climbing as they drove. Rhys had been driving since they'd left the city, so it would soon be Malachi's turn. Perhaps then he could think about something other than the tempting woman next to him.

Almost as if he'd heard Malachi's thoughts, Rhys said, "I'm going to pull over and fill up. Take a turn driving?"

"Of course."

They stopped at a small petrol station outside Ankara, and Ava went in to use the restroom as Malachi filled up the car. Rhys came back from paying the shopkeeper, giving Ava an appreciative glance on the way back to the car. Malachi gritted his teeth as his friend approached.

"So, what's got you all broody, Mal?"

"Don't call me Mal."

"Only the pretty girl gets to call you that, eh?"

"Be quiet."

"I like it." Rhys snickered. "She's got your number, as the Americans say. Is that why you're in such a foul mood?"

"No."

He narrowed his perceptive green eyes. "I thought you liked this woman. She's intelligent. Funny. Obviously very attractive. What's your problem?"

"She's Irina."

"Yes." His friend nodded. "Hard to explain how, but she certainly bears the most common markers. That's a good thing for you, remember?"

"But she was raised human, Rhys."

"And?"

He lowered his voice. "She was around humans all her life. She's never... She doesn't know about Irin relationships."

"What in heaven's name are you talking about?"

"I touch her, and..." He frowned. "For the first time, she feels one of her own kind. She says I help take the voices away. I can relax her. And *I* feel... well, you can imagine how I feel."

Rhys spoke as if to a small child. "Again, the problem is...?"

"What if it's not *me*?"

A look of understanding dawned. "You mean what if she'd react to any Irin male that way?"

"Yes! If she'd been raised like us, her mother and father would have hugged her and held her. She would have had a normal childhood. Not one where she was starved for contact with her own kind for twenty-eight years. It's not fair for me to take advantage of that, Rhys. How would you react, if it were you?"

A bitter smile touched his lips. "You mean if I'd been denied the comfort and strength of a mate for two hundred years? If I had little to no hope of ever achieving the kind of connection with another Irin that my parents had? I just can't imagine,

Malachi. Who would be able to imagine that, except… oh, ninety-five percent of us?"

"You know what I'm talking about."

"And you're being ridiculous. You had feelings for this woman when you thought she was still human, you idiot. This sounds like some nonsense Damien told you." Rhys only sneered when Malachi flushed in anger. "That's right, isn't it? Damien warned you off her. Filled your head with this rubbish."

"You think he's wrong?"

"I think he *has* a mate," Rhys hissed. "Even though they rarely see each other outside their dream walks. And I think he distrusts anything and everything he doesn't understand. I also think Ava has feelings for you, and you're being a right ass toward her."

Malachi stepped back and finished with the gas pump. Ava was still in the building. "I'm trying to do the right thing."

"You think the right thing is leaving her without a friend in this crazy new reality?"

"I think she deserves to find out what all this means for herself without being influenced by what I want!"

"Truly? Well, then…" Rhys smiled. "*Excellent.*"

Malachi's eyes narrowed. "What does that mean?"

"It means the first new Irina seen in two hundred years is riding in the back seat with me all the way to Göreme, and I'm suddenly feeling much happier about the journey. Thank you."

Malachi's face fell. "You wouldn't."

"You seem to think that she might be drawn to anyone, so I might as well give her the option, my friend."

A red haze fell over his vision, but just then, Ava stepped out of the shop, carrying three bottles of water and a bag of oranges. Rhys walked over with a smile, holding out his hands for the bag.

"Here, let me hold that. That was extraordinarily thoughtful, Ava. These look delicious."

She smiled up at Rhys. "Well, I wasn't sure what you guys

like to eat, but I'm assuming it's more than milk and honey. Or whatever the myths say."

"Clever girl." He slid an arm around Ava's shoulders, guiding her back to the car. "I assure you our appetites are very similar." He opened the car door and helped her inside. "And we always appreciate sweet things."

HE WAS GOING TO KILL RHYS. SLOWLY. IN SEVENTEEN DIFFERENT ways so far, and they were only two hours past Ankara. The man talked and flirted, drawing Ava out in ways that had her confessing childhood mischief and university adventures. He asked about her travels and told her about his, making himself the hero of every confrontation, the key to every success.

Malachi was going to kill him.

He touched her casually, a brush on the arm, a bump of the knee. Ways that Malachi knew must be killing him. Like most of the Irin, Rhys hadn't had regular contact with any woman since the Rending. He must have been as ravenous for Ava's touch as Malachi had been on that hill by the monastery, but unlike Malachi, he had his control clamped down.

Malachi had been overwhelmed. Even the memory of her lips left him in a painful state of arousal, which was rather inconvenient, considering he had four more hours of driving.

He saw Rhys brush his elbow against Ava's knee as he bent down to get something from his backpack. Malachi slammed on the brakes, sending Rhys's head crashing into the front seat.

"Sorry."

Rhys straightened, rubbing his forehead, murder in his eyes and a book in hand for Ava.

"No problem. Accidents happen."

"I thought I saw a dog run across the road. False alarm."

Ava said, "Rhys, are you okay?"

"I'm fine, Ava. I'm used to Malachi's driving. It's always been quite bad."

"Here, let me take a look."

Then she put a hand on his jaw and pulled Rhys's face down toward her neck so she could see the red bump on the man's hard head. From the corner of his eye, Malachi saw Rhys's eyes close in pleasure as Ava's small fingers traced over the nonexistent wound.

"Does it hurt?"

"Only a little. Did it break the skin at all?"

"Not that I can see, but let me…" She started to run her fingers through the hair at his temple, examining it for any blood.

Eighteen. There were eighteen ways that Rhys could die.

IT WAS NIGHTTIME WHEN THEY PULLED INTO THE OLD HOUSE IN Göreme. The small Cappadocian town was ancient, dug into the soft volcanic rock of the hills. Once an Irin retreat had thrived only a few miles away, but after the Rending, when most of the Irina and the children were gone, the remaining Irin took shelter in the scribe house. They dug farther into the cliffs, scribing spells into the rock that made the compound one of the most secure places in the world. The libraries were legendary, as were the skills of the scribes who had stayed.

Ava crawled out of the car, sleepy and stumbling on unused legs. They'd driven straight through without stopping after the last break for petrol. Rhys was still snoring in the back seat.

"We're here?"

"Yes." He opened the back of the car as she leaned against it.

"Anything I can do to help?"

"It's fine. I can get most of it, and the others are expecting us." Malachi could already see the gates that guarded the compound opening. Lights began to switch on all over the side of the hill and scribes climbed down from their solitary rooms to greet the visitors. "Everyone will be out in a minute. I'm sure they'll have rooms ready for us."

"This place is amazing." She looked up at the terraces and caves that had been carved into the hill. The scribe house had been a work in progress for hundreds of years. The oldest parts were near the base where the library had been dug down into the rock, the dry Cappadocian air perfect for the preservation of manuscripts. The rest of the compound stretched up and back into the hill. A series of gardens, terraces, and decorative metal-work gave the compound a stark beauty.

Ava said, "Rhys told me the scribes here are older."

"Yes." He set some of his bags in the dust, moving them out of the way to get to hers. She would want her things so she could sleep. "Most of the scribes here came after the Rending. Many of them stopped casting the spells that prolong their life, so they are aging. More slowly than humans, but still aging."

"How old are you?"

"Biologically?" He smiled. "Around thirty. But I've lived for over four hundred years."

Her eyes were saucers. "Wow."

"And you will live as long or longer than that." He tried not to think about it. Tried not to see the gold letters forming under his fingers as they trailed down her spine to the small of her back. Tried to block out the rush of desire the image brought. "The magic is shared by Irin couples so they can age together."

"Oh."

Ava stared up at the stars, her skin pale and milky in the moonlight.

"What did I do to piss you off, Malachi?"

"Nothing," he choked out. "You didn't do anything, Ava."

"Are you sure? It seems like you're mad at me, but I don't know why."

"I'm not mad at you. I'm... trying to be your friend."

"My friend?"

"Yes." He forced a smile. "You told me once we were friends, didn't you?"

"I guess I did." She turned her eyes to him, and Malachi wondered whether those dark pools could see through him. See through to the longing inside. "I guess, I thought there was something... I was probably imagining things, right?"

He cleared his throat. "You have so much to think about. So much to consider and learn. It's not that I don't want—"

"Are we here?" Rhys yelled from the back of the Range Rover. The door creaked open and he climbed out, unfolding his long legs from their cramped position. "Oh, Ava, love, do you need help with your bags?"

Malachi bristled. "I've got them, Rhys."

"Good man." His friend slapped him on the shoulder before he grabbed his own bag and hoisted it out.

Malachi saw some Irin walking through the old gates. An elderly scribe raised a hand and waved.

"Ms. Matheson?"

Ava stepped forward and held out her hand as Malachi and Rhys stopped to watch. Watch the old scribe take her hand delicately, then more confidently, his face breaking into a huge smile. Most of the Cappadocian scribes were older, having stopped their longevity spells after the Rending, but a few of the younger men gaped at Ava as Malachi and Rhys followed her into the scribe house with the luggage.

Rhys was still groggy. Sadly, he was also talking.

"She was pressed against me in the car, Malachi. Heaven, I'd forgotten what that felt like. Just to have the weight of a woman—"

"Really!" he burst out. "Just... shut up, Rhys."

Thirty-three. There were thirty-three ways Malachi could kill him.

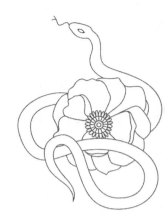

CHAPTER

TEN

He was avoiding her. It was the only explanation for the fact that Ava had been at the scribe house in Cappadocia for almost a week and had seen Malachi a grand total of two times. Fine. Whatever. If he was avoiding her, she refused to be sorry about it. She had other things to do.

For the first few days, she slept. For once in her life, sleep seemed to come easily. There was something about the inner voices of the Irin scribes that soothed her. Though none had the resonance that Malachi's did, the combined chorus of their souls blended into a soothing tapestry, almost like the white noise of ocean waves. She dreamed vivid dreams where she wandered in a dark wood. Nothing about it was frightening; it was profoundly peaceful.

Her days were spent with Rhys and the oldest scribe at the house, Evren. She'd met Evren the first night, and he seemed to take Ava under his wing. He told her he was seven hundred years old, but he looked around seventy. His dark hair was sprinkled with silver and curled at the neck. His skin was olive-toned, but pale. Ava suspected he spent most of his time among the books.

"And your mother's maiden name?" Evren asked quietly, taking notes with a pencil as Rhys typed on a computer in the library. Small windows, high in the walls, were the only bit of the outside world she saw. Like much of the oldest parts of the scribe house, the majority of the library had been dug underground into the soft volcanic rock.

"My mom was born Magdalena Russell. Lena."

"Ethnicity?"

Ava shrugged. "Honestly, I don't know. Her family has been in America for ages. I don't think I've ever heard her talk about relatives in another part of the world. I think I'm a mix of all sorts of stuff."

Evren nodded patiently, taking more notes she couldn't read. They were in the same rough script that marked his arms and the back of his hands. She could see similar markings peeking out from the collar of the loose shirt he wore. All the scribes were tattooed with what Rhys told her were spells to enhance different senses and control magic.

"You said she was from South Dakota originally. And your mother's mother?"

"Just her mom?"

Evren folded his hand in a way that reminded Ava of one of her favorite undergraduate professors. "When researching the Irina, it is the female line that is important. Irina power stems from their mother's magic. Even when tracing Irin bloodlines, we always start with the Irina. Irin scribes are the preservers of magic and knowledge, but Irina hold the creative force in our race."

"Oh. Okay, my mom's mom was Alice Cook. Her maiden name was Rutner. She was from Missouri. I think. I don't know much about her. My mom and she weren't close."

"Your mother's grandmother?"

"I think her first name was Sarah, but I'm not sure. We're not big on family history. Do you need to know about my dad?"

"Probably not." Evren smiled. "Though I'm sure that seems

backward to one used to human tradition, where male blood-lines are more thoroughly documented."

"I hadn't really thought about it, to be honest." At least they didn't need to know about her dad. Jasper's family was a total mystery.

Evren cocked his head. "Do women still take a husband's surname in America?"

"Not always, but it's pretty common. My mom did with Carl. That's why I'm legally a Matheson. He adopted me after they got married."

"Hmm."

Ava squirmed, feeling like she was under a microscope. "How about you guys? What's your last name?"

Rhys turned from the computer. "We don't have surnames in our culture."

"Isn't that confusing? I mean, you guys live a long time."

Both men chuckled.

"Well, I suppose it helps that we don't have many children," Evren said. "They're quite rare. If we were more prolific, I suppose it could be."

Rhys said, "We have our own ways of keeping track of family history." He reached down and pulled off the T-shirt he wore, then he rolled his office chair toward Ava and showed her his back, which was marked with more strange writing along with the first decorative tattoo work Ava had seen. Without thinking, she reached out and traced the intricate knot work that showed a distinct Celtic influence.

"This is beautiful." She felt his warm skin shiver underneath her fingertips, but she didn't take her hand away. Like any casual touch from one of the Irin, the contact was calming. "What is this? Is it magic, too?"

"Yes and no." Rhys cleared his throat. "The writing on my back is the only work I haven't done myself. My father did it. The names down the center are my family's. Mother first—"

"Always the mother first," Evren said. "Because we are protected by Irina magic when we are born."

Rhys continued. "Then my father's name. Then my maternal grandparents and then paternal."

"So it's like your whole family tree, written on your body. And the design?"

"From my mother." His voice was quiet. "It was her gift to me."

Evren said, "An Irin mother always designs something of beauty to add to her son's *talesm* when he leaves for his training at thirteen, then his father does the tattoo. It goes on his back, over the heart. To be matched on the front of his chest when he is mated as an adult." Then Evren's face fell a little. "Though my son has neither, as he was only a child when his mother died."

The look of sorrow on Evren's face was enough to make Ava's heart weep. His silent voice groaned at the mention of his wife as Ava waited for the words.

Vashamacanem, his soul whispered.

At least, that's what it sounded like. Ava had come to think of it as the universal mantra of the grieving. She didn't know what the phrase meant, only that she'd heard the same words from countless people around the globe. Funerals. Hospitals. It was one of the few phrases that was completely universal.

She pulled her hand away from Rhys's back and squeezed Evren's hand. "Where is your son? Does he live here, too?"

Evren squeezed her hand back and took a deep breath, forcing a smile. "He lives in Spain now. In a scribe house near Barcelona."

A young man walked into the library, staring at Ava with the tentative awe she'd come to expect from most of the men. He bent down and whispered to Evren, who nodded and turned to her.

"We will have to take more notes later, Ava. I do apologize, but there is something I must tend to this afternoon."

"Of course," she said. "Don't let me keep you."

"Is there anything you need before I go? There is an English section in the library. Not large, but there are some books about local history that might interest you."

Rhys said, "I'll show her around, Evren."

"Are you sure? I can find where Malachi—"

"I'm sure Rhys can keep me entertained." Ava said, winking at the young scribe, then turning to Rhys who offered her a mischievous smile. Evren smiled knowingly as he and the young man turned to go.

When they were alone, Rhys said, "You know, scribe houses are almost as bad as sororities when it comes to gossip."

"I'm counting on it."

"Bad, tempting woman, you are." He shook his head before he pulled on his shirt. "You're going to get me stabbed. Malachi is not a man accustomed to sharing."

"Well, then I guess he should be the one to keep me company. And you know about sororities, huh?"

"Sadly not through personal experience." Rhys grinned. "But modern movies can be quite the education."

"That was never my scene. Sorry. The popular girls don't hang out with the crazy ones very often. Unless it's to make fun of them."

"Ava, Ava," he muttered, throwing a casual arm around the back of her chair as they sat next to each other at the library table. "Don't you know you're not crazy? You're special." She felt him toying with an errant curl. "You're magic, love. Someday you'll understand how much."

A beam of light came through a high window, flooding the room with sudden light and illuminating a mural on the other side of the library. One old man sat in the far corner, staring at the beautiful scene depicting a village bustling with life. In the six days she'd spent in the library, Ava had seen the old man do nothing else. He looked to be in his eighties or nineties, though like all the Irin, she knew he must be far older. Suddenly, she knew exactly what she wanted to do.

"Rhys?"

"Hmm?" He was staring at the mural, too.

"Will you tell me about the Rending?"

"THERE'S A HUMAN SAYING: YOU DON'T KNOW WHAT YOU'VE got till it's gone. We Irin should have that tattooed on our foreheads."

Rhys led her past the mural, toward a long hall lit with candles. On the dark wall, more images flickered from a mosaic of intricate design, made with shards of glass and pieces of pottery. Bits of stone, both precious and common, interspersed with paint and cloth and plaster. It was a confusing mixture, but as Ava stepped back, the images became clearer. She said nothing, waiting for Rhys to speak.

"It happened in the early 1800s. Things had been turbulent in human years. Wars. Revolutions. Political and social uprising. But for the Irin..." He shrugged and took a step down the hallway. "It had been an oddly peaceful few decades. Time has always moved more slowly for us. We exist among humans, but separate. We had become isolated in our own communities, for the most part. The council decided it was necessary after the madness of the medieval period in Europe."

"Why?"

Rhys pointed to a section of the mosaic where a long-haired woman was laying hands on someone in a bed. "The Irina have always been healers. Before humans developed modern medicine, the Irina used their magic and their knowledge to help humanity. Herb lore. Wives' tales. Those little bits of knowledge that have passed down in human custom. Much of it came from the Irina. Sadly, many humans thought their magic was evil. Some Irina were captured and executed as witches. Their families were devastated, and their mates often took revenge, killing the ignorant who had murdered their wives. Inevitably, innocents were killed, too. The council finally made the decision to isolate families so the Irina and the children could be better protected."

"The council?"

The two had stopped near a depiction of an ominous Gothic building.

"The Irin council is in Vienna." Rhys smiled and nodded at the Gothic building. "Everyone has their politicians, don't they? They are ours. Once it was made up of seven scribes and seven singers—"

"Singers?"

"Irina." He smiled again. "Their magic is in their voice. The oldest and wisest Irina would sing—" His voice broke. "The most beautiful, powerful music you can imagine. Ethereal. Their voices *are* magic. The council was always even, but once they had decided that families needed to stay in the retreats… there was conflict. Many of the Irina felt as if they were being punished for their sisters' deaths. Many didn't want to be isolated in the retreats. Eventually, though, it settled down. The Irin and Irina who were mated—particularly those with children —would live in retreats. Irin without mates, or with mates who were in study and meditation, worked among the humans or manned the scribe houses that preserved ancient knowledge." He gestured around them. "Like this one. The Irin worked here. The retreats—small villages, really—were for families. There were also other Irina compounds where they went to train and study, but Irin weren't allowed there, so I know little of those. I was raised in a retreat in Cornwall."

"And Malachi?"

"He was born near here, actually." Rhys smiled. "Though I believe his parents moved when he was still a child and were living in Germany when the Rending happened."

"The Rending."

"Yes… the Rending." Rhys nudged her farther down the

hall as his inner voice took on a low, desperate tone. "One summer, there was a sudden rash of Grigori attacks in the cities. We learned later that it all happened within just a few weeks, but at the time, we had no idea. I was in London, about one hundred years old. I'd finished my training and was doing guardian work, as we all do. The Grigori, who had been relatively quiet for years, started attacking many human women. It was unexpected, and we couldn't keep up. We'd let our guard down." He let out a shaky breath. "My watcher followed protocol. When we needed help, we called for the mated men to come help us. They left the retreats to aid us in the city, because that was where the threat lay... we thought."

They took another step down the hall, and Ava saw the edge of chaos.

She whispered, "But they left the Irina in the retreats alone."

"Irina..." Rhys's fingers came up to trace the image of a woman, arms stretched out as dark figures ran toward her. "... have frightening magic of their own. Powerful. Deadly. But they were outnumbered, and they had to protect the children." Ava felt the tears wet her cheeks as she watched him trail his hands over the scenes of carnage the artist had rendered in frightening detail.

Bodies broken on the ground.

Homes burning.

Children's toys, bloody and abandoned.

Rhys stopped in front of the depiction of another woman, this one with a fearful gash on her throat. Rhys's finger traced down the woman's face, lingering near her neck as if to cover the wound. "Grigori will go for the throat first. If an Irina cannot speak, most of her magic is rendered mute as well. Their voices are..." Ava saw him blink away tears. "The Grigori soldiers overran retreats all over the world. The Irina protected as many children as they could, but most didn't survive. The girls, especially, were hunted."

A rushing began to fill her mind. Ava could almost hear it.

Hear the voices of the women, silenced forever. Their children, cries cut short by murder. A terrible pain began to throb in her chest.

"How many?" she whispered.

Rhys shook his head. "No one knows for certain. Thousands. It was a coordinated effort on the part of the Grigori to render us weak. They know we are most powerful when we are mated. And they have always feared the voices of the Irina. They fear magic they don't understand. So, they killed them. As many as they could, along with most of the children and the men who had stayed behind."

Ava felt the trembling start in her legs.

"The council estimates eighty percent of our women and children were wiped out within a matter of weeks in the summer of 1810. Our race was cut in half. That's why we call it the Rending."

The shaking grew. The horror was too much. The loss—barely comprehensible.

They halted at the end of the hall where a tapestry hung, woven with the same circle of Irin and Irina depicted in the book Malachi had shown her. But instead of a couple embracing, the tapestry was torn down the middle, forming a kind of curtain that Rhys pulled back.

Behind it, there were more words, written in the ancient script.

"These are names of the Irina and children from the retreat nearby," Rhys whispered. He pointed to one near the top. "This was Evren's wife."

Ava stifled a cry. Hundreds of names followed that first one. Column after column of names. Some worn smooth by fingers rubbing over them. Others sharp and jagged, as if the stone still held the anger of two hundred years.

She felt rage bubble up along with a primal grief she could barely comprehend. Words caught in her throat, and her hands clenched, her fingernails digging into her palms till she could feel the skin break and the blood run. She felt powerless. Strangled by her own pain. By Rhys's pain. By the pain lurking beneath every face she'd seen. She shook with it, knowing she was crying, but the tears weren't enough.

"Ava?" Rhys's voice seemed to come from a distance. "Ava, are you all right?"

Don't speak. Can't speak. Never speak again.

Shaking her head, Ava pulled her hair and closed her eyes. She dug her fingers into her temple, relieved by the bite of pain. Her tear-filled eyes rose to the wall of names, but there was only silence.

And Ava knew.

These *were* her people. And they were gone.

"No," she whispered.

The shivering took over, starting in her chest and spreading to her limbs. Her mind flew in a thousand directions as she closed her eyes again and rocked.

"Ava?"

She felt Rhys's hand on her shoulder. He tried to put an arm around her, but she shoved him back.

"*No!*"

"Ava, I'm sorry. I shouldn't have—"

Rhys broke off at the unexpected cry of grief that came from her throat. It was a groan. A shout. It was everything her soul didn't have the words to express. Ava leaned against the far wall, staring at the mosaic, feeling her legs start to give out. She felt locked in a pain she couldn't escape.

And then she felt him. Felt him running toward her. Heard his footsteps coming down the hall.

Closer.

"What did you do?" he shouted.

"She asked! Was I not supposed to tell her the truth?"

A shove. A punch. Ava reached out, her eyes still closed, grasping for something she couldn't name yet.

Hands met hers. Arms encircled her. And the calm followed.

The rage fled, and in its wake was a fierce grief for a thousand faces she would never know. A thousand voices she would never hear. Ava held on to Malachi and wept for a loss her mind could barely comprehend. He lifted her and took her away from the hall. Away from the flickering candles and the bloody stones. Ava closed her eyes and let him take her away.

"So many dead." She closed her eyes and whispered into his skin.

"I know."

"Women like me. They hated them. They killed them. Because they were afraid."

They were sitting in a quiet corner of the scribe house, in a room she hadn't seen before. Low lights flickered from sconces on the wall, and the room was lined with comfortable chairs and sofas. There was another mural on the wall, but this one was a picture of the sky, vividly blue against the light stone walls. Malachi was holding her on his lap, stroking her hair as she burrowed her face into his neck.

"Was your mother killed, too?"

He didn't answer for a moment. "Yes. And my father. He had remained behind at the retreat when the men in our village went to Hamburg to help the guardians. He was killed, too. Almost our entire village was wiped out. I was stationed in another city."

She fell silent again, focusing on the quiet comfort of his skin against hers. How could a people survive such a loss?

"You lost your wives. Your mothers. Your children."

"Most of us haven't even seen an Irina since the Rending." His voice held suppressed rage. "We are half a people."

"That's why you called me a miracle," she said.

She felt his arms tighten. "Nothing about your family says you can be Irina, but you *are*. We lost so many, but... I am willing to hold out hope that somehow, if you exist, then others might, too. That our race will survive. We are dying, Ava. We may live forever, but we are dying from the inside. Once there were so many of us. Families. Generations. Now there are almost no children. The Irina who still live hide away, angry with the rest of us for leaving them vulnerable. Enraged at the loss of their sisters and children. And who can blame them?"

"And the Grigori know who I am."

His arms squeezed a little tighter. "They will not get you. I will not allow it. None of us will."

She pressed her face into the skin of his neck and breathed deeply, allowing herself the comfort. Allowing herself to dream for a moment that there could be a future for her that didn't mean loneliness and isolation.

"Ava." She heard the reservation in Malachi's voice and felt him begin to draw away. She held his shoulders tightly.

"Just give me a few more minutes."

His shoulders tensed, then relaxed, and she felt his arms go around her even more tightly, pressing her into his chest as he took a deep breath. His voice was only a soft murmur in her mind, and no other intruded. Malachi began stroking her hair again, tentatively brushing his fingers along her neck and behind her ear.

He finally said, "A few more minutes."

And just like the moment in the hall, when grief and recognition slammed together, Ava knew. However it had happened, whatever strange twist of fate had caught her... these *were* her people.

And however he tried to deny it, Malachi was hers, too.

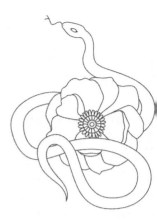

CHAPTER
ELEVEN

It was getting harder and harder to avoid her. Malachi sat
in the corner of the library, watching Rhys and Evren
interview Ava about her family again. He'd trusted his
brother to look after her, even if Rhys's behavior had irked him,
but Ava's collapse in the hallway had been unnecessary. Rhys
should have known. Irin scribes still struggled to talk about the
massacre that had taken most of their families. How did he
think Ava would react?

So Malachi was back to guarding her, this time from his own
people. He didn't know why he was so attuned to the woman,
but perhaps days of reading her expressions had given him
some insight the others didn't have. She was handling her new
reality well, but he knew she was still stressed at times. Like
when they asked her about her family...

"Listen... Yes, I have a lot of cousins on my mom's side."
Her voice was clipped, her hands clenched tight. "But no, as far
as I know, none of them hear voices. My mom doesn't hear
voices. Her mom didn't either. I don't know why you don't
understand this. There is no history of mental illness—"

"Not mental illness," he muttered from the chair at the far

end of the table, glancing up at her. "Stop calling it that. You're not mentally ill, Ava."

She rolled her eyes. "Fine. Whatever. Angel blood. Irin blood. Call it what you will. I'm the only one, okay? Lots and lots of girls all over my mom's side, and none of them hear voices. Or souls. Or whatever this is."

The rest of the world might have disappeared. Malachi and Ava glared only at each other.

"Are you always this sarcastic?" he asked.

"Are you always this taciturn?"

He picked up a book again and pretended to read.

Ava said, "I'll take that as a yes." She turned back to Evren. "Okay, next question."

Evren cleared his throat. "It seems improbable, but let's explore all genetic possibilities and look at your father's side."

"Now that could be difficult."

"Because?"

"I barely know my biological father."

Her father was a famous musician, Jasper Reed. He and Lena Matheson had never married. It was a brief relationship that only lasted until Lena became pregnant. From Malachi's research, he knew the father had stayed in the mother's life in a peripheral way, remaining friendly, but not an active part of his child's life. Malachi found little to admire about Reed, despite the human's legendary musical talent.

Children were rare to the Irin. A mated couple would probably only ever have one, possibly two, children in hundreds of years. No one knew why. Perhaps it was simply a divine trade for the unnaturally long life their race had been granted. For that reason, children were unreasonably cherished. Malachi might even say pampered, except for the rigorous magical training that started when Irin children reached the age of thirteen.

The thought of fathering a child and abandoning her was unheard of.

Evren asked questions carefully, but Malachi could tell Ava was becoming more upset. She twisted her ring in a nervous gesture, and the air around her became charged. He had the almost unbearable impulse to shove Rhys from his seat next to her so he could take her hand, just to calm her down. He quashed it. Damien's warning still rang in his ears. Ava wasn't a normal Irina who had been nurtured by a loving family. She had been subjected to the battery of human emotions her whole life. In that situation, any Irin male would be able to offer her comfort. It didn't mean she had a special bond with *him*, even if he felt drawn to her.

But...

Maybe it was more than just a normal attraction. She wouldn't let Rhys approach her when she broke down in the hallway. She'd reached for *him*. Even with her eyes closed, she'd sensed him. Almost as a mate would.

Reshon. The word had become a persistent whisper in his mind.

There had been an overwhelming feeling of comfort as he held her. Malachi knew he was soothing her, but the act of giving comfort fed his soul, as well. Not to mention the intoxicating feel of her skin against his. Then the memories of their kiss on the island—

"Shut up!"

He blinked and looked to her. Ava was glaring at him, and Malachi frowned.

"I wasn't saying anything!"

"Not out loud. But did you forget I can hear you? *You.* You're here, and all the other voices fade, and I just hear *you.* And there's this weird mix of pride and frustration and wanting —" Her voice caught. "And guilt and anger and I cannot take it anymore, Malachi. I can't deal with all this and you, so please just go."

If she had punched him in the gut, he couldn't have been as shocked.

"Ava—"

"*Go.*" He could see a sheen in her eyes. "I can't handle all your complicated shit and these questions, too. So I need you to leave."

He saw Rhys begin to rise, but one look from Malachi had the other man sinking to his seat again.

He set down the book. "Fine." He shoved back his chair and marched from the room, ignoring the voice inside that practically begged him to take her with him. He wouldn't stay where he wasn't wanted, even if everything in him said she was exactly where he belonged.

HE CALLED DAMIEN FROM THE GARDEN OUTSIDE THE SCRIBE house. Phone reception was spotty in Cappadocia, but there was a corner of one garden that seemed reliable.

"How is the woman?" his watcher asked, by way of greeting.

"Coping." He paced, frustrated and anxious for some activity after being cooped up in the scribe house for over a week. "Have you learned any more about Dr. Sadik?"

"The therapist seems to be on holiday, from what we can tell. No one is in the office, not even nurses or the receptionist. No sign on the door, either. Considering the summer months, it could be a coincidence—"

"Or it could be that his reason for remaining open left the city." Malachi drummed impatient fingers against his thigh. Part of him craved the energy of the city. Part of him knew he was only looking to escape his own temptation.

Damien said, "Tell me more about the human."

"She's not human, and you know it."

"She cannot have Irina blood. I spoke with Evren yesterday. There is no evidence from family history that she is anything but a normal human woman."

"A normal woman who can hear the voice of the soul? A normal woman who can bear our touch? Who craves it, even?"

There was silence on the other end of the phone.

"To answer the question you didn't ask...," Malachi said, "Yes, I've been keeping my distance. Even though it has been difficult."

There was still more silence.

"Rhys has been keeping an eye on her, though there was an incident where she became very upset yesterday. He told her about the Rending, and she... She became distraught, as you can imagine. I was eventually able to calm her."

"Completely understandable," Damien said quietly. "It is still upsetting for all of us."

"We have been without Irina influence for too long," he said. "We become too blunt. I don't think Rhys expected her to become so upset."

Another moment of silence, until the watcher said, "Rhys told her?"

"I told you, I have been trying to maintain my distance," he snapped. "She was curious, so she asked him."

"But you were the one to comfort her?"

"I sensed her distress."

"And she asked for you?"

"Not exactly. But she wouldn't let Rhys touch her, so... She reached for *me*. I held her until she calmed. Was I supposed to ignore her when I seemed to be the only one who could reach her? The only one who—"

Damien interrupted him with a low chuckle that grew into a longer laugh.

"What's so funny?" Malachi asked.

"You've really been staying away from her all this time?"

"Of course!"

"When have you *ever* followed my orders so precisely, brother? At most, you take them as suggestions."

"I was trying to do what was right for Ava. You told me—"

"I think you misinterpreted my advice."

Malachi stopped the drumming of his fingers. "What do you mean?"

"I only wanted you to slow down. I know how rash you can be. I advised you to give the woman space, not ignore her completely. She'd just had a huge shock, and you were hovering over her like a worried mate. But if you gave her space and she still showed interest in you, then what are you waiting for, you idiot?"

"I thought you said—"

"Do you care for the woman?" Damien asked. "That's the real question. Not just the thrill of a woman who can stand your touch, but *her*?"

Did he? Was it too soon to be feeling as strongly as he was? What did he know about Ava, really?

He knew she was intelligent and funny. She was independent. He knew that beneath the tough exterior lay a vulnerable soul, and he suspected a deeply sensuous nature. She was cautious, but unafraid of him, or any of the other scribes she had met. He remembered her, standing boldly among the Grigori, flush with wine and unafraid of the creatures she challenged. Eyes flashing with indignation. Eyes that swung to him, as Malachi saw...

Recognition.

There you are, reshon.

He'd known in that moment, but it had seemed like an impossible dream.

"Yes." He cleared his throat. "I care for her. Deeply."

"Then, Malachi, see her for the gift she is and cherish her." Damien's voice grew rough. "We know how unexpected life can be."

"You're right." He nodded, feeling a profound peace for the first time in weeks. "Thank you."

"Don't thank me yet. You've probably angered her thoroughly and will have to convince her to let you court her."

"I haven't courted an Irina in over two hundred years."

Malachi had begun pacing the garden without realizing it. Thinking of the volatile relationship between Damien and his mate, he asked, "Any advice?"

"You're asking me? My wife hasn't allowed me to see her face outside of our dreams for over ten years. Though Sari is unusually stubborn. Even for an Irina."

"Good point. Why did I listen to you in the first place?"

"I'm your superior. It's required. Now, I have to go."

"Sadik," Malachi said, remembering the reason he'd called. "I want to continue watching him. I'll ask Ava if she's called him. I think there's still something we're not seeing."

"I would agree with you. You said that his visits seemed to calm her? Release some of the tension she'd been having?"

"Yes. She always seemed calmer after a visit with him. She said he used acupressure. Nothing unusual. Mainly around the head and neck." He paused and thought. "If I didn't know any better, I'd say that she'd been in contact with—"

"An Irin."

"Yes."

"Someone siphoned off her energy enough for her to function more easily."

"It's possible."

"But he is not Irin; Leo was watching him. Following the doctor. He said he wasn't Grigori, either. Didn't appear to be anything other than a normal man."

A disturbing thought tickled the back of Malachi's mind. "Appearances can be deceiving, brother. Especially for certain beings."

"Only for…" Damien fell silent.

"Is it possible?"

"Anything is possible, as your human Irina proves. But is it probable? No."

"And yet, it seems there are all sorts of *improbable* things going on lately."

"If you're right, why? Why her?"

Malachi stopped pacing to look at the sun, setting west into the hills and painting the sky in vivid purples and reds. "She could be a miracle, Damien. The first Irina born from human bloodlines the world has ever seen. Why wouldn't she have attracted their attention?"

"It's worth looking into. If you're right, then her description, and Leo's eyes, mean nothing."

"He could be anyone."

"Not anyone... There aren't many."

"Keep me updated?"

"Of course. Keep her safe."

"I will."

BY THE TIME MALACHI MADE IT BACK INSIDE, EVREN HAD packed up his notes for the day and Rhys and Ava were chatting by the computer. Ava appeared to be checking her e-mail while Rhys read over her shoulder, laughing about something in a friendly way. Looking up, the scribe spotted Malachi coming into the library and the teasing look fell from his face. Stern grey eyes met narrowed green ones as Malachi approached. He glanced at Ava with a possessive gleam, then looked back to Rhys.

Cocking his head, the corner of Rhys's mouth lifted before he asked, "Hey, Ava?"

"Hmm?" She never turned to look at Malachi, even though he knew she must have sensed him.

"Where did you want to go for dinner tonight?"

"I don't know. You know the town better than I do."

Malachi stopped. Bastard. He'd planned on taking Ava out to dinner in the village to get her away from the scribe house, but apparently Rhys had already thought of that.

Continuing toward them, he took the seat on Ava's other side. "I'll join you. There's a place I know with a beautiful balcony I think you'd like."

Finally turning, Ava sighed. "Malachi, I don't…"

She trailed off as he picked up her right hand, casually playing with the ring on the middle finger the way he'd wanted to for weeks. It was her own nervous gesture, but he'd been fascinated with her hands every time she did it.

"Do you remember that coffee shop you liked near the Bosphorus?" he asked, continuing to play. "The owner of the restaurant is a cousin of the man who owns the coffee shop. We'll get a good table, I promise. And the food is excellent."

He didn't let go of her hand. Her cheeks flushed, and she pursed her lips as if she was holding back words.

Rhys said, "It's Friday night. Are you sure you can get a table for three?"

If Rhys wanted to tag along, Malachi could work with it. "I'm sure. Ava?"

He finally set her hand down, letting his fingers trail over hers as he drew back and crossed his arms across his chest, flexing his forearms and the intricate spells he'd worked over them. He'd seen her looking at his *talesm* many times. He knew she was fascinated by them. Her eyes grew wide before she looked away.

"Yeah, that sounds fine. Table for three?"

"Of course. I should have taken you out before. I'm sure you're tired of the kitchen here. It can be rather simple food."

"It's been fine." Her voice was a bit rough and the color on her cheeks was heightened. "Just give me a few minutes, and I'll put my stuff away. Meet you two in the garden?"

Rhys said, "Good idea."

They both watched as Ava gathered the bag with her laptop computer and left the library. When she was a suitable distance away, Rhys turned on him.

"I see someone has finally removed his head from his posterior. Congratulations. You've thoroughly pissed her off at this point. Hope you like a challenge."

He shrugged. "I've never backed away from one."

"Good." Rhys stood. "Neither have I."

"Rhys." His friend froze halfway to the door. "I'm not backing away again."

The scribe shook his head and grimaced. "You changeable bastard."

"She doesn't feel that way for you."

"How do you know?"

"Because I do." Malachi rose and walked toward him. "The same way I know she's for me."

"Are you sure about that?" Rhys's eyes met his in challenge.

"Absolutely sure."

THE THREE MET IN THE GARDEN AS THE SKY TOOK ON THE DEEP, midnight blue of the evening. It was late, but Malachi had already called the restaurant, reserving his favorite table in a corner of the balcony. They walked toward town, Ava between them, and Malachi forced himself to remain casual, even when the scent of her perfume drifted to him on the breeze. It held notes of jasmine and smoke, a sweet fragrance with hidden depths he knew would be even stronger at the curve of her neck where he had kissed her before. Kissed her neck. Her mouth. He imagined nibbling on the skin that peeked from above her waistband when she wore the green shirt he liked.

Malachi let his mind wander down sensuous paths, knowing she would hear the tone of his thoughts even if she couldn't understand them. Ava turned around, eyes wide and color high. He simply smiled before he shrugged and kept walking, letting their hands brush casually on the uneven sidewalk.

"What kind of food does this restaurant serve?" she asked, obviously trying to ignore him.

"Turkish, along with some Cappadocian dishes that are very good. There is a lamb dish I think you would like."

"I love lamb," Rhys said. "Quite the delicious fluffy animal, don't you think?"

Ava gave him a mock scowl. "Do you dine on kitten, too?"

"Only if they're prepared with the right sauce, love."

The two joked all the way to the restaurant. Malachi tried not to let it bother him, but they had obviously become familiar over the past week. It wasn't that he didn't want Ava to like Rhys. He was one of Malachi's closest friends, after all. But he also knew the look on Rhys's face, and it was one he hadn't seen in two hundred years. The Irin was infatuated with the woman. And Malachi had thrown them together.

He really was an idiot. He could only hope that his gut feeling was correct, that Ava didn't feel for Rhys the same way she felt for him. They had none of the electricity that charged the air between her and Malachi. When Ava gave Rhys's shoulder a friendly jab, Malachi tried to hide his smug expression.

The restaurant was bustling that night, but Malachi nodded to a waiter he recognized and they were shown to a private balcony looking out over the town. Low lights and candles flickered. It was an unmistakably romantic setting that he hoped would impress her.

It did.

"Oh! This is so beautiful. Look at that view!" Ava's eyes glittered with delight as the waiter held her chair for her. Rhys gave him a dirty look.

The table where they were sitting was private enough that he knew they didn't have to worry about being overheard, which let him relax as Rhys and Ava began chatting about Irin history in the region.

"You were born near here, weren't you?" Ava asked him. "I'm sure it's changed a lot over the years."

He smiled. "This area? No, but I remember visiting here with my father as a child. The cities change more, of course. Cappadocia can almost feel like a time capsule. I was born west of here. It's still a very rural area. The village where I was born in is no longer there."

Malachi thought he saw a troubled look filter across her face. He wondered if she was thinking about the Rending.

"I have many happy memories from that retreat and the one in Germany," he added, hoping to ease her mind. "Both were wonderful places to grow up."

Rhys distracted her with a joke about Malachi, and within moments, the troubled look left her face. He would have been resentful if he wasn't so grateful.

Malachi watched them at dinner, trying to discover her feelings. It was clear she liked Rhys, but Malachi was still convinced that his and Ava's connection was unique. It had to be. Even when he was young, he didn't remember being drawn to one woman the way Ava drew him. Of course, he'd had his flirtations and even a few brief relationships with suitable Irina when he'd been young, but nothing like this. He could spend hours just watching the subtle play of emotions across her face.

They'd been eating for over an hour, and the wine had brought a flush to her cheeks, and then she asked the question.

"Hey guys, I've been wondering. There's this phrase I hear repeated a lot in people's minds. It sounds kind of like... *Vasha*—"

Rhys slapped a panicked hand over her mouth as Ava's eyes widened. In the next second, it disappeared as Rhys's arm was twisted away and shoved to the side. Malachi bared his teeth as Ava gasped.

"You do not silence her. Ever."

"But the magic—"

"Never." Malachi's grip tightened around Rhys's wrist and the man winced. "Warn her if you will, but never attempt to silence her again."

"Let go of my arm," Rhys growled.

"No one is looking."

"They will be if you don't let go *now*." Rhys warned Malachi with a glare.

Malachi released him as Ava let out a breath.

"What on earth just happened?"

Rhys cleared his throat. "Forgive me, Ava. I was concerned and I overreacted." His eyes cut toward Malachi. "As did your defender."

"What did I do?"

"Nothing," Malachi said. "You asked a perfectly reasonable question."

"But you must be very careful, Ava," Rhys added, his voice dropping. "Remember that the words you hear are in the Old Language. The eternal one. It is the same language we use to cast spells. For scribes, those spells must be written down to have power. But for singers—"

"Ooooh." Her own eyes widened. "They speak them, right? So if I say something—"

"You could be performing magic you have not been trained for. Rhys is correct about that," Malachi said softly. "We start to manifest power near puberty. It is why we start training then. But for you, who has no training in magic, even repeating a simple phrase you hear from the mind of a human could be quite dangerous. You do not understand your own power yet."

He saw the curious gleam in her eye.

"But I can learn? Even though I'm older?"

Rhys and Malachi exchanged a look.

"Irina magic is always taught by other Irina," Rhys said. "What we don't know outweighs what we do. Still, there has to be a way. There are Irina in the world, though they are mostly in hiding. We will find a way to let you unlock your power, Ava. I promise."

"As do I." Their eyes met in the flickering candlelight, and Malachi had a vision of Ava, her arms spread, her voice raised in song. Magic poured from her. He imagined her voice whispering secrets in his ear, the ancient words a mate would share. The most beautiful power imaginable that bound two into one. The thought brought a rush of emotion he hoped she heard. From the flush of her cheeks, he was guessing she did.

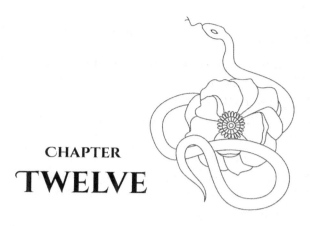

CHAPTER
TWELVE

Four days later, Ava was still thinking about Rhys's words.

We will find a way to let you unlock your power, Ava. I promise.

Power. They told her the manic energy that had stalked her wasn't illness or mania, it was power. For someone who had spent her life skirting around the edges of insanity, it was hard to fathom.

Excitable.

Emotional.

High-strung.

Hyperactive.

Troubled...

The descriptions from friends and doctors had slowly devolved as she'd gotten older. They'd gone from amusement to awkwardness. And though her mother had always cushioned the blow, Ava had known from the time she was a child that there was something different about her. Something that wasn't good. Something that made her "too much" to deal with. Carl had only confirmed it when she'd reached her teens. His constant stream of classes and camps and internships may have given her a résumé most twenty-somethings would kill for, but Ava knew it had little to do with concern. She was a problem, one he preferred to farm out.

"Evren?" She turned to the old scribe sitting across the table from her.

"Yes, my dear?"

"Would you say that I'm... normal? For an Irina?"

Evren gave her a slow smile. "But what is normal? For any man or woman?"

"You know what I mean."

"I know what you mean." He put down the pencil he'd been taking notes with and folded his hand. "You are who you were meant to be, Ava. I see nothing damaged or wrong with you. How you came to be who you are?" Evren lifted his shoulders in a helpless shrug. "Who can say? In Irin history, there is no incidence of any Irina being born in a human family. But you are here now. You are among your people. You are a wonder to us, not an oddity."

"My whole life, I've never fit in."

"Of course you haven't," he said. "I'm sure in the human world, you would stand out. Here? You are normal. You remind me very much of a girl I grew up with. She was so curious." A dimple touched Evren's cheek. "She was the favorite of our teachers in the village."

Ava was quiet for a long time, staring at the high, glowing windows of the library. When she finally spoke, she spoke softly.

"I thought I was crazy for a long time. My whole life, really. It's hard to leave that behind, even with all of you telling me that I'm not."

"Why?"

"Don't get me wrong." She shook her head. "I know it should be a relief. But there's a part of me that still doesn't believe it. A part that thinks I'm locked in a room somewhere because my delusions have finally taken over. The voices have finally won, and this is all a kind of dream that my mind is using to cope."

Evren opened his mouth, then closed it. Finally, he said, "I think…"

Pain bloomed in her knee when he kicked it under the table. Ava's mouth dropped open in shock.

"Ow! What the heck, Evren?"

He shrugged again. "That wouldn't hurt in a dream, so you're not dreaming."

She was speechless.

"What?" he asked. "You want me to come up with some deep, philosophical answer? You're not crazy. You're part of a race that is descended from the offspring of angels and human women. Is this so hard to believe? Look at your legends and myths. There are bits of truth all over. Pieces of the story that have been told for thousands of years. Wise women. Oracles. Heroes of ancient times. We've always been here. You just thought the stories were nothing more than stories. So your doctors hear you tell them about whispers, and they call you crazy. A thousand years ago, they might have called you a witch or an oracle." Evren curled his lip in disgust and turned back to his books. "Modern humans learn much, but they forget even more."

"Okay," she said. "Got it. Not crazy."

"It's insulting for you to say it."

"Cut me a little slack, will you?"

"You cripple yourself and your own power when you say this, Ava."

"I get it." She tried to turn back to her books, but then she looked up again. "So, these powers…"

"Yes?"

"How… I mean, what do I…" She frowned, unsure of what the right question was.

"What powers do you have?"

"I guess so."

Evren said, "It varies. All Irina have the capacity to speak and perform magic. Other gifts are rarer. A very few have the gift of foresight, which is directly from our angelic forefathers. Our magic expresses itself in similar ways. Some Irina spells are exactly like our own. For health and strength. Longevity. Physical or emotional strength for our mates. Others are uniquely Irina. We have no capacity for their magic."

"Like what?"

"Healing of humans. Creative spells. Much to do with the natural world that helps the plants grow or brings health to a baby in the womb. Bearing children—"

"My mom says there's nothing magical about that experience, Evren."

He chuckled. "But of course there is! Though it is not without pain. Irina have a unique talent for anything creative. Wonderful architects and artists. But their greatest magic is *listening*."

"Like the voices."

"It is not only the voices in their minds." Evren pinned her down with his stare. "There are seers, yes, but also those who hear what is unsaid. They listen and they *understand*. As we Irin are able to discern the tiniest marking on parchment, a gifted Irina hears what is said and also what is unsaid. They discern where others do not."

"Well… that makes sense."

Ava wondered if that was one of her gifts. After all, she'd always had a pretty good bullshit detector, because the inner voice, that no one else heard, couldn't lie. Sure, someone could say one thing, but the tone of their silent voice gave their true motive away. It was probably why she'd always had so few friends. It was also why she was still so confused about Malachi.

He had been quietly present ever since the night at the restaurant. She got the distinct feeling he was biding his time. For what? She had no idea. But the tone of his thoughts had taken on a decidedly heated air, even though she couldn't understand what he was saying.

And she could always hear him. Even when others were around, his voice shone through. With a little guidance from Evren, she'd begun to master control over the voices. Even casual contact with the scribes around her helped. Evren made it a point to pat her hand as they worked, and even the shyest scribe in the house, when he met her, greeted her with a warm handshake that enveloped her palm. They were quietly affectionate, all of them treating her like a treasured sister or daughter. Everyone except Rhys and Malachi.

With Rhys, it was a teasing grin, or a tug on her hair. A casual arm thrown around her shoulders as they walked to the village. A flirtatious nudge as they sat next to each other on the couch.

With Malachi, a pass in the hallway meant a shiver-inducing brush along her arm. He continued to taunt her fingers, letting his own linger when he handed her a book or sat next to her at the table. He didn't flirt with her. Didn't even speak to her much when others were around. But Malachi was always there. She could feel his eyes. She could sense his heat. Could feel his irritation every time Rhys came close.

The pressure was building, and Ava had no idea when things might boil over.

THE PHONE FELT HEAVY IN HER HAND. IT RANG AND RANG WITH no friendly secretary picking up. Finally, she heard the message for Dr. Sadik's office, but hung up. He'd given her his mobile number, so she used it. She had to tell the man something. She'd have missed two appointments by now. She hoped he hadn't worried. She'd already called her mother, and that had been bad enough. Dr. Sadik's mobile rang only twice before he picked it up.

"Hello?"

"Dr. Sadik?"

"Ava! How are you? I've been wondering what happened. I hope you are well. You've missed your appointments for two weeks. Did you go back to the States?"

"No." All of a sudden, the careful excuses she'd rehearsed flew from her mind. "I... I met some friends. We decided to travel for a while. I'm so sorry I forgot to call you."

"I'm only happy to hear you are well. I'll admit that I was worried. Where are you traveling? Are you still in Turkey?"

She took a deep breath and smiled. His calming voice always put her at ease. "I am. Traveling in Cappadocia, as a matter of fact."

"Ah. A very interesting part of the country. How do you find it?"

"Excuse me?"

"Are you enjoying yourself?"

"Yes." She saw Malachi enter the small room where she was using the landline. "Mostly."

"And your friends? Are they Turkish? From that region, perhaps?"

"Kinda."

Malachi stopped and listened for a moment, then his face became a very carefully composed mask.

Dr. Sadik said, "Pardon me?"

"Hey, Doctor, can I call you back? I'm going to return to Istanbul eventually, but I just wanted to let you know where I was and apologize for missing my appointments. If there's a charge, just let me know, okay? I really need to go." There was something wrong with Malachi. He'd gone entirely still, and he was staring at her.

"Ava, is there—"

"Really need to go." She felt her face flush. "I'm fine! I'll talk to you soon."

She hung up. Malachi stood carefully on the opposite side of the room, still staring.

"You called the doctor," he said quietly.

"Yes."

It wasn't a calm quiet.

"From the house phone."

She shrugged. "Um… yeah. What's the big—"

"The one that can be traced?"

Ava frowned. "By my psychologist?"

"We have no idea who he is, Ava."

She rolled her eyes. "Right. But I imagine he's calling the Turkish police to come raid the place right now."

"Don't make light of this."

"Yep! That Dr. Sadik, he's actually a… a spy who's into old—"

"Ava." He took a step toward her. "There is no Dr. J. Sadik operating in Istanbul."

A heavy silence filled the room, and a thread of anger uncurled in her chest.

"Of course there is. You've been to his office with me. You know, if you wanted an excuse to argue with me, how about—"

"He. Doesn't. Exist." Malachi crossed to her. "Do you understand me? He is a ghost. Rhys can find no documentation on him from Turkish medical boards. No trace of his practice. And he left his office in the city the same time we did."

A sick churning hit her stomach. "You were checking up on my psychologist?"

"Do you understand what I'm telling you? We don't even know what his connection is to your psychologist in Israel."

Her mouth dropped open. "You're unbelievable!"

"We're trying to keep you safe, as it's evident we're the only ones who—"

"Shut up!" Ava rose to her feet. "I understand there could be any number of logical explanations why a harmless man who was *helping* me might not be in Rhys's computer searches." The anger took over, begging her to slap at him for the intrusion. The doubt. For making her question everything and everyone she'd allowed herself to trust. "What I *can't* understand is why you felt you had the right to spy on me. What else have you been looking into? Checking out my trash? How about listening in on my phone calls like you did just now?"

"You're missing the point." He stepped closer.

"No, you are!" She pushed a finger in his chest. It hardly budged. "You come into my life. You lie to me. You follow me. You act like you're protecting me, then you… you kiss me!"

"Ava—"

"No! Shut up. I'm talking here, remember? You kiss me, and the next day you act like I don't even exist. You ask me to trust you, but who am I supposed to trust? You're hot and cold. You pawn me off on Rhys, and then you're mad at him when he's the only one who makes me feel slightly normal. And now? You're just *there*. All the time. And don't even get me started on what you've been thinking, because that—" She broke off when she saw a young scribe poke his head through the door. Malachi spun around and barked something in the Old Language that had the man scurrying back.

Ava snapped, "That's right, scare the nice scribe, why don't you? Jerk."

His eyes widened. "You're calling me… a *jerk*?"

"I could call you a lot worse."

"I have a few choice words myself. And everything I've done has been to protect you, so stop bitching at me."

"Bitching at you?"

"Yes, bitching. You kissed me as much as I kissed you. I backed away because I didn't want to overwhelm you, and what do you do?" He stepped closer and glared. "Rhys? After everything? Rhys! Where was he when the Grigori—"

"He's my friend!"

"He wants a hell of a lot more than friendship, *love*." The last word dropped with a sneer. "If you'd pay attention, you'd have figured that out by now."

"So what if he does? It's not like you have any claim on me. You act like you don't want anything to do with me."

"Is that what you think?" His voice fell, and he put his hand on the side of her neck. Immediately, her pulse roared. Her mind went silent. There was only him. His scent and touch. The rest of the world went quiet when his thumb stroked the base of her throat. "You really think I have no claim on you?"

She swallowed with effort; her eyes locked on the stormy grey in his. "None."

"Really, Ava?" He leaned down, his breath whispering across her cheek. "How do you feel when I touch you, *canım*?"

Her mind warred with her body. She ached to have him close the distance. Ached to feel his lips on hers again. But her protective instincts went on high alert.

Too close! Once he had her, he'd tire of her. He'd leave like the others. And if he left…

"You could be anyone," she whispered, the lie bitter on her tongue. "Any… any Irin man would feel like you."

Malachi froze. Then his head drew back and his hand left her neck. When she managed to meet his eyes, they were full of cold anger. His soul, however, whispered hurt. She said nothing, already hating herself for lying to him. No one felt like him. No one sounded like him. But she was tired of feeling jerked around, and her feelings—the depth of them—frightened her.

"I'm going for a run," he said. "We'll talk later about your Dr. Sadik. Don't call him again."

Ava was too bruised to argue. "Fine."

He left, and she was alone again.

"WHAT'S GNAWING AT YOU, LOVE?"

"Hmm?" She looked up. It was dark outside, and she and Rhys were sharing a drink in the garden. They'd eaten at the scribe house, the table a mesh of languages Ava had been able to disappear into. Turkish, English, German, the old Irin language, and a few more she hadn't recognized. Among them all, she'd felt comfortable being silent. Malachi hadn't been there. He'd disappeared in the afternoon and, as far as she knew, hadn't come back.

"Thinking about tall, dark, and brooding again?"

Annoyance flared. "My life doesn't revolve around him, you know?"

"I know it doesn't. Nor should it. So why don't you wipe the frown off your face and enjoy the wine? It's… well, it's not great. But it's not horrible, either." He smiled, a brilliant flash of white in the twilight.

"Don't tell me how to feel. I'll be annoyed if I want to."

"Oh, two hundred years was almost enough to make me forget the churlishness of an angry female." Rhys threw an arm around the back of her shoulder and leaned in. "Nothing quite like it. And all that anger sitting behind so much power? It's a wonder more Irin don't suffer from missing—"

"You talk too much." She pulled him down by the collar and kissed him. Hard. His lips were frozen in shock, and Ava released them almost immediately, pushing him back. "Sorry."

His voice was a rough growl. "Finished punishing him?"

"I said I was sorry."

"Don't be." His arm slipped lower, looping around her waist and pulling her into his chest. Then his mouth met hers in a yearning kiss. Hungry. Biting. Rhys's lips pressed against hers, and his tongue licked out, teasing along her bottom lip until she gasped. He danced along the edge of desire, his hands holding her carefully, his mouth doing wicked things to her own. After a few heated moments, he pulled away, his green eyes practically glowing in the moonlight.

"Well," he said. "That was…"

Her cheeks were flush with embarrassment. "It was definitely…"

"Fine." He sat back and his shoulders slumped a little. "It was fine."

And Ava felt exactly the same. "Totally and utterly... fine."

They both let the silence hang for a moment.

"Why wasn't it more than fine?" Rhys asked.

"It should have been. Good technique."

"Well, that's nice to hear, considering there's been a necessary lapse in practice."

She patted his thigh. "No, you're good."

"Just good?" The corner of his mouth lifted. "Maybe I should try again."

Ava couldn't stop the smile. "Please don't. It would just be weird at this point."

"Totally agree." He squeezed her shoulder.

Silence fell between them again, and Ava felt the depths of her own stupidity. Her kiss had been unfair to Rhys. Unfair to herself. Rhys was her friend. Would this change things? Would he resent her? She was mentally cataloguing her faults when she heard him speak.

"It's all right, love."

She whispered, "I wish it had been more than fine."

"I'm not him," Rhys said. "I think he'll figure it out soon. He's very bright, despite being an idiot. But he holds honor above self-interest, which is both wonderful and maddening."

"I don't know what you're talking about."

"Don't lie. We're past that now. And I'd be lying if I pretended not to know how he feels about you."

"I'm not..." She struggled to put it into words. "I'm not used to expecting happiness, Rhys. I'd probably punch it if it looked me in the face. So really, I'm as much of an idiot as he is."

"His voice sounds different to you, doesn't it?"

She blinked. "How did you know that?"

He seemed to draw away. "I didn't. Just a guess."

"What does that mean?"

A slow smile crept across his face. "I don't think I'm going to tell you. It'll be too fun to watch you find out on your own."

Pounding steps approached in the night. Malachi appeared out of the black, shirtless and dripping despite the cool evening air. His *talesm* seemed to glow when he caught sight of her, a low silver light in the darkness. He said nothing, shooting Rhys a glare as he walked past them and into the house.

"Has he kissed you?" Rhys asked when Malachi was gone.

"Yes. On the island."

"Was it more than fine?"

Her breath left her body in a rush of memories. "So much more than fine."

He nudged her shoulder with his own. "Then don't be stubborn. Go."

Fifteen minutes and another glass of wine later, Ava knocked on his door. Malachi opened it, holding a towel. He'd showered, and a few drops of water still clung to his tanned shoulders. He wore a pair of loose pants and a guarded expression.

"What do you want?"

"I kissed Rhys."

Now she knew she wasn't imagining it. The tattoos pulsed silver in the dim light of the hall. Ava forced her eyes back to Malachi's face, which was locked down tight. Only a tic in his jaw told Ava her words had even been heard.

His voice was low and thick with tension. "Get that out of your system?"

"Felt a little like kissing my brother."

He dropped the towel and tugged her into the room. "This won't."

CHAPTER
THIRTEEN

W ith one hand, he pulled her into the room, and with the other, Malachi slammed the door shut. He tugged her into his chest and captured her lips with his own. Desire roared through his body, thick with tension after two hundred years of fasting and a lifetime of waiting. For her. For Ava.

Reshon.

Malachi knew as he held her. He could feel the power pulsing through his *talesm*, the bare skin over his heart aching to be marked by Ava's magic. He could feel it singing over her skin, her touch igniting the fierce passion he'd buried for so long.

Backing Ava against the door, he curled his body over hers, bracing his arms on either side of her head, forcing her to look into his eyes.

"Do you want this? Say so now." He dangled on the edge of forever. All he needed was a word.

He saw the edges of doubt cloud her eyes, but behind it was a desperate hunger that mirrored his own. He pressed closer.

"Do you want me, Ava?"

Malachi saw her mouth form the word before he heard it. "Yes."

His control snapped.

Reaching down, he gripped her hips, lifting her against his chest as Ava wrapped her legs around his waist. A fierce possessiveness overtook him as Malachi pressed her against the wall and ravaged her mouth. He held her with one arm while the other tugged at the back of her hair, baring her neck to his kisses. He inhaled the heat of her skin as he trailed his tongue up the line of her throat, pausing to press a gentle kiss at her neck where he could feel her voice hum.

"More," she whispered.

"Yes."

"I need... Malachi—"

"I know." Groaning with desire, he swung her around and walked across the room. "Bed."

It was small, barely fitting his own tall frame, but it would have to do. He'd find more fitting accommodations later, but for now Ava was tearing at her clothes as he carried her, as desperate for contact as he was. He could feel the heat of her arms branding him. Feel the draw of energy as if touching a live wire. He lay her down and slid next to her, suddenly aware of the manic energy that hummed underneath her skin. It took everything in him to cage his own desire and think of her.

"Ava." He took a deep breath and pressed a hand over her heart, halting the fingers that were fumbling with the buttons. "Ava, wait."

She stopped, eyes narrowing. "You better not be backing out of this. If you've got some noble idea about being cautious or taking things slow—"

"Be quiet and let me undress you, woman." His low growl shocked Ava out of her anger. "I've been thinking about this for over two hundred years."

Brushing her hands away, he slipped open the first button, and Ava watched with wide eyes as he bent down and kissed the newly bare skin. A single finger trailed from her neck down, leaving a faint gold trail in its wake. Malachi traced a calming spell over her skin and felt her pulse stop racing. The urgency was still there, but as the magic took hold, the frantic energy was drawn into his own body, feeding his passion as he slowly stoked hers.

"Beautiful," he whispered, slipping another button open. His lips tasted again as he trailed another charm between her breasts. His tongue followed the gold letters that bloomed there, and Ava's back arched in silent pleasure.

"Malachi…"

"Tell me what you're feeling," he whispered. "I want to hear."

"Hot."

"Yes?" He flicked open another button, spreading her shirt and flicking open the lace that bound her breasts.

"Aches… Keep touching me. Don't stop."

"Never." Her skin bared to his eyes, Malachi stopped for a moment to stare. With a groan, he closed his mouth over one sensitive peak as Ava clutched the hair on the back of his head. He closed his eyes and lost himself in the taste of her. The salty bite of her skin and the lingering scent she wore intoxicated him. He would never get enough.

"Too much!" she finally gasped. "It's too much."

"Shhh." He soothed her, laying his forehead in the smooth valley between her breasts. He forced his mouth away from her skin as his fingers made quick work of the rest of her shirt. Slipping it off, he took a moment to gaze at the beauty spread before him.

Ava's skin still glowed with the traces of magic he'd written over her heart. A small bruise was forming on the rise of her left breast where his mouth had taken her skin. Malachi forced back the urge to mark her. There would be time. For her, he had eternity.

Shaking his head in wonder, he said, "For you? It is never too much."

"Faster," she urged.

"No." He bent his head again, fighting back his own desire to take and claim and spend himself in the cradle of her body. He loosened the button of her jeans before he slid them down over her legs. Each newly revealed limb received the attention of his lips. His fingers. Magic flowed between them. He could feel her energy and smiled, knowing one day she would mark him too.

"When you find your power," he murmured in her ear as he stretched out beside her on the narrow bed, "you will sing to me. And I will feel your magic as you feel mine."

"Is that what I'm feeling?" she said with a smile, throwing one leg over his thigh and pulling him closer. "That's a lot of magic."

He grinned, pleased by the laughter in her eyes.

"Ava," he whispered again. "*Reshon.*"

Her voice dropped to a whisper. "I can hear you. Inside. All I hear is you."

He stilled his hands. "And what do I sound like?"

"Perfect," she choked out. "You sound… perfect."

He saw the tears forming, so he came to her, knowing there was no pleasure she could ask for that he would not give. He ran a hand from the nape of her neck, down her spine, picturing the spells he would mark her with. Spells to strengthen her. Claim her. Mark her as his mate as she would mark him as hers.

"What do you want?" he asked.

"You."

Now it was his breath that was coming faster as she reached down and took him in her hand. His head fell back and Malachi felt Ava press kisses along the line of his jaw as she worked his pants down over his hips. Then her lips trailed over the markings on his collarbone. His shoulder. Her delicate teeth closed over his nipple for a moment before she continued across his chest. He was on the edge of losing control.

"Ava, stop." His head swam with the rush of sensation.

"Really?"

"Uh... no, not really."

He was light-headed with desire. Intoxicated by her touch. She might not have been able to use Irina magic, but Ava had a power all her own. Her energy was mounting again, feeding him, stoking the fire that built between them. They were face-to-face, staring into each other's eyes while Malachi's fingers moved over her skin.

"So warm." He buried his face in her neck and she wrapped her arms around his shoulders, holding him there. "I need you."

"Then take me," she whispered. "And don't let go."

He lifted her thigh and drew her forward, sliding into her body with aching slowness as he drank in the sensations. Heat. Pleasure. His instincts roused, and he groaned into her mouth as they rocked together. Skin against skin. Lips melded together. Push. Pull. He felt the blood rushing in his veins. Felt their breath mingle as their pleasure built. And when he felt Ava begin to fall over the edge, he followed.

He would follow her anywhere.

"WHAT DOES 'JAH-NUM' MEAN?"

"Hmm?" He was drowsy after the third time he'd taken her. Sex energized Irin men, but eventually, even the strongest man tired. Ava was like a loose rag draped across his chest. She had tried to move away when she started to fall asleep, but he wouldn't allow it, pulling her closer, still needing the contact.

"You say it sometimes. When we're together. 'Jah—'"

"Oh, *canim*. It means... my darling." He pressed a kiss to her forehead. "My life." More kisses along her cheek, ignoring the slight tension his words evoked. He didn't hold back. "It means 'my soul.'" The shell of her ear. Loose lazy brushes of his lips that soothed her and fed his need. He had forgotten what it meant to be held.

"*Canim.*" She tried the word out, whispering as her fingers traced over the *talesm* on his chest. She circled down to the blank area on the skin over his heart. "There's nothing here."

"I've never taken a mate."

"Never?" A slow smile curved her lips. "You don't make love like a virgin, Malachi."

He could feel the quiet laugh from her, and he reached down, pinching her thigh before his hand spread to soothe the sting.

"There was an Irina… before the Rending, there was someone. We were planning on a union. Our families liked each other. We liked each other very much. We were very compatible. And yes, we had been together. But she broke it off."

"What?" She picked her head up and frowned. "Don't tell me you weren't good enough for her. That's ridiculous."

He shook his head, smiling at her annoyance that another had found him lacking. It made him want to crow with pride. "No. She found her *reshon*. Her true mate."

"*Reshon?*"

He nodded slowly, sliding his hands down to lie along her waist. Ava was extraordinary. He could already feel her energy mounting—even away from humans in the isolation of the scribe house, she shone.

"It doesn't always happen, but it's something we all hope for. She found her *reshon*, so I let her go. It would have been foolish to continue courting her when her heart had already left."

"That cheating—"

He covered her mouth with his own. When he drew back, her eyes were blinking with languor again, and the irritation had fled. "It wasn't like that. It hurt her to break off our relationship, because she did care for me. But I did not fight it, even though it pained me, too. A *reshon* is a blessing. Your destiny in another person. The perfect complement to yourself. Not everyone finds a *reshon*, but those who do are considered doubly blessed. And very, very powerful."

"Why?" Her gaze fell to his chest again, and Malachi wondered what she would ask him to create there. The mating mark was dictated by the Irina, a visible expression of her mate's dedication and love. She traced the smooth bare skin and said, "Why more powerful?"

"Imagine…" He drew her up so they were face-to-face on the narrow bed. "Imagine a person created for you. Another being so in tune with you that their voice is the clearest you've ever heard in your mind." He saw her eyes widen, so he looked away and trailed a finger over her shoulder. "Her touch sharpens your senses. Her lips…" He pressed a light kiss to her open mouth. "…feed your soul. A bond like that strengthens both. One magic feeds the other. Within it, Irin and Irina become who we are meant to be."

Malachi could feel Ava's hands tighten on his shoulders. Knew she was quietly absorbing the words he'd said. He didn't want to push her. He knew she was his *reshon*. Looking back, it had been evident from their first kiss. But he was heeding his watcher's advice in another way. He could give her time. He would let Ava come to the knowledge herself. Patience. He would seduce her body and mind until her soul compelled her to accept him. It would be his most pleasurable hunt ever.

"What are you smiling about?" Ava teased him, snuggling into his chest. "You look like the cat who ate the cream."

His laugh was low and satisfied. "I'm quite sure that I did. More than once."

Malachi laughed again when she elbowed his side, then he pulled her close and said, "Sleep, Ava. Rest with me."

"I don't think I've ever felt this exhausted."

"Sleep," he whispered. "I will see you in your dreams."

WHEN HE DREAMED, IT WAS OF HER. A SHADOW HE CHASED through a dark wood. She eluded him for a time, but eventually a faint outline walked to him out of a fog. He could not see her face, but when her lips touched his, he knew her. And she was his.

He blinked awake. Ava was still sleeping next to him, boneless in her exhaustion. Malachi slipped out of the narrow bed, wishing he had someplace more private to take her. The newly awakened magic did not want to share its mate. And though his room in the scribe house was one of the most isolated, it still lacked the privacy he craved.

He threw on some clothes and left the room, needing some water. Ava, too, would be hungry when she woke. Her metabolism, which was typically fast, would probably wake her with hunger before long. Though expending energy during sex was one of the most effective ways to calm her, it was also draining. They couldn't stay in his room forever.

Not that the idea wasn't appealing.

He ran into Rhys halfway to the kitchens. The other man backed away for a moment, then seeing Malachi's expression, relaxed.

"I was wondering whether you were going to hit me or not," he said. "But you've obviously found another way of marking your territory."

Malachi grunted and crossed his arms. "If she'd been more complimentary about you, I'd be more offended."

"I'm letting that pass since you're in a postcoital haze."

"Ava is my *reshon*."

Rhys was speechless for a few moments, instinctive rebellion evident in his eyes. But finally he said, "Of course she is. I probably knew that before you did, you idiot. Does she know what it means?"

"Not completely. She's smart. She'll figure it out."

Rhys fell silent again. "She's not had an easy time of things, brother. Her relationships, from what I can tell, have been... difficult. She may fight it."

Malachi's lips curled. "She won't win."

"If you expect me to bet against fate, you're wrong." A shadow of sorrow passed over Rhys's face. Then the expression cleared and his acerbic wit resurfaced. "Heaven, you're going to be more insufferable than Damien when Sari agrees to see him. I swear, you even look taller."

"I *feel* taller."

For the first time, Malachi understood why mated Irin were on the front lines in all battles and held the highest positions. Union with his mate had given him the kind of energy even magic couldn't accomplish. He felt stronger. Sharper. The after-glow of Ava's touch made him feel as if he could take on a hundred Grigori and win without a scratch.

"Mated Irin," Rhys muttered. "You're an insufferable lot." He started back in the direction of the library. "I'll see you later. Next month, maybe."

"I want to take her away from here. The research, all the questions... It's been tiring."

"Don't make excuses," Rhys called back. "You're being selfish with the pretty girl." A hint of wicked humor came back. "Besides, these beds... I can only imagine the frustration."

"Don't imagine." He glared. "Even though you're right."

His friend laughed. "Take her to Kuşadası. No one is using the house there. It's not fancy, but it's private. You can blend in with the tourists. She might like the beach."

Malachi frowned, thinking of the crowded tourist port where the Irin kept a small safe house. "It's too busy."

"Not as busy as Istanbul. And she'll be with you. The voices will be more controllable for her now, but other senses will waken. It might be a good idea to ease her into things before you go back to Istanbul. Otherwise, it'll affect both of you now."

"Maybe." He finally conceded, "Yes, that is a good idea."

"I have lots of them. Now go find some food for the woman. She's going to be starving."

With that, the scribe turned and left. Malachi watched him

go, a spear of sorrow piercing through his own joy. He wanted his friend to find the same happiness. Wanted it for his people. They had lived in isolation for too long.

Gathering up some water, bread, and apricots, Malachi returned to his room to find Ava sitting up in bed, a thin blanket wrapped around her. Her eyes were still sleepy, but they brightened when she saw him walk in.

"Hey."

"Hello." He smiled. "How do you feel?"

"Amazingly rested. Oooh." Her eyes settled on the bottle of water. "For me?"

"Yes." He opened it and handed it to her, then set the basket of fruit on the small table beside his bed. He sat on the edge while she emptied half the bottle in one gulp. "Make sure you eat, too. Your body will be recharging for some time."

"Mmmm." She smiled. "I'm not going to complain about your workouts."

"I'm glad." He leaned over and kissed her lips, taking lazy pleasure in drawing a satisfied sigh from his mate.

"Oh, you're so good at—" There was a rustle in the hallway outside the room, and Ava's eyes widened in shock. "There's someone close."

He frowned. "There are more bedrooms past mine, but I'm sure—"

"I didn't hear them." He heard her pulse pick up, and she clutched the blanket around her. "I didn't hear their voices, Malachi. What's wrong with me?"

Suddenly understanding, he said, "Nothing." He took care to smooth a tendril of hair away from her face and kissed away the frown between her eyebrows. "There's nothing wrong with you. You're not hearing them because we made love."

"So... sex with you..."

"When we're together, I draw away much of your energy. It's the reason Irin can't be with human women. The energy we draw during sex is too much. But you..."

"I have more than average."

"Far more. For you, your energy becomes balanced. It makes *both* of us stronger. But since our relationship is new, I expect you may not hear voices for some hours, even days. I know older couples have more control over it, but until we become more accustomed to…" Suddenly wary, he asked, "Are you all right? I didn't think to warn you about this."

As much as the voices had tormented Ava, they were still one of her senses. He couldn't imagine what it would feel like if part of his hearing suddenly dropped out. Would he feel vulnerable? Broken? He shouldn't have worried. A glorious smile spread over her face and Ava fell back into the pillows on the bed.

"Best. Afterglow. Ever."

Chuckling, Malachi stripped off his shirt and lay beside her, still craving contact with her skin. He absently wrote on her back as she curled into his body again.

"What are you writing on me?"

"Property of Malachi."

"Haha. Seriously, what is it?"

Well, it wasn't as if he'd lied. "Mostly charms to help you sleep. For good dreams."

"I had the wildest dreams last night. So vivid."

"Really?" His lips curled in satisfaction. She was already dream-walking with him. Soon, she'd know what it meant.

"Mmhmm. I don't really remember what they were, but they were good."

"I'm glad." He paused. "What would you say about going to the sea, *canim*? There is a house near the shore that we use for a retreat. It's safe."

"No Grigori?"

"No Grigori."

"No endless questions?"

"Only you and I would be there."

"Does it have bigger beds?" She wiggled against him, trying to stay on the mattress.

"Most definitely."

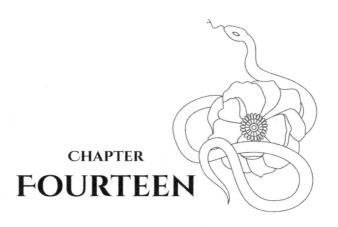

CHAPTER
FOURTEEN

Kuşadası was a busy port town home to cruise ships, tourists, and more cruise ships. Ava smiled as she and Malachi held hands, walking down the pedestrian walkway leading to the smaller marina where sailboats moored and nightclubs flourished. It could have been any number of port cities along the Mediterranean. Turkey. Greece. Spain. There was an odd kind of familiarity that was soothing, despite the crowds.

She squeezed his hand and smiled at the family with the sleepy toddler who was nodding off in his stroller. An older couple passed by, holding hands, the woman smiling at Ava after she'd glanced up at Malachi's striking figure. The sun had set and the humid heat of the day had given way to a soothing breeze that wrapped around her, twisting her skirt around her ankles and lifting pieces of her hair. Malachi leaned down and captured one curl that brushed in her face, stopping to tuck it behind her ear and steal a kiss.

"Are you having fun?" he asked quietly. "Do you want to go back to the house for dinner? There's food there. And you spent all day on the beach."

"No," she demurred. "I'm fine. The beach was nice."

"Honestly?"

"Honestly."

For the first time in her life, it was true. Malachi had been right, the days and nights of intimacy notwithstanding, a few days after their first frenzied coupling in the scribe house, she had started to hear the familiar voices again, whispering over her mind and filling her thoughts. Unlike before, she had someone to hold on to. Someone who understood.

Imagine a person created for you. Another being so in tune with you that their voice was the clearest you've ever heard in your mind.

Reshon, he'd called her. He thought she didn't remember, but in the heat of passion, the word had escaped his lips. The thought was frightening and thrilling all at once. Malachi thought she was his *reshon*. Every shield she'd built over a lifetime of solitude rebelled at the thought. She didn't want to be anyone's perfect match. She had no idea what he wanted from her, and a small voice whispered it was simply too good to be true. Eventually, he would grow tired and leave her. Everyone did.

A quick squeeze of his hand made her look up. He was watching her with suspicious eyes.

"What?" There was no way he knew what she was thinking. It wasn't as if he could read her thoughts.

"You're worried about something," he said. "What is it?"

"Nothing." She started walking again, but he wouldn't let her hand go.

"Me?" His silent thoughts were a swirl of confusion and concern. She hated hearing that from him. As big and tough as Malachi appeared, she knew there was a gentle part of him, and Ava suspected she was the only one allowed to see it. The thought of damaging that trust chilled her.

"I'm fine. I just—Whoa!" He picked her up and lifted her in his arms, smiling as the passing tourists laughed. Then he hopped over the rock wall and over to some deserted beach chairs near the lapping waves. He sat in one and positioned her so that her legs straddled his.

Reaching up to frame her face with both hands, he asked again, "What is it?"

"You're being pushy."

"This is new to me," he said urgently. "I worry I no longer know how to care for a woman. It has been too long. I cannot care for you if you don't tell me what is wrong, Ava."

"Malachi..."

"You must be patient with me. And tell me what you're thinking. You know my thoughts, but I do not know yours." A small smile lifted the corner of his mouth. "You have me at a disadvantage."

She couldn't look away. His grey eyes bored into hers. His skin was illuminated by the full moon that rose over the black Aegean Sea and his dark hair lifted in the breeze.

"It's too good," she finally whispered.

An understanding look passed over his face, but he said, "What is too good?"

"I... This. Us. It's too easy."

"It should be difficult?"

"It always has been."

He took a deep breath, then let it out slowly. "Other men are not me."

"Because you're Irin."

"Because I am me." He kissed her chin. "And you are you." Another kiss at her temple as his hands began soothing strokes up and down her back. She could feel his fingers playing along the delicate skin over her spine. "There are others like us in the world, but they are not us. We decide who we want to be."

"And you really want to be with me?" A thread of doubt worked its way into her voice, even though she willed it away.

A slow smile crossed his face. "Do you think me a martyr? That I do things I don't want to do?"

"No. I can tell that already." She had already seen his stubborn personality—it was apparent. It was hard to argue against it when iron control was so much of who he had to be. She could feel it under her fingers as she began to stroke his arms. Unbelievably powerful, Malachi had to show the strictest control among human beings. She saw it walking with him through the bazaar. At the shops. Among the more gentle scribes in Cappadocia.

She'd recognized it even when they first met so many weeks before in Istanbul. He was one of the most controlled men she'd ever met, his power on a very short leash. The fact that he loosed it when he held her, let his power wash over her in a gentle wave when they made love, caused her heart to soften dangerously toward him. It would be easy to put her heart in his hands. Easy to let him take care of her. But what would he take in return? Ava didn't know if she was hanging on to enough of herself to share.

"Are you worried about the Grigori?"

Sensing an escape, she answered, "Yes. This seems like a place they'd hang out."

He smiled. "Normally, yes. They love the tourist women. But I think so many of them were drawn to Istanbul when you were there, they may have left their usual hunting grounds. I haven't seen a single one since we've been here."

"And what would you do if you saw one here?"

"Kill it."

The flat certainty in his voice chilled her. "But how... They're like you. Not exactly, but didn't you say——"

"The Grigori may have had similar origins, but they chose their path long ago. They are predators. We are protectors. Once, the Irin helped humanity. We shared our knowledge and secrets until it became too dangerous. When we were no longer wanted, we withdrew. The Grigori continued to feed. Now our job is to stop them from killing. It is the only way we can still serve the humans we were meant to guide and protect."

Ava's back stiffened. "You act like humans are inferior."

"Not inferior. Different."

"I'm human."

He stifled a laugh. "No. You're not."

She stood up and glared at him. "My mother is Lena Matheson. A human woman. My father is Jasper Reed. A man. I am human. However this happened to me, I'm still human."

Irritation colored his voice. "Ava—"

"Do you think I'm inferior?"

"Of course I don't!"

"Then why—?"

"Why are you trying to start a fight?"

It brought her up short. What was she doing? She knew Malachi didn't see her as an inferior. If anything, she felt like he put her on some frightening pedestal. He stood and brushed off his slacks, slowly straightening his clothes before he met her eyes. He was angry.

"Do you think I'm going to get tired of you? Walk away?"

He turned with a glare and started toward the pathway while Ava stood frozen in the sand, the ocean breeze unable to warm the chill that reached toward her heart as she watched him retreat. Just before he reached the stairs, he turned and held out a hand.

"You can piss me off and twist me around, Ava, but you're not going to get rid of me."

She started toward him, and when she got close enough, his hand curled around hers. She swallowed the lump in her throat as he carefully ushered her up the steps.

"I want to go back to the house," she said as they reached the path along the main road. "I know you're mad at me—"

"Good."

They were silent on the long walk back, the cars and scooters honking as they darted across the main road. Ava had the distinct feeling that Malachi could have stopped them with a single glare if any got too close. They walked up the hill and toward the small, nondescript house they'd been sharing the past four days. It was nothing fancy, but at the end of a dead-end road, it was private and the beds were more comfortable than the ones in Cappadocia.

They didn't make it to the bed.

As soon as Malachi shut the door, he spun her around, desire and anger lighting up his eyes. Before a word could leave her, he had captured her lips, pulling her to his chest as she grasped the nape of his neck, digging in her nails when she heard him groan.

"Not. Leaving. You," he muttered between biting kisses, backing her toward a gathering of low couches and pillows in one corner.

"Okay." She could barely keep up, overwhelmed by his fierce possession. She held on to his neck, her teeth nipping at the softer skin there as she tore at the buttons on his shirt until he lifted it and pulled it off with an irritated scowl, as if the fabric itself was offensive. He carefully took off the twin daggers strapped to his torso, then he glared at her own clothes and knelt to strip them off.

"Do you understand me?" He pulled off her skirt, her blouse, finally slowing when he reached the fevered flesh beneath. Malachi bent down to the low couch, kneeling before her and pressing his face to the soft skin of her abdomen, his arms wrapping around her hips. Her whole body shuddered in awareness of the power at her feet. "I will not abandon you. I will not leave you. Ever."

She wanted to believe him. Wanted to be worthy of the devotion he offered. She reached a tentative hand out and brushed at the hair falling over his forehead, her pale fingers threading through the thick locks that teased her skin. His breath was hot against her belly when she tilted his chin up to meet her eyes. She traced the tip of one finger around the sculpted beauty of his mouth before she pressed it between his lips, and his tongue darted out to taste her.

"Show me."

. . .

HOURS LATER, AVA DECIDED THE FIGHT HAD BEEN WORTH IT. Lying against Malachi's chest in the lone extravagance of the house, the marble-clad bathroom, she looked over his shoulder.

"I think I like fighting with you."

He pinched her ass under the water.

"Hey!"

"I do *not* like fighting with you. Don't start fights."

"Some fights are going to happen."

He closed his eyes and shrugged, the water lapping against his chest. "Don't start unnecessary fights."

After a few silent minutes, she said, "I know you don't see humans as inferior."

"So what were you really worried about? The Grigori?"

She knew she should be. The shadowed hunters were still stalking her, as far as anyone would tell her. Damien, Leo, and Maxim were still tracking them in Istanbul. Rhys said Dr. Sadik was still suspicious and out of contact. They would have to return to the city at some point, and she really had no idea what she'd be walking into.

"Hmm?" He touched her face, tilting it toward him.

"I'm worried… about lots of things."

"The Grigori?"

"Yes."

"Dr. Sadik?"

"Yes."

He paused for a moment. "Me?"

"I can't help it," she said, her shoulders stiff. "Nothing is this… There's a reason I've been alone my whole life, Malachi."

He lifted his hands to her shoulders and Ava knew he was letting his magic soothe her. She'd only suspected it before, but there was a tingling kind of hum that she felt when he used magic.

"Don't use—"

"Shhh." His head dipped down and his lips teased behind her ear. "Just to relax your muscles. I won't touch your emotions, canım. Just let me help you."

Giving in, she leaned back and felt his arousal pressed against her, but he continued massaging her shoulders and arms. Her neck. The base of her skull.

"You're really good at that." He grabbed a silk washcloth from the side of the bath and rubbed some soap on it. The smell of orange blossom and fig filled the steaming room. "The bathroom here is amazing."

Though the house may have been modest, the bath was not. Clad floor to ceiling in grey marble, it was a picture of indulgence. A deep soaking tub filled one corner, and a rain-shower was in the other. There were steam vents and heated floors. Fragrant soaps and oils to condition the skin. Ava decided she might not ever leave as long as Malachi would keep her company.

"We Turks like our baths," he said as he brought the soap to her skin, the bubbles coating her shoulders before he began massaging her again.

"I can tell."

"And for Irin, too, touch is very important. Especially between... lovers."

Reshon. The word whispered in his mind.

Ava cleared her throat and said, "That makes sense."

"We're a very affectionate people," he said, lifting one arm and repeating the massage. Soap. Slick skin. Deep, soothing strokes. He brought her arm up to lie over his shoulder, and she twisted her fingers in his hair as he covered her with the rich scent. "When we are young, we are coddled. Children are so rare, they are fussed over. I was cuddled and played with constantly as a child. I could barely get any time alone." His voice held no resentment, only a hint of laughter.

"I spent most of my time alone," she whispered, her eyes half-closed. "I liked it that way."

"Did you like it?" he asked, washing and massaging her other arm. "Or were you simply accustomed to it? Was it easier without the voices?"

Both her arms stretched around his neck, baring her body to him as Malachi moved on from her arms to brush the silken cloth over the rise of her breasts.

Her voice hitched. "It was easier. I didn't have to concentrate on blocking the voices when I was alone. It was peaceful."

"Are you peaceful now?" he whispered, the cloth ducking lower, stroking over her breasts, circling her navel, until her body was trembling.

"Malachi—"

"Relax," he murmured, leaving the cloth and using his hands to stroke over her flesh. Slowly, deliberately teasing her. His tattooed arm slid under the water and toward the lush heat of her. His fingers dipped to the juncture of her thighs, feathering touch along the crease before he dipped into her slick heat. Her body soft with pleasure, she arched back and felt his lips tracing down her neck.

"I love touching you, Ava." His breath whispered across her neck. "You were meant to be touched and kissed. To feel pleasure."

She felt it rising. His fingers moved deliberately, his other hand on her breast as he played Ava's body, and her sighs echoed off the marble walls.

"You..." She gasped, looking down to see his black-scribed arms cradling her, one hand teasing her breasts as the other disappeared into the water, driving her slowly mad. "Come in me. I want you..."

"I love watching you." He turned her head, swallowing her cries of pleasure in a kiss as she came against his hand. Her skin was alive. She felt him behind her, the hair on his chest brushing against her back, his legs cradling her. Every sense was alive. Every instinct pulled her toward him.

Reshon.

The voice hadn't come from Malachi. The word whispered through her own mind as he kissed her over and over, his arms banded around her, dark ink against pale skin. She could see the faint silver glow as his *talesm* reacted to her.

Reshon.

He slowly worked her down, her pulse calming under his hands. There were tears in her eyes when they slipped closed.

"Sleep, Ava," he whispered as she laid her cheek against his shoulder. "I will hold you."

THE NEXT WEEK PASSED IN RELATIVE PEACE. MALACHI continued with his dogged patience, diffusing the fights Ava seemed unable to stop instigating, even when she tried. Try as she might, she couldn't seem to combat his steady affection. She snapped; he joked. She sneered; he smiled. It was maddening.

It was wonderful.

And with each small conflict, each new resolution, Ava felt a growing current of devotion and loyalty. Their chemistry was undeniable, but every time she turned from him and Malachi pulled her back with a simple hug or teasing kiss, a little bit of her walls crumbled, rolling toward a growing foundation of something she could barely acknowledge.

Love.

She was falling in love with him.

They were sitting across from each other, sipping two beers at a café as Malachi watched one of the cruise ships with amusement.

"There are so many of them." He played with her fingers as he stared at the massive cruise ship that had just docked, travelers pouring off like ants. "How do they even see the country with so many—"

"I'm falling in love with you."

He stopped speaking immediately, a smile teasing the corners of his mouth. "Hmm."

Ava narrowed her eyes. "Hmm? I say I think I'm falling in love with you and all you say is 'Hmm'?"

Grabbing her hand and holding on when she tried to pull it away, he said, "What did you want me to say?"

Her mouth dropped open. "I... Maybe that you... You know what? Never mind. I changed my mind."

"So you're not in love with me?"

"I never said I was!"

"Exactly." He winked and pulled her hand to his lips, kissing each finger deliberately. "If you had..."

"If I had?" She knew she was holding her breath, but she didn't know why.

Malachi leaned closer. "How do you think I feel about you?"

How did he feel about her? She didn't even need to ask, really. She knew without asking that he loved her. It was in every kiss. Every embrace. Every teasing comment. Every patient smile. His dogged affection had worn her down. In that moment, her heart tumbled, and she could feel the flush on her skin.

"I think..." Her eyes were drawn to a man who had just walked around the corner. "Grigori."

He frowned. "You think Grigori?"

She clutched his hand. "Grigori. There's a Grigori coming up the sidewalk. He's—"

"Another one just came in the back. He's by the bar."

Grabbing his wallet and throwing a fifty-lira note on the table, Malachi rose. "Walk calmly."

"He's already looking at me." Her heart raced. "Malachi, he's already—"

"This one spotted us, too. They're not here hunting. They're here for us."

They walked toward the sidewalk, nodding at the host who looked at them in confusion. Malachi muttered something in Turkish as they passed and the man nodded. He kept his hand on the small of Ava's back, walking quickly in the other direction. Ava chanced a look over her shoulder. Both Grigori were following them. Another melted into the foot traffic as they passed another café.

"There's three. Three of them are behind us."

"I'm leading them away from the humans."

"Should I—?"

"Stay with me. Keep yourself behind me when we get there."

"Get where?"

They were speed-walking up the hill until Malachi ducked into a side street. Houses rose on either side, the street dead-ending into a hill covered by pink oleander and trash. Ava tripped over a scattering of cans that littered the ground as Malachi leaned down for a quick kiss, his eyes gleaming.

"I love you. Of course I love you. Now stay behind me while I take care of these nuisances."

He turned his back to her and drew two silver daggers from the sheaths against his skin just as six Grigori soldiers turned the corner.

CHAPTER
FIFTEEN

S ix? Where had the other three come from?

No matter, Malachi grinned in anticipation. Playing lovers' games for the past week had been more than satisfying, but the hunter in him craved this fight. He paced across the alleyway, letting the Grigori come closer. Let them grow more confident. It would make them more fun to kill. The one in front could have been his brother, so alike were they in height and physique. But the soldier didn't have what Malachi had—years of experience and the strength of his *reshon* flowing through his body.

Malachi faked to the right, more pleased than irritated when the Grigori wasn't fooled. Their eyes met for a brief moment before the soldier's eyes flicked to Ava standing behind him. He heard Ava let out a small sound of panic.

Enough. He'd forgotten she would be frightened.

Crossing his arms and brushing both hands along his tattoos, Malachi felt the preternatural strength flood his body. His eyes grew stronger in the early evening gloom. His hearing more acute. He could track the soldiers' movements almost as if the men were moving in slow motion. And he could hear the two soldiers the Grigori had stationed at the mouth of the alley to warn away any passersby. Ava's pulse hammered behind him. The rush of blood filled his ears.

By the time Malachi pulled his knife, he'd already darted to the left, pulling one soldier by his arm, spinning him around and plunging the silver knife into the base of his skull. He shoved the body away as it began to disintegrate, only to grab another, his movements so fast he saw Grigori eyes blur.

Spinning around, he caught one with a swift kick to the jaw, sending him to the ground as he knifed the second Grigori in the neck. He could feel the gold, sand-like dust coat his hands before the wind lifted it, shielding him from the view of the fallen soldier's compatriots. Through it all, his senses were tuned to Ava, who continued to stay directly behind him, not cowering in a corner, but shadowing him, keeping Malachi between her and the monsters.

Clever girl.

The Grigori in front came toward him, ignoring the scrambling of the other soldiers. The man's eyes flicked to Ava again, and he moved as if to approach her, drawing Malachi's attention from the soldier he'd been about to knife. He sliced at the man's neck and threw him to the ground, only to have the Grigori's foot whip toward him unexpectedly.

The kick surprised Malachi, causing him to lose the knife he'd used on three of the men. It clattered to the ground, but Malachi did not pick it up, instead shoving it behind him with his boot, toward Ava, while he grabbed for his second dagger with his left hand. In the seconds he was distracted, the Grigori had come within a few feet, attacking with far more skill than the other soldiers.

But just before he reached Malachi, he darted to the left and toward Ava. From over his shoulder, he saw a flash of silver. Then the powerful Grigori stopped in his tracks as the knife plunged into his eye.

Malachi seized the opportunity, grabbing the man as he screamed in pain, spinning him around, then smashing his dagger into the base of his skull. He grabbed the other knife as the man's corpse disintegrated in a river of gold sand before it was gathered by the wind and lifted toward the heavens. The three remaining soldiers stood stunned as their captain drifted away, then one ran while the other made a last attempt at his mission.

It wasn't successful.

Malachi kicked him to the ground with a boot to his knee, then crouched on top of the soldier. Turning the Grigori face-down, he slammed the dagger home.

In the back of his mind, he heard the cries of the children left in his village, hidden by the Irina who had been slaughtered. He blinked at the memory of a little girl, her arm riddled with bites from her own teeth as she forced herself to remain quiet in the hiding space under the floorboards. Her hollow eyes and blood-stained lips haunted him as he moved to the last soldier on the ground, blood still pouring from the gash in his neck where Malachi had slashed him.

The Grigori stared up at the stars, dead eyes unseeing, bubbles of air bursting at his throat. His lips formed the words over and over.

"Please. Please. Please."

With a swift jerk, Malachi flipped the soldier over and ended his life.

Bowing over the corpse as it dissolved, he let his head hang as he opened his senses. The last soldier had fled with the other two who'd been standing guard. He could hear them fleeing toward the main road. Then car doors slammed shut and an engine roared to life before speeding away. Whoever had sent the soldiers would know where they were and that the attempt had not been successful.

He finally turned to Ava, who was standing stunned and wide-eyed, staring at the ground.

Roused from the fight, he blinked and tried to read her expression.

"Ava?"

"I…" She swallowed. "I killed it. Him. Well, I stabbed him and you killed him. And then… he melted."

"It's a kind of dust." Malachi wiped phantom sand from his hands. "Irin and Grigori both—"

"I killed him," she choked out. "He was coming toward me and I just…" Tears started to roll down her face. She clutched her arms around her body. "And you killed, like… lots of them."

"There were four." And he could have killed more. He'd wanted to. He still felt high from the thrill of the battle, but his mate's reaction was starting to scare him. It was easy to forget in the heat of battle that Ava was a stranger to violence.

The shivers started in her shoulders but spread down her back.

"Ava." He held out a hand and she just looked at it as if he was a stranger. The pain was swift and sure. "Ava, please."

With a sob, she came to him, and Malachi wrapped his arms around her shoulders while the fist around his heart loosened. "I'm sorry. I'd forgotten. You're not accustomed to violence."

"Were they trying to kill me?"

"No," he soothed her. "Just kill me. I think they were probably trying to capture you."

She cried harder. Perhaps that wasn't the right thing to say.

"K…kill you?"

"Shhh." He stroked her hair, glad that Grigori didn't leave messy corpses. "I only have a few bruises. They'll be gone in minutes." Then he tilted her head up with a smile. "And my fierce love has her own defenses after all. Where did you learn to throw knives?"

"C…circus camp." She hiccupped. "Summer I was fourteen."

The smile grew wider. "Circus camp?"

"I can walk a decent tightrope, too, but knives were my favorite. I liked throwing, so I kept practicing. Mom bought me a set and Carl's gardener made me a big target." Her eyes were wide and glassy. Her lip was still trembling. But Ava smiled through the tears. "It was fun."

"I'll keep that in mind." Sensing the tension in her shoulders had eased, Malachi sheathed both knives before he turned and tucked her under his arm and they started back to the house. They'd have to leave that night. He'd need to call Rhys and let him know. Call Istanbul and tell Damien to expect them back. Call—

"Your knives are much better balanced than my set, though." Her voice was growing steadier as they walked. "Can I get some for myself? They might come in handy."

"Are you going to use them on me?"

"Probably not."

"We'll see. What other camps did you go to?"

"Um... circus camp. Art camp. Surf camp. Photography. Wilderness skills. Horseback riding. More photography. Sailing."

"You're very well-rounded."

"You should see me start a fire."

THE CAR RIDE BACK TO ISTANBUL WAS QUIET. AVA SLEPT SINCE Malachi was still jumping with energy. Even their adrenaline-fueled sex back at the house had done nothing to take the edge off. He was beginning to think the woman had more energy than any Irina he'd ever met. It might have simply been a conse-quence of too many years with no Irin contact, but he was starting to suspect that, with training, her powers would be formidable. It made him want to thump his chest like a Nean-derthal. His woman, his *reshon*, would be a force to be reckoned with.

His phone rang.

"Hello?"

Damien asked, "Is anyone following you?"

He glanced in the rearview mirror, but it was still empty. The only traffic had been scattered, though he knew it would become heavier the closer they got to the city. Here, they sped through countryside populated by more tractors than immortal assassins.

"We're fine. Nothing suspicious."

"Maxim said he's picked up more activity in the last couple of days than what he'd expect for this time of year. More outsiders than he's seen before. Something is definitely happening with the Grigori in the city. And Leo says that the elusive Dr. Sadik seems to be back in his office. Says the secretary showed up this morning, even though no patients came."

"No sightings of the doctor?"

"No, but if the secretary has come back from her holiday…"

"The doctor could be expected soon." He paused, adding the fact to the mosaic of information he'd been building about Ava. "Has Maxim heard anything?"

The young scribe was the best information merchant they had. While Rhys could command the computer systems, sometimes nothing beat having ears to the ground. And the quietly charming Maxim had become a favorite among some of the more… legally challenged elements of Istanbul. His love of gambling probably helped.

"Maxim claims your Dr. Sadik hasn't rung any bells with the human element, though a Grigori he captured went stubbornly silent when the name was mentioned."

"So he is Grigori. Or connected in some way."

"Or the soldier knew he was going to die and didn't feel like giving Maxim the answer to his question. It's all speculation at this point, brother."

He thought for a moment, wishing he could just be back in Istanbul without the long drive. Ava's breathing changed slightly and she let out a soft murmur but didn't wake.

"You and the woman," Damien asked. "You're together?"

"Yes. She's mine."

"You're certain?"

"Yes."

There was a long pause, and when Damien's voice came back, he sounded amused. "It'll be good not to be the only one tormented by a mate. Congratulations."

Malachi grinned, reaching over to play with a piece of hair that was tickling her nose. "My Ava adores me. I don't know what you're talking about."

"Ha!"

He bit his lip to hold in the laughter when she frowned in her sleep and batted at his hand. Adoration, indeed.

"I'll let you off the phone. Drive carefully. Rhys should be back tomorrow night. He left Göreme just a little bit after you left Kuşadası."

"It will be good to see him. Has he made any progress with Ava's genealogy?"

"He sounded like he'd made some kind of breakthrough, but he didn't say what. Just that he had a few more questions for her."

Malachi frowned. "Fine."

"And I'm going to suggest she go see the mysterious Dr. Sadik."

"Not without me."

Damien paused, then said, "We'll talk about it when you get back."

"Not without me, Damien. It's not going to happen."

"She saw him for weeks with no danger."

"We don't know that. How do you think they found us tonight?"

"It's hardly out of their normal hunting grounds. Perhaps it was a coincidence?"

"I don't believe in a coincidence that leads six Grigori to corner me in an alley while I happen to have Ava with me."

"You're newly mated, and thus you're paranoid. It's completely understandable."

"And I'm completely right. She's not going to his office without me."

"We'll talk more tomorrow. Until then, take care."

"I'll see you later."

As he hung up the phone, the question plagued him. How had the Grigori found them? Not just in Kuşadası, but in that particular restaurant at that particular hour? It couldn't be a coincidence. He glanced at Ava, still sleeping securely. He didn't think she'd called Dr. Sadik again, so how had it happened?

He slowed the car and pulled over near a roadside market, then he grabbed her mobile phone from the center console. Could Sadik have tapped into the network somehow? Doing so would indicate he was far more connected than Malachi or Rhys had initially suspected. Perhaps it was simpler. A tracker of some kind. A simple GPS chip would have allowed him to track Ava anywhere she went. He flipped her phone over, looking for any indication it had been tampered with.

"What are you doing?" Her sleepy voice didn't distract him as he looked at the edges of her mobile. No scratches or marks indicated that the case had been manipulated or modified.

"Do you have one of those location apps on your phone so you can find it online if you lose it?"

"No. I turned off all the location services except for maps. Carl put one on and it pissed me off, so I shut all of them off. Why?"

He muttered, "How did the Grigori find us?"

"What?"

"At the restaurant tonight. How did they find us?"

She sat up straight. "I don't know."

"You haven't called Sadik, have you?"

Ava rolled her eyes. "I still don't buy your suspicion of him, but no, I haven't."

Another thought occurred to him. "Did Dr. Sadik ever give you anything?"

"What?" She rubbed at her eyes. "No. I don't think so."

"Think, Ava. It might have looked innocent. Like a trinket."

"Well... nothing he could use to—"

"What did he give you?" His interest spiked. "Something harmless. What was it, love?"

She shrugged and reached into the purse near her feet. "It's nothing. I'd kind of forgotten about it. It's one of those nazar-amulet key chains. To ward off the evil eye, you know? Dr. Sadik told me to keep it with me. For luck."

From a pocket, she pulled out the vivid blue glass. Around four centimeters wide, it looked like any of the tourist trinkets hanging from every shop in Turkey, only it was backed with metal he suspected doubled as an antennae. The white and blue circles stared back at him, accusing him of paranoia. Malachi held it up to the light.

"I thought it was kind of silly, but I put it in my bag and I haven't really thought about it since."

"I'm sure he was counting on that."

In the darkest blue of the glass, there was an almost translucent chip with a wire leading toward the metal frame.

"There." He held it out so Ava could see. "Do you see? I think it's a chip."

She blinked. "Like they put in dog collars to find them if they're lost?"

"A simple GPS chip. As long as you have this with you, he could track you."

He saw the color rise on her cheeks, but her eyes were cold. "Son of a bitch…"

Malachi grabbed her hand. "You trusted him. I know. It's not—"

"That asshole!"

"He betrayed you, and you're—"

"I'm gonna *kill* him."

Now it was Malachi cautioning patience. "We need to find out more before you do."

"This thing—" She tried to grab the nazar, but Malachi closed his fingers over it.

"No."

"Give it to me! I want to smash it to pieces!" She was already opening her car door. "I want it as far away from me as—"

"Do you want him to think you're in the middle of nowhere on the side of the road?" He shook the hand she was trying to pry open. "Think."

Ava blinked, coming out of her rage. "He'd know I found it."

"Exactly. We're not going to take it back to the house, but we don't want him to know we've found it."

She took a deep breath and nodded. "Okay, so what do we do?"

"We're going to take it back to Istanbul, and we're going to leave it someplace very safe." An idea sprang to his mind, and Malachi smiled. "Someplace that will confuse the hell out of him."

IT WAS MORNING WHEN THEY WALKED INTO THE LOBBY OF AVA'S old hotel. The streets of the Sultanahmet were almost deserted as they made their way past the sleepy young man at the front desk and toward the courtyard near her old room. The young man raised his head in a quick smile, recognized Ava, then put his head down again, not realizing she no longer had a room there.

"This way," she said softly. "I think this is where they keep the carts."

Malachi spotted a maid turning the corner with one of the narrow cleaning carts, so he tugged Ava toward it, engaging the girl in a conversation about finding a razor because his luggage had been lost. Malachi trapped the young woman in conversation while he passed the nazar to Ava. She palmed it, took out the gum she'd been chewing, and stuck it to the glass-and-metal amulet. Then she pressed the blue circle into a corner, out of the line of sight, but hopefully secure enough to remain on the cart. Malachi saw her stuff a rag under the nazar to hold it in place, then she tugged on his hand.

"You know what? I totally forgot, honey. I have an extra razor in my bag." Ava put on a big smile as she shook her head. "Can't believe I forgot about that. I was surprised they let it on the plane."

Malachi switched to English. "Is that so? I won't bother her anymore then." He turned to the confused maid with an apologetic smile and thanked her. Then he and Ava turned back toward the lobby and slipped out of the hotel.

"Hopefully, the cart will move enough that he won't be immediately suspicious. Plus, you've stayed there before. So while he'll know you're back in the city, he won't realize you're at our house."

"I can't believe I stuck gum to the corner of her cart." Ava shuddered. "The well-behaved schoolgirl in me is appalled by my behavior."

"You were really a well-behaved schoolgirl?"

"Of course not. I was the crazy chick with a reputation to uphold."

"That's what I was hoping for."

CHAPTER
SIXTEEN

B y the time they arrived at the scribe house on the other side of the bridge, morning traffic had started. Cafés and shops were stirring, and the corner market near the old wooden house in Beyoğlu was opening its doors. Ava held Malachi's hand as they walked from the car park. She had slept in the car, but not deeply. She needed quiet, food, and warm arms surrounding her while she slept.

I love you. Of course I love you.

He said it like it was the most natural thing in the world. And Ava, despite a lifetime's worth of disappointment, was starting to believe it.

"Malachi." She tugged on his arm a few steps away from the front door. The sun was rising, painting the side of the house a warm red-brown. It touched his hair, and Ava was blinded for a moment by the planes of his face. The warmth in his eyes as he looked down on her. He was becoming the most handsome man in the world to her. Just the sight of him stole her breath.

"What?"

"What happens now?"

He smiled and touched her cheek with a finger. "Now my brothers will greet us, and we will both get some rest. We eat something. We take things one step at a time, Ava. We will find who is after you and what they want. Then, we will make you safe."

"It sounds pretty simple when you put it like that." She felt her head swimming and knew she'd reached the end of her rope. She was five steps from the door, but minutes away from collapse.

Malachi squeezed her hand and reached over to knock, but the green door was already opening. Damien stood in the doorway, a fierce, intimidating figure, his torso bare save for the markings across his chest, shoulders, and arms. A linen cloth hung around his waist, and Ava saw black stains on his hands. His hair hung past his shoulders, and Ava could see the ancient warrior in his eyes as he stared.

"Morning greetings, brother," he said quietly, opening the door farther and holding out his hand. Malachi put a hand at the small of her back and grasped Damien's forearm with his hand.

Malachi asked, "Does the fire still burn in this house?"

"It does, and you are welcome to its light." Then the stern expression melted, and Damien looked down at her. "You and your own."

With that, some kind of wall was breached, and she heard Malachi's thoughts swell with pride and excitement. He held her with one arm while grabbing his friend in a fierce embrace. The two men's quiet laughter enveloped her as they ushered Ava through the door, and she saw Leo and Maxim standing behind Damien, both wearing the same joyful expressions. They lined up to greet her. Damien was first, leaning down to put both hands on her shoulders and kissing her cheeks, right and left.

"You are welcome, sister." Damien's voice held a slight waver. "You honor us with your voice."

Aware that there was some meaning she didn't quite grasp, Ava only said, "Thank you."

Maxim was next. His vivid blue eyes held a devious glint,

but his smile was warm. "Welcome, sister." He leaned down and also kissed her cheeks in greeting.

"Thank you."

Leo was the last to say hello, but Ava was grateful to see his familiar, playful expression. "Welcome home, Ava. I'm so happy you're back."

She was almost ready to burst into tears when his lips touched her cheek. She felt Malachi's hand at her back a moment before he pulled her back and into his chest.

"Rhys?" he asked as she tried to recover her composure. She had never felt so welcomed in her life. A small, abandoned corner of her heart sighed and whispered, *Home*.

"He arrived a few hours ago. Still sleeping."

"Is our room ready? We both need sleep."

"Of course," Damien said. "Leo?"

The smiling man stepped forward. "We moved you to the second floor. The east room has the most space, and it's coolest in the afternoon."

"Thank you," Malachi said.

"Wait." She put a hand on his arm. "They moved your room?"

"Our room," he said softly, leading her toward the stairs. "Thank you, Leo. We'll see you later."

"Rest well." Without a whisper, he disappeared, along with every other man who'd been there a minute ago. Ava blinked back the blurriness in her eyes and followed Malachi.

"Wait... so, what? They moved me in?"

"I believe Maxim collected your things from your hotel after we left Istanbul. They simply moved them to a new room along with my things."

"Isn't that—" She couldn't stop the yawn. "—a little premature? I mean, we've been... whatever-we-are for—"

"They don't think like that," he said with a smile. "They see the truth."

"Oh?" She yawned again, walking through the door he held

open for her. She entered a dim room surrounded by bookcases on three walls. There was a window shielded by wooden blinds and a beautiful mural painted around it. But all Ava saw was the bed. Low, covered with pillows, with the bedspread turned down. It was the most beautiful thing she'd ever seen. She collapsed face-first onto the pillows, barely registering Malachi's quiet chuckle.

"A little tired?"

"You haven't let me get much sleep the past week, you insatiable man."

"I think you've worn me out, too," he said as he tugged off her shoes and jeans. Then he rolled her over and eased off the button-down shirt she'd worn, leaving her in a lightweight tank and her panties. The cotton sheets were a cool kiss against her skin, and Ava burrowed into the pillows as he pulled the bedspread up to her chin. "Sleep, my love."

"You, too. Come to bed." She pulled at his hand, rolling toward him with her eyes closed when she felt the other side of the bed dip. Then his arm was around her, and his skin pressed against her own. Leg to leg. Chest to back. His arms encircled her as oblivion descended.

"Malachi?"

"Hmm?"

"Your brothers… what do you mean, 'they see the truth'?"

"About you and me."

"And?"

"We belong to each other," he murmured, his voice growing dim. "The Irin know how precious love is. How quickly it can be taken from us."

"Still, so fast…"

"Perhaps… we have learned not to wait."

Reshon, reshon, reshon.

She didn't know whether the whispers were coming from his mind or her own. And for the first time, Ava didn't care.

. . .

She woke slowly, the knowledge of *who* reaching her before the *where*. Malachi was with her, arm still wrapped securely around her waist. As her eyes blinked open, she realized they were back in Istanbul, in the wooden house with the green door, where she'd been greeted like family before falling asleep with the man she loved.

Loved to distraction.

She turned carefully, wanting to watch him as he slept. His face was covered with dark stubble, and his hair fell across his forehead, a frown on his face as he dreamed. His full lips pursed in disapproval at whatever visions he saw, and long lashes curled on his cheeks. He really did have the most beautiful eyes; his lashes would be the envy of women everywhere.

"Angels would weep," she whispered, only realizing after she'd said it how truly ironic it was. Angels probably had wept.

The Forgiven. The angelic ancestors of the Irin. In the story Rhys told her, the Forgiven had been the ones who left. Leaving behind their women and children to return to heaven when they were called. And in return, their descendants had been blessed with knowledge and magic in exchange for their sacrifice. Ava traced the stern line of Malachi's lip.

"I think I'd pull down heaven," she said, "if that's what it took to keep you here with me."

A slow smile curved his lips. "And I'd abandon it if you weren't there." His eyes flickered open. "Good morning."

"I'm pretty sure it's afternoon."

"Oh well." He rolled over, dragging her with him so she lay over his chest. "Let's go back to sleep and forget them all."

Ava giggled and squirmed as he held her. "We should get up."

"I'm well on the way. Can't you tell?"

"Clearly." She managed to wiggle to his side. "But I have some questions."

"Oh…" He groaned and buried his face in her neck,

nipping at the soft skin with gentle teeth. "Do I get a prize if I answer correctly?"

"Not those kind of questions."

"What kind then?"

"Last night…" She shook her head. "This morning. When we got here. The things they said… That meant something, didn't it?"

"Yes." His voice held an abundance of caution.

"What did it mean?" When he didn't answer, she rolled over. "Well?"

She started to sit up, but he grabbed her and pulled her down, curling around her as he spoke.

"When we went to Cappadocia, the scribes there greeted us as guests. You might not have noticed, as they're not as formal there."

"You were speaking in the Old Language, too."

"Yes. But here… When we arrived this morning, Damien greeted us as family. In the old way, the way the head of a household would greet a mated couple returning to a retreat. He called you sister. He called you my own."

A quiet suspicion began to take shape. "They moved us into this room. Which is quite obviously intended for two people."

"Yes."

"And all your stuff is here. And my stuff."

"Ava, I—"

"Are you telling me they think we're married or something?" Her heart started pounding.

"Irin don't marry," he said, just a little too quickly. "So, no."

"But they think something."

"They know we're together. That's all. I told them we were together. Aren't we?"

"I guess…" Ava felt like she was trying to find her way in a dark room that everyone could see but her. "Yes, we're together. I just want to know what's going on. This is all happening really fast. Do they think I'm going to live here forever or something?"

She felt him stiffen, and his face went blank. "Are you planning to leave?"

"Not right now. But... I don't know." She knew her words caused him pain, but they had to be said. "I have a life, Malachi."

He drew back, and Ava hated the distance immediately. "Yes, you have a life."

"And I can't just—"

"A life where you travel from place to place every few months, never putting down roots." His voice was brittle. "You don't speak of any close friends. You have a mother who loves you but doesn't understand you. A stepfather who protects you but doesn't love you."

His words stung, even though Ava knew they were true. "You have no right—"

"You were alone," he said, grabbing her hand and stopping her from leaving the bed. "Like I was. Even more than I was. We were alone, but now we're not."

The urgency in his voice, the raw honesty of it, cooled her anger. "Malachi—"

"Why do you want to leave that? I need you, as you need me." He drew her back down and placed a lingering kiss on her lips. "We can stay here. We can go another place. We can seek out the Irina who have hidden themselves and ask them to train you in magic. We can hide from the world if we must. I don't know what we'll do for money, but we'll find—"

"I have plenty of money," Ava said. "Money for a lifetime. I'm not worried about that."

"Then why?" He kissed her again. "Why leave? I don't care where we go, as long as we're together."

Her heart swelled, and she tried to swallow the lump in her throat. "Is this real?"

He smiled a glorious smile and kissed her again. "Of course it is. We can live forever. The two of us. Forever. Have a family. A life."

"I love you." Ava kissed him back, her heart pounding out of her chest with a mad hope. She believed him, and it scared her. "I love you so much."

"I love you, too."

He held her on the bed, rocking back and forth as Ava bit her lip and tentatively allowed the dreams he shared to take root in her heart. She could see it. For the first time in her life, she caught a glimpse of a life that didn't end in loneliness and pain. She wanted to be cautious, but her reckless heart ran toward him.

"To be completely honest, however..." He glanced down. "Some might consider us... mated."

Ava sat up. "That's the Irin version of married, isn't it?"

"It's not exactly..." He was fiddling with the fingers on her right hand in what had become his own nervous gesture. "Yes."

"I knew it!"

AVA AND RHYS WERE LOOKING THROUGH OLD RECORD BOOKS, trying to identify the Grigori she and Malachi had seen in Kuşadası. Unlike police lineup books, which Ava had been acquainted with due to her kidnapping as a child, the Irin records were a mix of pictures and sketches. The profiles she paged through were only for the longest-lived and most dangerous soldiers, which meant it read more like an encyclopedia of evil than a suspect book.

Ulrich, son of Grimold. 1734. Took part in Rending near Stockholm.

Finn, son of Volund. 1856. Known kills in Barcelona, Madrid, and Rabat.

Michael, son of Svarog. 1699. Took part in attack of Prague prior to Rending.

Kemal, son of Jaron. 1955. Known kills, multiple victims in Istanbul, Athens, and throughout Romania.

Joseph, son of Volund. 1902. Known kills in London, Edinburgh, Manchester, Brittany, Lyon, and Milan.

Some of the names had been crossed out, usually with a notation about who had killed them. There were also notes about how each Grigori fought or who their associates were. Certain names kept popping up over and over.

Volund.

Jaron.

Svarog.

Galal.

"Hey, Rhys?"

"Hmm?" He looked up from his computer.

"These names—the fathers of the Grigori listed—so are these...?"

"Fallen angels," he said. "The real kind. Not offspring like us, and definitely not the nice fluffy variety you see on the television. The Fallen never left Earth, and they're incredibly powerful. Incredibly cruel. We've killed a few over the years, but it's very difficult. They can shapeshift and cloak their power, so more than one Irin scribe has lost his life thinking one of the Fallen is a harmless old woman or child in need of help. It's more common they kill each other than we're able to kill them."

"How do you kill an angel?" she whispered to herself.

"There are only a few weapons that can do it. Most are in the possession of the Council in Vienna. They have an ancient armory they loan out to very specific people. One of their daggers showed up on a Grigori soldier last month, which has everyone scrambling. Damien was up in arms when he called Vienna, wanted to know how the bastard had obtained it."

"Does anyone know?"

Rhys shrugged. "It's possible an assassin they sent to kill one of the Fallen failed. Brage—that's the one who had it—is one of Volund's most trusted children. Volund controls most of Northern Europe and Russia. He might have given it to him, but if he did, he'd have a very specific purpose for it. It's not something you'd give away lightly or carry every day."

"Is it weird that one of Volund's Grigori is here in Istanbul?"

"It could be, but then, it may be nothing. Most go back and forth despite some rivalry."

"Huh."

"Though… there's a lot of strange happenings lately," he muttered, still searching for something online. "Like your Dr. Sadik."

Ava burned just thinking about him. Bastard. She'd trusted him, and now she had no idea who the doctor was, or even if he was a doctor at all. Rhys was still trying to track him down. They worked in silence for several more minutes, but Ava could feel Rhys's eyes keep coming back to her.

"What?"

"I'm curious about something." Rhys handed her a book written in what looked like Farsi just as Malachi entered the room. Ava tried to push down her own annoyance at seeing him.

"I can't read this," she protested, looking through the book. "I can speak a little Farsi, but—"

"Just look at the pictures," Rhys said. "See if you recognize anyone."

Malachi walked toward her, but she shot him a look. She was irritated about the whole "mated-not-married" thing, and she wasn't going to try to make him feel better. He could have at least warned her. And the fact that everyone around her was so damn happy only irked her more. Would it have killed him to keep her informed?

"If you want to punish him, you're doing a bang-up job," Rhys said when Malachi crossed the room to speak to Maxim about something. The two conferred for a moment before heading toward the library door, leaving her and Rhys alone. Ava turned to him.

"I'll get over it eventually, but right now I'm pissed."

"He didn't mean to anger you. I'm sure of it."

"But he didn't exactly keep me informed, did he? Did Malachi tell *you* we were mated?"

Rhys's mouth did a little gasping-fish thing. "Not in those words... exactly."

"Really? When?"

He muttered something that sounded like "Captain Donkey."

"What?"

He cleared his throat. "Cappadocia."

"Oh really?" She glared at the door. "We were there *one night* after we... you know."

"I think the whole valley knew. Caves echo." Rhys kept talking, even though her face reddened. "Honestly, love, the two of you had been dancing around each other for weeks. Stop being such a fussbudget."

"A...a what?" She tried to hold in the laugh as Rhys blushed.

"Nothing."

"Did you just call me a...a *fussbudget*?" The snicker turned into a laugh.

"I... well, you are. Being very fussy about all this. You're—"

"Showing your age, old man." Ava couldn't stop laughing.

"And you're being annoyed for the sake of being annoyed." At least Rhys was laughing, too. His eyes were lighter than they had been since the disastrous night she'd kissed him. "So just stop." The laughter left his voice and Ava wiped the tears from her eyes. "You two have what most of us have only dreamed of for over two hundred years. A mate. A partner. We can all see it, even when you're annoyed and he's exasperated."

She sighed. "I do exasperate him."

"And he loves it. He loves you. And you're clearly besotted with him." Rhys grabbed her hand and squeezed it for a second. "So stop trying to be sensible about it. Grab love when you can. It doesn't come around for everyone."

"I'll try."

"You'll try…" He shook his head and turned back to the computer screen. "You know what? Keep fighting the inevitable. It makes for very entertaining—"

"Oh my God," she breathed out, staring at the face on the page. The vivid green eyes were rendered in black and white, but the shape was exactly as she remembered. The sketch looked old, maybe from the turn of the century or earlier. It was hard to tell. After all, that particular style of glasses was classic. "It's him."

Rhys whipped around. "Who?"

"Him." She pointed to the angular face on the page. "It's him. Dr. Sadik."

"You're positive, Ava?"

"I'm sure! It looks just like him. Exactly." She looked at the other pictures on the page. Even though she couldn't read the writing, it was clearly an extensive entry. "You're saying my therapist is really a Grigori soldier?"

"No, he isn't." Rhys reached over and closed the book, swiping a thumb over the title. For a moment, the letters shimmered and shifted, then the characters reshaped into the more recognizable Roman alphabet.

"That spell is incredibly…" Ava blinked when she read the title. "Oh. My—"

"Your therapist isn't a Grigori," Rhys said, pulling away the book. For a moment the letters held, then the title shifted back to the original Farsi. But the name was branded onto her mind.

JARON.

"Your Dr. Sadik is a fallen angel."

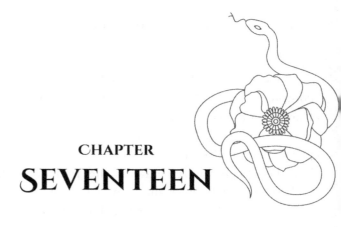

M alachi shivered just thinking about it. She had been
alone with him for weeks. The monster had touched
her. Touched his mate. The fact that she was still so
silent probably meant she was in shock.

"Absolutely not," Malachi said, pulling Ava closer as they sat
on the couch in the library.

Maxim said, "But surely you can see the value of—"

"You will not put her at risk," he barked, unable to comprehend why they were even considering his brother's suggestion.

Ava's doctor was Jaron. Jaron was Sadik. The fact that his
mate was still in the city drove him to distraction. He wanted to
board a plane. No, not a plane, the bastard could fly. A boat?
Water was safer. A car would do. Anything to get Ava away. Get
her as far away from the monster as he could. For the first time,
he completely understood why the Irina had fled.

"Malachi, calm yourself," Damien said, standing in the
doorway.

"I want to know more." Ava spoke for the first time since the
brothers had gathered.

Rhys sat near the computer. Leo sat next to him, looking

through more books, everything they had on record about the fallen angel known as Jaron. Maxim was sitting across from Malachi and Ava, and Damien was waiting for a callback from Vienna.

"I want to know more about the Fallen," Ava said again. "This makes no sense. How did Jaron know about me? Why was he even interested? Malachi acts like the Fallen are more powerful than you guys——"

"They are," Maxim said.

"So, what did he want with me? And why didn't he hurt me when he could have?"

The set of her jaw told Malachi he'd be answering questions whether he liked it or not. When his mate set her mind on something, she was impossible to budge. Part of him loved it. The other part wanted to tear his hair out.

But then, there was no such thing as a biddable Irina.

Maxim crossed his arms and leaned toward them. "Ava, the first thing you must understand about the Fallen is this: They are not human."

"I understand."

"No, you don't." Malachi ignored the clipped manner his brother took with Ava. For such a young scribe, Maxim had more knowledge of Fallen and Grigori society than he did. Malachi had a tendency to stab first and question later.

"You don't truly understand what they are," Maxim continued. "It's impossible. The Fallen are angels; beings with no place in this world. Completely and entirely foreign. Irin are at least partly human."

"The Fallen are bad; I know that."

"Don't make the mistake of assigning moral judgment to them," Maxim said. "Good. Bad. These have no meaning to them. They do not live by human mores. They were never intended to."

"But…" He saw her frown. "I thought angels were meant to be good."

"No, they were meant to serve. That is their sole purpose. Servants of the Creator."

Ava leaned forward, away from Malachi's arm. "But the Forgiven…"

"The angels fell from the heavens, tempted by the beauty of human women, curious about the interest their Master had in this new race. Remember that: They *all* fell."

"Because they fell in love?"

Maxim shrugged. "Don't assume so. Don't assume any human emotion when it comes to angels. They wanted and they took. They're curious creatures. Human women would have been stunned by their appearance. They probably thought they gave themselves to gods. Their children were powerful and magical. Heroes and seers. The first offspring were imbued with the powers of their fathers, but they were uncontrolled. Unpredictable."

"So what happened? Where did the Irin come from?"

"We are the children of the Forgiven. Fallen angels who returned to heaven."

"Why? Why did they leave?"

"The Creator offered forgiveness. They took it. We don't know why or how."

"But they left," Ava said. "They left their wives. Their children. How could they?"

Malachi said, "Angels were never meant to live here. The Fallen were heavenly creatures who turned their back on their purpose. And as Max said, their offspring were frightening. Some were thought to be gods. Others became so powerful their own fathers were forced to destroy them. The Irin believe the Forgiven returned to heaven because—though they realized they could rule over the Earth—that power was contrary to everything they had been created for. So they left us and returned. They sacrificed their own power for the good of humanity and were redeemed."

"And their children?" Ava's voice wavered, and Malachi took

her hand when her eyes filled with tears. "You said some were destroyed, but the Irin are still here. Even with the Irina mostly gone—"

Damien broke in. "The Creator took mercy on the mates of the Forgiven and on their children. He protected the offspring who were not destructive. Allowed them the strength and knowledge of their fathers, but on the condition they would watch over this new race of humans. That is where we came from, Ava. We are of the race of angels. Neither wholly human, nor wholly heavenly. The Irin were meant to guide humanity and guard it. Servants on Earth as our fathers were servants in the heavens. That became our purpose."

"And the Fallen?"

"The Fallen are an abomination in every sense," Damien said. "Beings meant to serve who repudiated their Creator and desired to rule. They didn't leave, because they sought to conquer. They saw humanity as sheep. Lesser beings. They break every law of the universe, simply by their rebellion. The Fallen cannot be trusted. Their very presence on Earth is evidence of their dishonor. That is why their children are cursed."

"The Grigori," she said.

"Yes," Malachi drew her closer. "They became predators like their fathers, the Fallen. They prey on the humans we seek to protect. It has always been so."

Ava asked, "How many fallen angels are there?"

"We don't know," Rhys said from the desk. "There are nine prominent ones, scattered across the globe. Each rules over an area, but there are minor Fallen as well. They kill each other off occasionally. Fight their own wars, which we only pay attention to when it affects us or the humans."

Leo muttered, "It's not as black and white as you all believe. There are variations. Subtle shifts in power that—"

"We all know your fascination with them," Rhys said.

"Trying to understand the Fallen doesn't make them any less evil."

Leo and Maxim simultaneously bared their teeth, and Malachi was reminded, again, how young the two cousins were. Only around two hundred, they were babes when the Rending happened, hidden by their mothers somewhere in the cold North. No one knew how, exactly, the boys had survived. They had been delivered to a scribe house in rural Finland weeks after their families had been destroyed.

"Fallen society is, in its own way, as complicated as ours," Maxim growled. "I've studied it. Jaron is—"

Malachi finally broke in, exasperated by the bickering. "Can we please stop the history lesson and return to how we're going to protect Ava?"

Maxim said, "I'm just saying that Jaron is not easy to classify. The fact is he had access to your mate for weeks when no one suspected him. He could have harmed Ava at any time, but he didn't. Clearly, he has some interest in her that is not wholly understood. It may be beneficial for her to meet with him and try to get more information."

"It's not safe," Rhys said. "He may have not moved then, but how do you explain the clear aggression in Kuşadası? They were trying to hurt her. Or capture her at the very least."

"Malachi," Maxim asked. "You said the Grigori in Kuşadası looked like Brage?"

He nodded. "Not the captain, but the rest of them were lighter skinned and light haired. Most likely not Jaron's children. More Northern-looking. Maybe Volund's or Grimold's, if I had to guess."

"And Brage has been seen in Istanbul," Leo said. "With an angelic blade."

Damien nodded. "In Jaron's territory. He may have other alliances. We may be seeing a move from the North that would upset Jaron's rule here in the region."

Rhys asked, "A coup? Volund moving against Jaron, and

using his most trusted Grigori to kill him? He could have been the one to give him the blade. There were rumors he had one."

"They all have them," Maxim grumbled. "Don't let the council in Vienna fool you."

Damien barked out a reprimand in the Old Language, and Maxim shut up.

"If there is a coup in the works, then having Ava collect more information from Jaron could be crucial," Leo said. "She's smart. And she's in the perfect position to—"

"She's not a bloody soldier!" Malachi said.

"And I'm not a china doll, either." Ava stood, looking around the room, glaring at every man in sight. "You guys keep talking about me like I'm not here. Enough."

Malachi stood with her. "*Canım*—"

"I'm going to the garden to think for a while," she said. "Alone. I need some quiet, so don't follow me. Any of you." She left the room, and Malachi could hear her climbing the stairs, all the way to the roof garden that looked toward Galata Tower.

He turned to Rhys. "Are there security cameras up there?"

"Yes." His brother clicked a few times on the computer, then tilted the monitor toward Malachi. "She's covered from every angle. And the alarms will go off if there is any movement on the sides of the house."

He pointed toward Rhys's chair as Maxim and Leo drifted from the room. "I'll watch her. At least give her some privacy."

Rhys looked like he wanted to object, but a quick word from Damien called him from the library, leaving Malachi alone with only the image of his mate in black and white, staring off into the distance with haunted eyes.

MAXIM CREPT INTO THE LIBRARY AN HOUR LATER, AT SUNSET, AS Malachi was watching Ava.

"You have a lovely mate, brother."

"I do."

"An unexpected blessing to our kind."

Malachi had the urge to cover the computer so his fellow scribe could not see her. But Maxim only glanced at Ava briefly before turning to Malachi.

"He was with her for weeks, and no harm came to her."

His voice held a warning note. "Maxim…"

"I believe there is something happening," Maxim said. "There are shifts in Vienna. Then Ava appeared like this. Strangers are showing up in Istanbul. So many rumors among my associates. I hear them, Malachi. I know everyone thinks me a gambler and a rogue, but—"

"Max—"

"Something is happening." He leaned forward. "And I think she is the key. There is something she is or has that Jaron has an interest in."

"Of course he does!" Malachi finally burst. "She's the first new Irina in centuries! However she came to be, she could be the key to restoring our race. And if the Irin are made whole again, the Fallen could be conquered."

"Is that what we're truly fighting for? Don't be like Damien and follow the Council blindly."

Malachi narrowed his eyes. "You speak rashly, Scribe. And you make assumptions that betray your years."

"Just because I'm young doesn't mean I don't see things. Damien is wise, but he never questions orders from Vienna."

"And you question them too often."

"I only seek to see our people whole again," Maxim said. "We are constantly at war, but where are the Irina? Why are there none on the council any longer? When did the future of our race become the will of eight old men? There are too many secrets."

"The Irina retreated of their own will," Malachi said. "Were we to force them to stay?"

Maxim sat back, no argument rising to his lips as he turned his eyes back to Ava. "She is the key. And Jaron showed her no aggression. She should meet with him and find out why. He is not an unreasonable creature."

"He's a Fallen."

"Now who's making assumptions?" Maxim said. "You admitted that the angel was helping her cope with her abilities before we knew what she was. Perhaps there is more to him than you think."

Malachi sat back, staring toward the screen. Ava wrapped her arms around herself as the evening breeze picked up. A slight shiver shook her frame. He immediately rose to go to her. She'd left her sweater in their room.

"I must go," he said. "We'll talk more later."

"It's really rather simple," Maxim said as Malachi reached the door. "Why don't you ask Ava what she wants to do?"

He turned. "She's mine to protect."

The young scribe shook his head. "She's all of ours to protect, brother, but she has a will of her own. Ask her."

Malachi went to their room first, grabbing a blanket from the closet before he climbed the twisting staircase to the tiled garden on the roof. The sun was setting over the city, and the sky was painted a lush golden red. Ava turned when she heard him, then silently held out her hand.

He went to her, sliding behind her on the chaise where she sat and pulling her back into his body as he wrapped the blanket around them both. Ava leaned against him, their earlier argument seemingly forgotten as she took a deep breath and tucked her face against his neck.

"What were we fighting about before?" she asked quietly.

"You going to Jaron's office? All of us speaking for you, instead of with you?" He tucked a curl behind her ear as the breeze tossed her hair into his face. "Or me stupidly not telling you the implications of coming back here together?"

"To be fair, I probably would have run screaming at the thought of a lifetime commitment, so I understand why you didn't."

"I think the phrase 'stupidly in love' applies. I'm very out of practice handling women."

He felt her laugh against his skin, and she turned until she'd wrapped her arms around his waist as he laid back.

"I don't need to be handled. Just informed."

"I'll remember from now on. I promise."

Night descended, cool wind sweeping up from the water and over the city as lights lit up the evening sky. The cries of the muezzin came and went, echoing from all corners before the call to prayer drifted into the night, leaving them in a cocoon of darkness and warmth as they huddled together.

"There's no going back," she finally whispered. "I know that. I…I don't even want to. You were right about what you said before, even if the truth hurt. I was alone. Plus, I'm stupidly in love with you, too, so I guess we'll have to figure this out together."

He thought his heart would beat out of his chest with joy. "I love you, Ava." He squeezed her tighter. *Reshon.*

She tensed for a moment, then relaxed, and Malachi suspected she'd heard his soul speak the word. She'd probably been hearing it for days. Weeks? And despite that, she'd stayed with him. He'd been a fool to doubt her.

"But if these are my people," she started, "then this is my struggle, too. My responsibility."

"Don't—"

"I want to meet with Dr. Sadik. With Jaron. Maybe he knows where I came from. Maybe he knows what this all means. Why those Grigori were after me. I know you always suspected him, but looking back, I never felt unsafe. I could hear his voice, Malachi." She turned her face up to his. "And I know he didn't mean to harm me. So, why? If he was only a predator, why?"

"I don't know."

"I want to find out. And I also want to know if he was telling the truth about there being others like me."

Malachi sat up. "What do you mean, others?"

"He'd said he'd helped others with my same symptoms. Maybe he was lying, but maybe he was telling the truth. I didn't hear any dishonesty in him. And if there are others out there, other women like me…"

"There could be more Irina," he said softly.

"It's possible. We still don't know why I am the way I am. Where my powers came from. But maybe Jaron knows."

"But would he tell us?"

"He might not." Ava shrugged, and a glint of excitement lit her eyes. "But there's only one way to find out."

THE WAITING ROOM LOOKED LIKE ANY OTHER WAITING ROOM OF any other office in the city. Bright. Modern. Framed art on the walls and an efficient secretary quietly making calls.

Malachi thought nothing had seemed as menacing. He abhorred masks. And that, no matter what Ava thought, was what this office was. A few minutes later, a cheerful nurse poked her head in.

"Ava?"

"Hello," she said, rising with Malachi's hand grasped in her own. "Good to see you again."

"So happy to see you back. How did you like Cappadocia?"

The two women chatted as they walked down the hall and were ushered into a comfortable office. Malachi's daggers burned against his skin. He would be able to reach them in seconds, even though they would do nothing against a fallen angel. His brothers surrounded the office building, watching from all angles while Malachi and Ava were inside.

A few minutes later, a seemingly harmless middle-aged man entered the office. His green eyes flicked to Malachi for a moment before he greeted Ava.

"My dear," he said warmly. "So good to see you back. And this is your friend you were telling me about?"

"Yes, my… fiancé." Ava glanced at him, but Malachi didn't

take his eyes off the doctor. The disguise was seamless. He could sense no extraordinary power from the creature. No flicker of otherworldly strength. No wonder they'd all been fooled.

The angel, pretending to be harmless, held out a hand. "So good to meet you, Mister…"

"My name is Malachi," he said, ignoring the offered hand. "And you know what I am."

A slight waver in the mask. "You'll have to pardon me, but—"

"We also know who you are," Ava said quietly. "So no more lies. No more disguises. Let's speak plainly… Jaron."

Green eyes widened for a heartbeat before the doctor stepped back. And Malachi watched, never letting Ava's hand leave his own as Dr. Sadik stood behind his desk with a small smile flickering over his lips.

His eyes darkened to near black, then lightened to a glowing gold color as the mask dissolved. Jaron's shoulders grew wide and thick. His frame lengthened before them until the being was at least a foot taller than he'd been before, almost seven feet. There was a faint gold shimmer that covered his skin as the mask of the harmless doctor fell away and the heavenly being emerged.

His hair grew longer until thick ebony strands brushed past his shoulders. His human clothes disappeared, and the angel stood before them in nothing but a pair of loose pants. The bronze skin of his torso glowed in the afternoon light and raised *talesm* rose like shimmering brands on his skin.

He was radiant.

Glorious.

Terrible.

The only other time Malachi had beheld an angel, the creature had been cloaked. Jaron was probably still cloaked, but he was letting Ava see him far closer to his true form, if Malachi had to guess. It was little wonder that early humans had thought the creatures were gods. No classical sculpture could compare with the utter perfection of the angel's form.

And throughout the transformation, Jaron's eyes never left Ava's. He stared at her as if Malachi didn't exist, his eyes glowing with a gold light as he watched Malachi's mate. When he glanced over, he could sense Ava's awe. She stood, her heart racing, clutching his hand, but her eyes never left Jaron's.

"I am Jaron," he said. The Fallen's voice was low and resonant. Malachi could feel it pressing against his mind. It wrapped around his body, and he had to fight the urge to flee. "Now you see my true face. Hear my voice. *Ava.*"

"I...I didn't know." She stammered as tears came to her eyes. "*I didn't know.*"

"Child, you should not have come back."

CHAPTER

EIGHTEEN

Ava couldn't speak. Her eyes locked with Jaron's as image after image flooded her mind. Bright, glaring, as if seen through eyes that took in every shadow and color in preternatural detail. The pictures flickering like an old film reel, she saw herself as a child, stumbling through her first steps. Splashing in a wading pool in front of a tiny house in Santa Monica. Riding a horse at Carl's ranch.

Darkness.

Then images from her first days in Istanbul. Wandering through the spice market. Buying chestnuts from a vendor near Galata Bridge. Drinking tea with Malachi. Their kiss on the island.

Malachi.

Utter black. Pain. Despair.

She clutched Malachi's hand tighter, gasping when the next images flew past.

Two dark-haired children. A girl with a golden gaze, laughing as butterflies swirled around her. A boy, staring back at her with his father's eyes. An ink-black jaguar curled around the children protectively as a wolf and a tiger paced behind. The tiger bent to the girl, opening his mouth. Ava felt her heart race, but the great beast closed his jaw around the girl's nape gently as she continued to smile and pet its cheek. The image flickered away as a great circle rose in the sky, like a sun twisted with gold and silver. Higher and higher it rose, until the sun faded away to stars, a million scattered points of light dotting the heavens, dancing in concert to a growing song.

Darkness.

Ava felt Malachi's arms around her. Heard Jaron's whisper in her mind. Not in the Old Language, but in her own.

I show you what has been. What will be. And what could be. Do not fear the darkness.

Her eyes came back into focus, staring into Malachi's as he looked down on her. She must have stumbled, because he was holding her in his lap, sitting in a chair in the doctor's office.

"Ava?"

She couldn't speak for a moment, still lost in the eyes of the boy as her mate's eyes stared back at her. She reached up, brushing away the dark hair that had fallen across his face.

"I will not fear the darkness," she whispered. Turning her head, she looked at Jaron again, but the radiance had grown dim and the Fallen appeared more human, though no less frightening. "Who are you?"

"You ask the wrong question, child."

"Who am I, then?" She blinked and sat up, trying to fight the wave of nausea that swept over her. The instinctive fear that hummed in her blood.

"A better question, but one I have already answered."

"No, you haven't." She frowned when she saw the angel's lip curl slightly at the corner.

"You're right. It's better to say that I've answered it as much as I want to right now."

"I don't understand any of this."

"You will." He shrugged. "Or you won't. Try to understand, as more fates than yours rest in your song."

Ava stood, vibrating with anger. "Why don't you tell me more, then? What am I?"

She felt Malachi rise behind her, putting a calming hand on her shoulder. "Ava—"

"I'm not scared of you, Dr. Sadik. Or Jaron. Or whatever your name is."

The angel looked amused. "You should be scared. Wiser ones usually are."

Malachi growled behind her, trying to push forward to stand between Ava and Jaron. Ava wouldn't let him; she pushed forward.

"Ava, stop—"

"If I'd wanted her dead, Scribe, she would be," Jaron said, his voice growing more resonant and his face starting to glow again. "If I'd wanted to harm her, she would be gone. Wiped from the Earth and your memory as if she had never existed."

"Impossible," her mate murmured, drawing Ava back to the safety of his arms.

"Very possible," Jaron whispered. "Never underestimate my kind, Scribe. She has chosen you, yes. But I am not convinced you are equal to the task. What darkness have you truly battled?"

She felt him draw one of the daggers from under his arm. It glinted in the light from the window as he held it between Jaron and herself.

"I have battled evil like you before."

In the space of a heartbeat, the angel towered over them. Ava trembled, but Malachi stood firm, his arm across her chest never wavering. His hand on the dagger didn't tremble.

Jaron spoke, and his voice moved over them like a wave. "You have never battled one like me. You will meet the darkness, and it will overwhelm you." His gaze flickered down to Ava. "She knows what could be now. Protect your woman, Scribe. Get her out of this city. It is no longer under my domain. Others seek to take her from you. They will show you no mercy. Even now, your brothers battle children who are not of my blood, and one carries a heavenly blade."

Then Jaron spoke something in the Old Language, and the writing that covered his body, even more intricate and beautiful than Malachi's *talesm*, glowed with a burnished-gold light. Ava had to shield her eyes, and when she opened them, the angel had disappeared.

"We have to get out of here," Malachi said, tugging her away from the gold glow where Jaron had been.

"Where did he go?"

"I don't know. I don't care. We have to move, Ava. Now."

Bursting through the door, Ava could hear them. Silent physically, but their dark minds scratched at her own. Vicious whispers of violence and blood. She ran after Malachi, halting briefly when she saw the blood.

The receptionist and the nurse were dead, their necks split open, blood pooling on the tiled floor and staining the intricate carpet in the waiting room. Malachi cursed under his breath and pulled her from her shocked stupor.

"Th...they killed them. Why didn't Jaron—"

"Tools," he hissed. "I told you. They were nothing to him. He's left here. Possibly left the city. Whatever protection he was granting you is gone. I have to get you away."

Malachi and Ava ran down the stairs, leaving the vicious whispers behind, only to be slapped by shouting voices when they left the building.

"This way!" She pointed toward an alley where she sensed them, running toward it and pulling Malachi with her.

"Ava, no!"

"But Rhys and Leo are there! I can hear them."

With another muttered curse, he followed her, shoving her behind him as they ran. "Stay back, but stay close." He dropped her hand and pulled out his other dagger when they'd left the foot traffic behind. Ava could hear the humans around them, chattering about the man with the weapons. A few wondered if a movie was being filmed. Their inner voices buzzed with excitement and curiosity, but no fear.

As they reached the back of the building, Rhys and Leo emerged. Leo was bent over, holding his side as Rhys held him up.

"Angelic blade," Rhys panted. "Damien distracted him. They're still fighting. There were... so many. Heavens, Mal. Too many. There are too many. Even Max looked shocked. I have to get Leo out of here. He won't heal unless I can get him back to the fire."

"The fire?" Ava's eyes flew to the wound at Leo's side. It was deep and weeping. The blood was clotted and black around the wound.

Malachi grabbed Leo's other arm, and the young scribe groaned as the two men lifted him. "Any Grigori left?"

"We killed the six that were here. That blond bastard, Brage, was leading them, but Damien drew him off after he'd wounded Leo. Maxim has seven or so more on the other side, but none of them carried any serious weapons. He'll be fine."

They stumbled to the car, easing Leo in the back. Rhys pulled out the keys and opened the front door for Ava. "You keep him steady in the back. Ava, in the front seat."

"Why does he need a fire?" Ava asked as she slid in the car. They were only a few blocks from the scribe house, but Leo had fallen silent, and Malachi looked grim as he held him.

"Not just any fire," Rhys said as he drove through the twisting streets. "We need a flame from the ritual fire at the scribe house to cauterize the wound. I can stitch it up, but without that flame, it will never heal. What happened with Jaron? I'm going to assume this is some angelic shite we didn't know about."

"Apparently..." Malachi started speaking the Old Language and Ava tried not to scream. They were doing it again, withholding information she knew was important. She wanted to yell at them, but Leo's low groan interrupted her.

"Malachi…"

"Almost home." He brushed the blond hair from Leo's face, holding the man as he would a child. "You'll feel better soon."

"Hurts." Leo's voice was brittle with pain. "Won't… Tried all my spells. Won't heal."

Malachi held his hand over Leo's forehead, tracing letters Ava couldn't read, then the young man fell silent, soothed into a restless sleep.

"Rhys, how much longer?"

"There's a protest near the square again." More muttered curses as Rhys turned right, then left, trying to maneuver around the crowds gathered near Taksim Square.

"We could get out. Carry him?"

"Too many police. Too many questions."

The smell of smoke drifted through the windows, causing Rhys to look over to her. "Close it! There could be tear gas if there are protests."

Night was descending on the city, and the shops were lit up, taking advantage of the increased foot traffic, even as the police tried to herd pedestrians from the square. Ava could hear the chaotic shouts mixed with laughter and music blaring from the passing cars. The smell of smoke only grew stronger as they turned a corner that Ava finally recognized.

Rhys breathed out. "No…"

"What?" Ava turned her head from watching Leo and Malachi in the back of the car and her stomach dropped.

The scribe house was burning.

"WHAT ARE WE GOING TO DO?" AVA ASKED AS THEY WATCHED the old wooden house being licked by flames. Firefighters were already there, the spray of hoses and shouts filling the already chaotic night. "Malachi?"

Rhys barked something in the Old Language and got out of the car, keys still in the ignition. Malachi followed, the two arguing as Leo began to moan from the back seat again. After a few tense moments, Malachi slammed the back door shut and got in the front seat, putting the car in reverse and backing away from the scene.

"What are you doing?" she said. "You can't just—"

"I'm taking you and Leo to a safe house, but if Rhys can't get a piece of the fire, Leo won't survive the night. Rhys has to save a part of it, Ava. Even if the house survives, the firefighters will douse the fire. He has to keep part of it going for Leo."

"How on earth is he even going to—?"

"He'll find a way," Malachi said. "He has to."

Ava looked over her shoulder, but Rhys had already entered the house, slipping past the crowds that watched in fascination and horror as the old house burned.

"This is my fault," she said. "I brought this."

"This is a war, and it's been going on far longer than either of us have been alive, *canim*. Everything happens for a reason. Rhys will be fine."

Despite his comforting words, Ava couldn't escape the grim tone of his voice.

"You guys are practically indestructible, right?"

"Exactly."

AVA STILL HAD SMOKE IN HER NOSE WHEN THEY PULLED UP TO the modest carpet shop on the other side of the bridge. It was dark from the outside, but Ava could see a light glowing dimly on the second floor.

"Stay here," he said, pulling the car into a deserted alley.

Malachi got out and walked around the corner, returning after only a few minutes with a set of keys and a determined expression. He opened the back door and started to ease Leo out of the seat. The young man winced and Ava saw the blood start seeping from the wound again, black and thick.

"Help me," Malachi grunted. "You'll need to get the door." He tossed her a set of keys and Ava rushed to pick them up.

A few minutes later, the three were climbing a narrow staircase next to the rug shop. Ava opened the door to a deserted apartment with a small sitting room and a kitchenette.

"There's a bedroom in back." Malachi was carrying Leo, the tall man cradled like a child in his arms. Considering Leo was the tallest in the house, Ava wasn't quite sure how Malachi was even standing, but she didn't question it. She opened the door to the back to see a bed, narrow but clean. She knocked off the pillows and stripped off the covers, clearing the bed for the wounded man. Malachi laid him down gently, and Leo immediately curled to the side. Ava saw him bite his lip so hard that it bled.

"Rhys?" she asked.

"I lost my mobile. Do you have yours?"

"In my purse in the car."

"I'll get it. Stay with him and stay away from the windows."

"Can I turn on some lights?" The house wasn't pitch-black, but close. The windows let in light from the street lamp on the corner, but other than that, the low light in the front room was all that shone in the small apartment.

"Wait for now. There are more in the rooms upstairs and the windows are blacked out on that floor."

He ducked out of the room, and Ava heard him on the stairs as she sat next to Leo and stroked his forehead. His skin was starting to burn with fever, so she got up and looked for a washcloth or rag to cool him. She found a towel in the kitchen and returned to him, placing it on his forehead as he relaxed under her touch.

For the first time all day, Ava tried to gather her thoughts.

Jaron had been protecting her; she was almost sure of it. He might be evil—and nothing about their conversation had convinced her otherwise—but he had been protecting her for some reason.

Something very bad was happening among the fallen angels and the Grigori, and something in the city had shifted. Was it a coup like Maxim had predicted? If so, any protection Jaron had offered her was gone. There seemed to be countless Grigori in Istanbul, and they were bold enough to have burned the scribe house.

Ava had no idea where they would go. Did they have other safe houses? Should she go back to Los Angeles and take shelter in Carl's fortress of a house? Somehow, she doubted even her stepfather's hired guns could get her out of this mess. Besides, the thought of leaving Malachi was unthinkable at this point.

Reshon. She was the one saying it this time. The vision Jaron had given her only confirmed it.

I show you what has been. What will be. And what could be.

"What could be...," she whispered, still holding the cool rag to Leo's forehead.

They were her children. Hers and his. With her dark curls and Malachi's grey eyes.

"Do not fear the darkness."

Jaron's words caused her to shiver, even in the over-warm room. What had he shown her? Was it his vision or hers? And why had she seen her childhood? Had he been watching her since then?

Questions still swirled in her head as she heard Malachi climbing the stairs, talking quietly on the phone. He was just hanging up as he entered the room.

"Well?"

"Rhys is on his way. No car, so he's going to have to walk. They won't let him on a tram carrying coals in a clay cooking pot he stole from a restaurant, but they should last until he gets here and can stoke the fire again."

She heard Leo mutter something that sounded like relief.

"And that will heal him?"

Malachi winced, but his eyes did seem less strained. "How good are you at sewing?"

"Horrible."

Malachi opened the small closet and pulled out a black bag that he tossed on the end of the bed. "You can hold him down or sew him up. Sounds like our stitching's about the same. Leo, you have a preference?"

"I'll hold still," he muttered. "You do it, Mal. I'd rather curse at you than Ava."

Ava's stomach began to churn as Malachi stripped off Leo's shirt, peeling the cloth away from the clotted wound. "Can't we wait for Rhys?"

"He's bringing the fire to cauterize it," Malachi said. "We'll stitch it up, and Rhys will seal it. Has to be done, Ava."

"Just get it over with," Leo said. "If I'm lucky, I'll pass out again."

MALACHI AND AVA WERE AS PALE AS LEO BY THE TIME RHYS showed up. The wound was over eight inches in length, and it seemed like it took Malachi forever to stitch it after Ava had helped clear the blood as much as she could. According to Malachi, infection wouldn't be a problem. Once the fire cleansed the wound, Leo's own magic would heal him, and having Ava's hands on Leo during the stitches would boost his energy, since she was Irina.

"Irina are the best healers," Leo said, gritting his teeth as Rhys placed glowing coals on the mottled skin at his side. "My father said my m…mother could heal any wound. She studied medicine at university, even." A tight smile. "She dressed like a man so she could go. My father said he laughed and laughed, but really, he liked her wearing pants."

Malachi smiled, brushing back the young man's hair. "That's a good story, Leo. When did your father find you?"

"When Max and I were seven, he just showed up." He closed his eyes as a growl of pain rumbled from his chest. After another gasping breath, he said, "He didn't know we'd survived the Rending. He'd been in Russia killing Grigori. He was… a bit mad, to tell the truth. But he got better eventually."

"Ava, put your palm on his neck," Rhys said, grabbing her hand and placing it over Leo's rapid pulse. "Hold it there."

"What else can I do?" she asked, tears threatening. She felt helpless in the face of the young scribe's pain.

Rhys shook his head, singed hair falling in his eyes. "I don't know how it works. Think about making him well, maybe? I don't know Irina magic."

"There's a song," Leo said, his voice sounding dazed. "My father sang it when we were young. A song to make you feel better…" He started mumbling under his breath as his eyes drifted closed.

"She can't sing it yet," Malachi murmured. "Not yet, Leo. Soon she'll know the words. It's too dangerous for her now."

Too dangerous because she couldn't control her magic. For the first time, Ava felt the sting of resentment. Maybe if the Irina hadn't run away, she would know. If they hadn't run away, Leo wouldn't be suffering as much. Maybe she wouldn't have spent years thinking she was a freak for hearing voices. A bitter seed took root in her heart as she thought about all the Irin had lost.

"Ava," Malachi whispered, pulling her hand away. "He's sleeping now. Enough. You need to save your strength, too."

She was feeling it. For the first time since her night in Cappadocia with Malachi, the voices around her were completely silent. She must have expended far more energy than she realized, helping Leo to heal.

"Take her upstairs to rest," Rhys said. "I'll stay with Leo and keep the fire burning."

"Have we heard from Damien and Max yet?"

"Not yet. I'll keep Ava's phone, if that's all right. Hers is the only one working."

She nodded and let Malachi lead her up the stairs to a tiny bedroom with a small lamp. He turned it on and began to peel off her clothes as she sank into the mattress. She felt Malachi lay behind her as she curled on her side.

"Sleep, my love. Leo will be fine, and you need rest."

"Sleep with me," she said, half asleep before her head hit the pillow. "*Reshon.*"

CHAPTER
NINETEEN

R *eshon.*

　　She called him *reshon*, and his heart soared. Despite the fear. Despite the loss. She called him *"reshon,"* and he was content. Malachi slept a few hours by her side, hand planted firmly on her soft skin, drawing and offering strength as she rested. But by the time he woke, he couldn't ignore the words Jaron had whispered in the Old Language before he shimmered out of sight.

"Thousands of you, Scribe. One of her. Remember."

Remember? How could he forget? The angel's meaning had been clear: Protect the Irina at all costs.

Whatever Jaron had showed her, Malachi hadn't seen. But clearly he'd been communicating with his mate in some way. The scene in the office flashed back to him. Jaron's transformation. Ava's awe. Their locked gazes held a secret that teased the edge of his mind. There was something...

"I didn't know. I didn't know..."

What had Jaron told her? Why had he been protecting her? There had to be a reason, but Malachi couldn't see what it was. As always, the motivations of the Fallen were incomprehensible. He wished Damien were here to counsel him, but he knew if the Watcher still lived after battling Brage's angelic sword, he was probably in a different safe house. It was better that they weren't all in one place. Had Damien already contacted Vienna? Did the Council know what was going on?

He had to get Ava out of Istanbul. He could drive across the country to Cappadocia, but getting her to Vienna would be better. He wished he knew where Sari was hiding. There was no fiercer Irina than Damien's mate. She would help him protect Ava; he knew it. Would Damien take them to Sari? Malachi felt like he was wandering in the dark forest of his dreams, stumbling through the fog and chasing answers to questions he didn't know. The house was utterly silent, but his mind was filled with disturbing and conflicting thoughts.

Ava stirred beside him.

"I can hear you thinking," she murmured. "Go back to sleep."

"Can't."

She pulled his hand up to her breast. "Then do something more entertaining than brooding."

Despite everything, she still made him smile. He bent down, kissing along her neck and caressing the skin of her breast, toying with her as his energy built.

Reshon.

A thought occurred to him. Ava wasn't in control of her magic, but there *was* a way to make her stronger. To lend her his own. She wouldn't be able to perform her half of the ritual— she didn't know the songs—but he could perform his half, lending her his power and protection. She would heal faster. She wouldn't tire. Her mind would be clearer and her sight better. If they were attacked again, it could mean the difference between life and death for her.

But not for you..., a small voice whispered. It would weaken him, because Ava couldn't lend her own magic.

Thousands of you, Scribe. One of her.

She turned to him, lifting her face for a kiss. He met her

mouth with eager lips, delving in to taste and tease. She responded by pulling him closer, melding her body to his in the small bed as his skin sang where she touched it. More. He had to have more of her. Malachi pulled off his shirt and hers until their bodies were pressed together. He'd never felt more whole. More alive.

Reshon.

He pulled away with a gasp. Protecting Ava was imperative. He knew she was the key. And as her mate, Malachi was the only one who could offer her the strength.

"Malachi?" She sat up, her hair spilling over her shoulders in the low light.

"Wait here. I'll be right back." He whispered a kiss across her mouth before he stood and walked downstairs, all the way to the old rug shop. He walked past the showroom, looking into the back room where they stored the new pieces for shipment and also the tools to do repairs.

There, on the workbench, he found what he was looking for. He grabbed the dye and then looked for a brush but couldn't find one. Just then, he spied a child's painting in the corner, sitting on top of a small wooden box. Opening it, he saw a mess of watercolor paints and... He smiled. A brush. Not the best quality to touch his mate's skin, but it would have to do. Someday, they would complete the ritual, then he would brush her skin with sable and decorate her from head to toe. The mental image was unspeakably arousing, so he grabbed the vegetable dye and the child's brush before he headed back upstairs.

When he entered their small room, Ava was sitting in bed with a frown on her face.

"Where did you go?"

He placed the brush and dye on the side table and knelt beside her. "I wish we were not here. I wish we were someplace beautiful where I could stand with you before my mother and father and speak the old vows declaring you mine."

Her eyes filled with tears, but they didn't look sad. "Malachi—"

"I can't do that, Ava. But I want you to know, I would. I will, someday. And before another hour passes, I want to say the words I can. Words that will mark you as my mate." He ran the tips of his fingers up her bare spine. "Write on your skin the spells that will bind us together." His fingers reached the nape of her neck as he bowed his face and kissed over her heart. "Will you let me, *reshon*? Will you take me, wholly and completely?"

"Tonight?"

"Right now."

"Your... mate?" She still hesitated at the word, but Malachi smiled.

"Yes."

"Forever?"

He looked up. "Forever. No turning away until death parts us."

A tentative smile crossed her lips. "I thought you guys were immortal."

He kissed her. "We're all immortal, Ava, as long as our stories are told." A small frown creased between her eyebrows, so he kissed her again. "Say yes."

"Yes."

"Yes?" He smiled.

"Yes, *reshon*." She placed her hands on his cheeks, stroking them despite the rasp of stubble. "You're mine. I knew it weeks ago. So yes."

Desire roared to life, but Malachi clamped down on it and said, "Take off your clothes. All of them."

"Every stitch?" The teasing light came back.

"Every. Single. Stitch." He pulled back the cover and reached for the jar of dye.

"What is that?" she asked as she pulled off her underthings.

"Henna dye. It's actually what we've always used, but I apologize for the brush." He shook up the dye and then uncapped it, dipping the rough brush into the jar before he looked up. "It should be much nicer than this."

"What do I do?" she asked, her voice tentative in the silence.

"Turn around," Malachi said. "Hold still. And let me mark you."

Ava pulled up her legs and turned her back to him. Malachi sat on the edge of the bed and took a deep breath. He'd dreamed of this moment for hundreds of years. Granted, the surroundings were usually a little more luxurious, but the sight before him…

Ava's smooth back, pale and glowing in the lamplight. The fine bones of her spine guiding him from the base of her skull to the swell of her buttocks. She was more than he'd dreamt. More than he deserved.

Malachi leaned forward, whispering the ancient vows against her skin, and his breath cast a golden glow as the magic took hold. He lifted the brush and began.

He wrote the spells across her body, the dye taking hold as the magic did. And though the henna would fade with time, the magic would remain, imbued in her skin. Protecting her. Strengthening her. For the rest of her life, his words would mark her. He took care as he wrote, hundreds of years of practice suddenly making sense. Countless hours of instruction. No mistakes were allowed in this; it was the most important *talesm* he would ever scribe.

Protective spells formed down her back. Whispered aloud as he felt the magic leave his body and enter hers. His lips trailed after his brush, kissing along her backbone as her heart raced beneath his mouth.

"Is it…" She arched her back when she felt the brush trail low. "Is it supposed to feel like this?"

He couldn't stop the smile of satisfaction. "This is the ritual performed on the mating night. Does it please you?"

She gasped as the brush moved over the base of her spine. She said, "That would be a yes."

Ava's scent bloomed and Malachi had to pause, breathing deeply as his forehead rested on her shoulder. "*Reshon*. Ava…"

"Keep going," she said, desire lacing her voice. "Don't stop."

Minutes turned to hours. She turned when he told her, baring the front of her body when her back and neck were covered with spells.

The spells for longevity were next, arching along her fine collarbone. Malachi groaned when he saw the golden flush across her throat. Her breasts. Her belly. The brush dipped and traced over and over, the ink darkening and drying as the magic glowed beneath it. She appeared lit from within. He bent his head and let his mouth suckle her breast, giving in to the arousal that had become almost unbearable.

She moaned and leaned back. "Malachi?"

"Almost done."

Spells for increased strength along her arms. Speed on her thighs. Spells for healing across her breasts and belly. He felt the magic leave him, knew he was giving almost dangerously of his own power, but he couldn't stop.

Her energy spilled over, and he felt the hum begin to build in the air.

"Soon?" She panted.

"Soon."

The last spells were over her heart, circling around as he pledged himself to her. He dipped in the dye again, then the brush met her skin as Malachi marked her as his mate. The balance of his soul. The bearer of his young. No other would mark her like this. No one but him. The possessive instinct swamped him as he finished the last stroke of the mating ritual. He braced himself over her, allowing the ink to dry as he drank from her lips. Over and over, she met him, as hungry for him as he was for her.

Patience.

Malachi was aroused to the point of pain. His breath came in rasps as her kisses drugged him, making his head spin. He clenched his hands in the loose sheets, allowing the magic to build and grow until her body was covered in a gold glow answered by his own *talesm*, which shone with a low silver light in the darkness. His magic swelled in recognition of its twin, even without the songs the Irina usually sang. Though untrained, Ava's magic was powerful. It called to him as their mouths met in aching hunger.

"Do you hear that?" she said, tearing her lips from his, bracing her hands on his shoulders.

"What?"

"That note. I…" Tears touched her eyes, but she smiled. "It's beautiful. Perfect. It's… us."

Complete.

Silver met gold when he tackled her to the bed.

Finally.

His body sang in recognition. Here was desire. Here was beauty. Here was completion. He reached down to test her, but Ava was as ready as he was, her body primed from hours of waiting.

"Yes!" She gripped his arms. "Now, *please.*"

He entered her with one thrust, halting when he was seated to the hilt, his forehead pressed to hers as they groaned in unison.

"Yes," she whispered. "Like this. Always like this."

He took her mouth again, leisurely tasting as he began a slow rhythm. She embraced him, arms wrapped around his chest, legs around his hips. The urgency was there, but Malachi didn't want to rush.

"Faster," she said.

He smiled. "No."

She dug her nails in his shoulders, and he bit back a moan. Then he reached down, gripping her hip and changing the angle until her head fell back and her body bowed. He took his time, ignoring her pleas to rush, delighting in her response as he tested their new connection. Her pleasure was his own. Her desire fed his. He held back—barely—when she came the first time. Then his body picked up a faster rhythm as the world narrowed to her.

"Again," he whispered.

"Can't."

"Yes, you can." He could feel it. Feel her body around him. The slow tightening. The catch in her breath. The pressure built as he flipped them over, letting her arch back over him as he watched her skin luminesce gold, alive with the ancient magic of their race.

This.

There was no greater beauty in heaven or earth.

"Again."

"Yes!"

Ava cried out as she came and Malachi's mind flew, her body pulling the long-awaited climax from him as he came in a roar of heat and light, his hands gripping her hips as his own back arched. His *talesm* shone bright silver in the darkness, then his mate fell forward, panting against his chest as he wrapped his arms around her and closed his eyes.

This is why the angels fell.

He woke slowly; the sun shining through the blacked-out windows cast eerie shadows in the room. Ava was still draped over his torso, exhausted by their lovemaking. Most of the dye had rubbed off during the night, leaving the red-brown henna patterns that mirrored his tattoos. His immediate reaction was to wake her and claim her body again, but he knew she needed sleep. He covered her with a light blanket and wrapped a towel around his body before he walked downstairs.

"Any change?" he asked Rhys, who still sat by Leo's bedside, drowsy in the brighter light of the second-story room.

"He's cooler. The wound is healing. He started getting some real sleep after you two quieted down."

"We weren't that loud."

"It wasn't the sound, it was the energy, for heaven's sake. You forget how young he is. If his body had let him, he would have gone charging into the night, desperate to find a woman."

"Sorry." Malachi pulled up a chair opposite his friend.

"No, you're not." Rhys's gaze flickered down to Malachi's hands, still stained from the henna dye. His eyes widened. "You marked her."

"I did."

"Malachi—"

"It was necessary."

"No, it wasn't. She doesn't know the other half of the ritual. You've given her half your magic with nothing in return."

"Don't say that." He glared. "Don't ever say that. If she was yours, you'd understand."

Rhys opened his mouth to speak but closed it again. After a few tense moments, he said, "You'll be weak."

"And she'll be strong."

"This is the worst time for you to indulge in sentimental—"

"It was necessary, Rhys." He bit back the urge to yell. "When we spoke to Jaron, he said something."

"What could he possibly have said that would make you risk your life—?"

"It was a warning. One of her, Rhys." His friend fell silent as Malachi spoke. "One of her. Thousands of us. She was sent to me for a reason. I have to protect her."

"We will all protect her, brother."

"I'm counting on that. If anything happens to me... I'm counting on that. Do you understand?"

Rhys's eyes finally met his intense gaze. "I understand. I would treat her as my own blood. You know this."

"Thank you."

"But seeing as you're her one true love, you'd better make this promise unnecessary. Do *you* understand?"

Malachi grinned. "You think I want to give her up after I've just found her? Think again. You'd have her forgetting me in no time."

His brother cleared his throat and forced a smile. "No, I wouldn't."

"No, you wouldn't."

"You need to get her out of the city."

"Has Maxim called?"

"No, but I know he keeps an extra car not far from here. With unknown Fallen activity and so many Grigori in the city, that's probably the safest route. If you can just get her out of the city, you'll buy yourself some time."

"Vienna?"

Rhys shrugged. "For now? Yes. But she needs to find someone to train her. After her safety, that's the first priority. Even untrained, her magic is powerful. She's like a loaded gun. She's been good about not speaking in the Old Language, but with your magic running through her veins now, the temptation to use it is going to be stronger. She might not even be able to control it."

"Irina, then."

"Irina. You need to find a group of them. Sari's faction would be the best, if Damien would tell you where they are."

"She's forbidden it. You know how she feels about males now."

Rhys nodded toward the stairs. "But you're not a lone male looking for a woman. You're bringing your mate with you for help. She won't leave an Irina unable to use her magic. It goes against everything she stands for."

Malachi nodded, thinking about their options. "She's rumored to be in Scandinavia somewhere."

"Somewhere. It's a big region."

"And Brage is on the hunt. He's Volund's offspring. If Volund is behind this aggression, Scandinavia may be the last place I want to take her."

"Or it may be the last place he'd look." Rhys leaned over

and wiped at Leo's brow, which was still dotted with perspiration. "If you get her out of the city, you two will have time to think. You'll have to find documents for her, anyway. Though if you can find Maxim, it's possible he already has them prepared."

"He's cautious like that."

"He is."

As if called by the gods, Ava's phone rang. Rhys smiled and handed it to Malachi. "Speak of the devil."

Malachi took the phone and saw Maxim's number on the screen. "Hello?"

"Finding unlisted mobile numbers is a pain in the ass, Malachi. Add her to the contact list, will you?"

He let out a sigh of relief and walked upstairs. "As if you already haven't."

"You are correct, old man. How's my cousin?" A slight hitch in his throat was the only clue how worried Maxim was.

"He'll be fine. Do you know about the house?"

"Yes. Did anyone retrieve the fire for him?"

"Rhys managed, but his hair's a bit shorter."

"We both owe him a debt."

"Which I'm sure he'll collect. How badly damaged was the house?"

"Not as much as we thought. The firefighters did an excellent job. I'm guessing whoever set it was trying to scatter us."

"So they succeeded."

"To an extent. Damien and I got hit with tear gas of all things after we got away last night. He's mad as hell this morning, but not damaged."

"We're lucky."

"You need a way out of the city. Damien has already called Vienna about the house, so they know some of what is happening. He was very closemouthed about your mate, though."

For some reason, Malachi was relieved. He didn't know why, but he felt like the less people knew about Ava, the better. "I'm not sure where we should go. Rhys said Scandinavia, but I need to speak to Damien about that."

"You're looking for Sari?"

"If she'll allow us sanctuary."

Maxim's low whistle was all the response Malachi expected.

"I'd tread carefully there. Luckily, I have obtained new documents for both of you. British passports, so you'll have no trouble traveling, but you'll have to be quick about it. Tonight. The row of hotels by the Theodosius Cistern. Go there. I have a spare vehicle at the Antea Hotel, right across from the entrance. The cistern is closed for renovation, so that area is quiet. Your keys and documents should be waiting at the front desk by seven o'clock."

"And if they're not?"

"Find a room. I'm sure you two will be able to keep yourselves occupied."

Malachi smiled when he saw Ava's eyes flicker open. "You'd be correct."

"You're not nice when you gloat, brother. I have to go."

"Wait, Maxim. Is Brage still in the city?"

"As far as I know."

Malachi sat on the edge of the bed, and Ava leaned over his shoulder, her ear to the phone.

Maxim said, "Damien wounded him, but not seriously. He'll be healed by tonight, if not sooner."

"Does he still have the blade?"

"He does," Maxim said. "Damn thing nearly hit one of my arms. I really have to go. Keep this phone with you. Tell Rhys to keep the fire burning. We'll find him and Leo later."

"I will."

He hit the End Call button and tossed the phone on the bedside table, turning so that Ava was pressed against his chest. Then he lay back, taking her with him.

"You've got to stop wandering off after we have mind-blowing sex," she said, snuggling into his chest.

"So… every morning then?"

She pinched his arm. "Cocky."

"Yes." Malachi pressed a kiss to her hair. "Did you hear Max?"

"Yes." Her eyes widened. "Every word, actually. My hearing is super strong right now."

"It's super strong forever, *canim*."

"And my eyes…" She looked around the dark room and frowned. "What did you do?"

He shrugged. "It's part of the mating ritual. I gave you some of my magic. And you'll give me yours. Eventually."

"But until then?" Ava sat up, eyes racing over his chest. "What do you mean, you gave me your magic? Does that mean you're not as strong?"

He reached for her cheek, but she pushed his hand away. "Ava—"

"No! Is that what it means?"

"I'm still very, very strong. We'll be fine. Do you really doubt me?"

Her face fell, and her eyes took on a faraway look. "I can't lose you, Mal."

"You won't."

"Trusting you—trusting *us*—was it for me. If something happened to you—"

"Nothing will happen to me. I'm too greedy. I'll never leave you." He sat up and pulled her into his arms. "We're almost there. Max has a car for us. Documents. We'll leave the city tonight. Sleep today and leave tonight. We'll be away before they can find us, and then we'll be safe." He brushed a hand over her curls, soothing her as she trembled in his arms. "Trust me, Ava. You'll be safe."

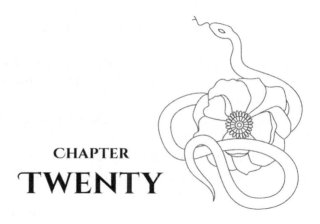

CHAPTER

TWENTY

T he Antea Hotel sat on the corner of the Piyerloti Caddesi, just at the end of a quiet string of hotels. A few hundred meters from the tourist center, the old street was sheltered by tall trees and staid municipal buildings. A quiet street in the Sultanahmet, but still central enough to the main thoroughfare, it was the perfect place to store an emergency vehicle.

Malachi held Ava's hand as they crossed the intersection, passing the empty cistern and the fountain in the center of the square. Pigeons startled from the sidewalk, but no other pedestrians interrupted them as they made their way into the lobby.

The young woman at the front desk eyed Malachi, causing an unexpected flair of possessiveness in Ava that caught her by surprise. Since the night before, she'd been on edge, bristling with borrowed energy and heightened senses. The passing cars distracted her. The lights were too bright. But her voices, thankfully, had become easier to ignore. The only one she heard clearly was Malachi.

"Good afternoon, sir," the woman said in perfect British English. "How may I help you?"

Malachi lowered his voice and switched to Turkish as Ava

took in the gold-accented lobby. It wasn't the fanciest hotel she'd seen, but it was clean and bright. The ground floor was quiet.

Almost too quiet.

Instincts pricked when Malachi took her hand and led her out toward the sidewalk.

"The car is here, but she said our package hasn't arrived yet. She suggested waiting in their restaurant, but I'd rather be out here."

"Me too." Ava looked around at the peaceful street that suddenly seemed ominous. "I don't like it here."

He frowned and smoothed a hand over her cheek. "What do you hear?"

"Nothing specific."

"Then we have to—"

"Not enough," she said in a low voice. "It's too quiet. Where are the other guests? There aren't even any tourists around here."

"It's the middle of the week, *canım*. I think you may be over-reacting." He raised a hand when she opened her mouth. "Which is completely normal considering your new senses."

She shook her head but couldn't find anything to argue with in his reasoning. He was probably right.

Since the mating ritual, Ava had been flooded with power. She was stronger. Quicker. She healed faster. She'd deliberately taken a knife to her forearm that afternoon while Malachi had been napping, just to see what would happen. The cut she'd made on her forearm had healed within minutes.

He was stroking her hair, leading them to the bench by the locked cistern. Ava looked at the sign announcing the renovations. It was in Turkish, but she could see the future plans for the new tourist attraction around the historic site.

"Did you get the car keys?" she asked when they'd sat.

"Yes. She said the messenger already called to say he'd be late. She said he'd probably arrive in the next half an hour."

"And Damien? Max?"

"Headed over to the rug shop right now. We'll call them once we get on the highway."

Ava nodded, a sense of unease still heavy in her belly.

"It's fine, *reshon*. Everything will be fine."

MALACHI WATCHED HER, WONDERING WHAT HAD HAPPENED TO the confident, fearless woman he loved. Since the night before, she was jumpy. A cloud seemed to hang over her shoulders. Was she truly that worried, or was their new intimacy making him more aware of her moods?

It wasn't uncommon for Irin mated for years to be almost telepathic with each other. Though they couldn't speak to each other's minds, the awareness of mood was hard to ignore. He'd know when she was angry or happy. Upset. Worried. He felt them all now as her emotions flooded the magic he'd given her. It was both intoxicating and distracting, and for the first time, he wondered whether the ritual had been the right thing to do.

Too late to second-guess himself.

Malachi watched the front of the hotel as two men exited. They looked up and down the street, then sauntered off in the direction of the Sultanahmet tram station. A few minutes later, a couple entered the hotel from the opposite side. Normal traffic on a quiet afternoon.

And still Ava sat, a silent knot of tension at his side.

"Tell me a story," she finally said.

"What kind of story?"

"Something not serious. What's your favorite childhood memory?"

He broke into a smile. "Swimming at the beach. We'd go to the North Sea in the summer when we lived in Germany."

"Wasn't that cold?"

"Freezing." He put an arm around her, thankful for the distraction. "My father had a good friend with a cabin there. I think it's still there, probably. It was quite old, but very nice. My mother and father and I would stay for two months in the summer. Living in a retreat can be very hectic sometimes. Families live in their own homes, but the children go to school together, the adults all work together. Even meals are communal. So my parents tried to make some time for only the three of us. That was our family time. I would play in the water even though it was frigid. My mother thought I was crazy."

A tentative smile crossed her face. "You were."

"We should go there," he said. "When we have children, we'll take them there."

There was a smile on her face. "We should." Ava took a deep breath. "We'll really have children, Malachi?"

"Hopefully." He squeezed her. "Irin don't have many children. One is normal. Two is fortunate. But I hope we have two."

THE VISION OF CHILDREN JARON HAD SENT HER FLASHED IN HER mind again. A dark-haired boy with his father's eyes. A golden-eyed girl laughing. It should have warmed her, but there was a dark side to the vision, as well. The animals had stood at attention, prowling around the girl and boy. Clearly guarding them, but from what?

"Do not fear the darkness."

The memory of Jaron's voice calmed her as she sat. Then she tensed again when she felt Malachi's arm tighten.

"What is it?"

"Grigori," he said, freezing as he watched two men enter the hotel lobby. "Two of them just walked in. Damn it."

Ava looked around them. They were completely exposed in the center of the square. There were no barricades to hide behind, no buildings they could duck into without being conspicuous.

"I can't kill them in the hotel lobby or out in the open here," Malachi said. "We'll have to wait for them to come out. Draw them somewhere isolated."

"Is it just the two?" Ava's eyes landed on the grated door of the Theodosius Cistern. Though it was locked, it was only with a simple padlock. No guards stood nearby. And the dark passageway had a view of the hotel.

"More coming this way," he murmured, taking her hand. "From the direction of the mosque."

Looking uphill, Ava spotted two attractive men strolling down the street toward them. They were looking toward the hotel, not at Ava and Malachi, but Ava knew as soon as they saw their friends leave the lobby, the Grigori would start looking for them.

"More from that street, too." Malachi pulled out Ava's phone and sent a quick text to someone. Somehow the drop location had been compromised.

"We have to get out of here," he said.

"How?" Ava's heart raced. Six streets converged at the cistern park, and from each direction, a group of men strolled toward them. There were two there. Three there. "Malachi, they've cornered us."

"No," he muttered. "There has to be a way..." His eyes landed on the locked grate leading to the cistern entry just as the call to prayer started and birds scattered in flight. The Grigori converging on the square turned their heads toward the mosque on Divan Yolu, and Malachi used the distraction to drag Ava toward the cistern. "This way."

"That goes underground!" she hissed. It was one thing to stroll through the Basilica Cistern with its dramatic columns and modern walkways, but the Theodosius Cistern looked like nothing but a black cave. "Malachi..."

"We'll watch and wait for now," he said, twisting off the lock that held the grate closed. He opened the door, and Ava was grateful the calls of the muezzin hid the rusty groan. "We can see the entrance of the hotel from here. There are too many to fight alone while I'm not at full strength. If we run, they'll catch us. Until Max and Damien get here, we need to hide."

She knew that ritual had been a bad idea. The thought of a weakened Malachi sent her heart into overdrive. "Did you text them already?"

"Yes." He shoved her farther into the shadowed passageway, and Ava almost tripped over the heavy rubber boots covered in mud that the workmen had left on the platform. "They should come soon. They'll create a distraction, and we'll grab the car. We can figure out documents later. Right now, I just want you out of this city."

"Okay."

Malachi sucked in his breath and darted back from the door. "Brage."

Ava's heart sank. From the darkness of the metal walkway, she could see the blond Grigori soldier walking out of the Antea Hotel and turning his head to look up and down the street. His eyes were narrowed with purpose.

The soldiers knew they were nearby.

MALACHI SHOT OFF ANOTHER TEXT TO MAX, WHO HAD YET TO respond. Where the hell was he? Annoyance and worry competed in his mind. What had happened to the documents? Had Maxim been set up? And further, how could Malachi get the car from the hotel while avoiding the dozen or more Grigori who had taken up residence at the intersection?

When he realized who the blond Grigori outside the hotel was, thoughts of the car fled. He had to get Ava away. Eyes darting into the blackness, he racked his memories for every-thing he knew about the cistern where they were hiding. It was an old one, and he suspected it connected to the Valens Aque-duct, the ancient waterway the Romans had built to transport water throughout the city. Many of the cisterns still had tunnels leading between them. Was the Theodosius one of them?

Malachi tossed one last look toward the square. The sky was growing dim, and the street lights in front of the hotel had switched on. He could see Brage and the other Grigori milling in front of the hotel. He could wait for them to leave the square, or he could look for another way out.

He looked down to the boots at their feet, then bent down to slip on the biggest pair, handing another to Ava.

"Put these on."

"Where are we going?"

"Down." He saw a small flashlight near the edge of the platform. Flicking it on and hoping the light wouldn't be seen from outside, he peered over the edge. "We're going to see if there's a tunnel."

"What?" Ava squeaked. She might have protested, but she was already pulling on the boots. "We're going farther down? Shouldn't we wait here for Max and Damien?"

"And wait for Brage to notice the broken lock on the gate?" Standing in the boots, he tested them, finding himself not unbearably clumsy in the yellow rubber footwear. "There could be a tunnel out of here. There often are in these old places. And if they do find us in here, I want a wall to my back and you behind me. It'll be easier to kill them if I don't have to worry about them coming from all directions."

He didn't mention Brage wielding an angelic blade. That was the real problem.

"I knew you shouldn't have given me a bunch of your magic," she said, pulling on the second boot.

Malachi was doubly glad that he had. If she was injured in all this, improved healing could be the difference between life and death for her. And with Ava's improved eyesight, they barely had to use the flashlight.

"Come on." He took her hand and started down the creaking staircase.

"Are you sure this thing is safe?"

"Workmen have been climbing up and down on this for months, so I hope so." He paused when one of the steps wobbled under his feet. Then he started climbing at a slower pace. "We're not that heavy. We'll be fine."

Once they'd safely reached the bottom, Malachi turned on the light. Sweeping it from side to side, he could see the soaring columns belted by steel bands for reinforcement, marching like grey soldiers into the black. The domes of the cistern towered over them, the ancient brick causing the slightest noise to echo. He could hear water dripping overhead and the splash of muddy water as Ava walked behind him.

"They're renovating it right now," he whispered, "but it used to have as much water as the Basilica Cistern."

"Looks more like mud to me." She almost tripped over a shovel leaning against the wall. "Holy cow, it stinks."

"People throw all sorts of things down here. Try not to think about it."

Malachi carefully led them around the periphery of the cavern, but he couldn't spot a tunnel or other exit. If there had been one, it was closed off or under mud or brick. The water grew deeper the farther they went, and thick mud sucked at their feet.

"Anything from Max or Damien?" she whispered behind him.

He glanced at the phone. "I can't get any reception down here. I told them where we were hiding. I just hope they get the message."

"If they don't... then what?"

Then what? He had no idea.

AVA'S SENSE OF DREAD GREW WITH EVERY STEP THEY TOOK INTO the dark cavern. The water sloshed at their feet, and the flashlight seemed unbearably bright in the pitch-black underground. She was certain anyone looking in from outside would see it.

"You know," she whispered, glad her voice didn't waver, "of

all the sights for us to see, this is one I probably could have skipped."

"I did promise to show you an authentic side of the city." He scooped up a dead fish and tossed it to the side.

"Malachi?"

"Yes?"

"I love you, even though you're dragging me through really stinky water and mud right now."

He turned and she could see his smile even in the darkness. "I love you, too. I say we deserve a vacation after this is over. Didn't you mention you were rich?"

"Extremely."

"Know any places with better water and less dead fish?"

"I just might."

She saw his shoulders shake with laughter as they continued working their way around the walls of the cistern. Despite careful inspection, no tunnel appeared. No alternate exit presented itself.

Finally, Ava sighed and said, "It's been a while. Maybe they're gone. Or some have left and we could sneak away. We should go check to see if they're——"

The sound of the door creaking stopped her. All ease fled as she heard the whispered voices from the platform above.

It wasn't Damien or Max.

HEART RACING, MALACHI TRACED OVER HIS *TALESM PRIM*, activating the magic that remained. He was still strong. Still able. He would be able to defend her. He felt the creep of magic and took her hand, slowly moving behind one pillar and out of the line of sight from the door. He listened.

"——gate open."

"Is this cistern linked through the tunnels?"

"I don't think so."

They were speaking German, the rough syllables echoing

over the water as he and Ava stood as statues in the dark. Even a ripple in the water would give them away. She was pressed against him, her heart racing against his chest, but her breathing was deliberately slow. She was concentrating on not panicking.

Good girl.

If they could just remain silent enough…

"There are lights."

Malachi heard a fumbling on the platform, and then the cistern was flooded with work lights hanging from various pillars.

Damn.

Another, heavier step sounded on the metal platform. The other Grigori fell silent.

"I can smell your fear, Scribe."

Brage's deep voice didn't boom. It curled and twisted in the darkness, seeking them where they hid. Malachi felt Ava tremble.

"The scribe and the woman are here," Brage said. "Spread out. Find them."

As soon as he heard the splashes, Malachi moved. Carefully stepping in the shadows, he went farther into the cistern, toward the deeper water where the mud lay thick on the bottom of the floor.

The Grigori were as slow as Malachi and Ava were, their normal speed negated by the pulling mud. He wrapped an arm around Ava to still her so he could listen.

One.

Two. Three.

Four in the water.

Splash!

Five.

A louder splash as one jumped from the railing and into the water.

Six.

"Matteus. Alfred. Stand watch with Mikael by the fountain. If any of the others scribes approach, alert me."

Brage. Three by the fountain. By Malachi's calculations, that meant eight in the cistern. Two more splashes confirmed his estimate, then the water fell silent, save for the isolated curses as the Grigori tripped over each other and the detritus of the work site.

Ava's hand squeezed his own, and he had to force her to release it so he could grab the silver daggers he wore under his shirt. He frowned. Weaponless. His mate was weaponless.

That is, she was weaponless until he saw her pick up the crowbar from a niche in the wall.

He smiled proudly.

"I think I saw some ripples in the water over there!" one said.

"Where?"

"Are there fish in this water? It could be fish."

"Yes. I feel them."

They moved deeper, Ava had sunk to the waist, but was still moving slowly, deliberately, behind him. He'd spotted a corner earlier where he thought she'd be best protected. A round, half dome carved into the wall. He suspected it had once been a walled-off exit, but nothing remained except a few steps. He didn't have time to investigate more.

Once they got there, he drew up her arm and started writing with his finger. The low luminescent writing was hidden in the shadows.

He hoped.

Stay here. I'm going to even the odds.

She shook her head violently, but he kept writing.

Use the crowbar.

He had to wait for the letters to fade before he wrote again.

Swing for the neck and the groin. Don't hesitate. If you can sink the clawed end into a neck, PULL. Do as much damage as possible and stay as quiet as you can. I'll be back.

She shook her head again, tears at the corners of her eyes. Malachi bent down, kissing them away before he whispered, "Don't worry. I told you, I'll be back."

Then he slipped into the darkness.

AVA WANTED TO SCREAM. SHE FELT HELPLESS. CHOKED BY silence, mysterious words whispered in her mind, teasing her as she waited in the darkness. The Old Language called her, the magic begging at her lips.

Powerless.

She was stronger. Faster. Healed more quickly. But she knew nothing about how to protect herself or make her mate stronger. She gripped the cold, gritty handle of the crowbar and lifted it against the dark, tensing when she heard the first sounds of struggle.

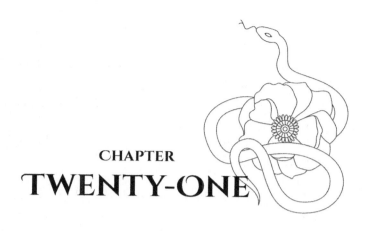

CHAPTER
TWENTY-ONE

Malachi slid through the shadows of the cistern, sneaking behind the first soldier and sliding a hand to cover his mouth as the dagger plunged into the monster's spine. The Grigori stiffened, arched, then began to dissolve. The dust lifted in the darkness, pulled by an unseen wind. He spun and darted behind the next pillar, waiting for the other Grigori to react.

"I see dust!"

"He's here."

"Where?"

"In the cistern."

"We already knew that, you idiot."

They were speaking a mix of German, Turkish, and Danish, with muttered curses in at least two other languages. These Grigori were not from Istanbul. Who had sent them? Who was pulling Brage's strings?

Malachi hid behind another pillar, darting out to grab another. He quickly dispatched him as the others scrambled in the water. Two down, six to go. His legs, long used to the strength of his immortal power, ached in the cold water, but pure adrenaline pushed him. He had to keep them away from his mate.

"Work along the walls," Brage said. "You idiots! Forget him. We want the woman. Drive her to me."

Eyes narrowing, Malachi stepped into the light, drawing their attention to him and away from Ava.

"There!"

Two Grigori rushed him, and Malachi was soon lost to the battle. Splashes sounded from overhead as more soldiers fell into the water, heading toward him. Then more shouting as he slashed and stabbed.

Another to dust. Another.

He ducked and twisted, using them against each other in the confusion of the dark water. Many ended up stabbing each other, their blades diverted from his skin by the spells that still protected him. The ones that did land hurt, but not enough to make him pause. It was their numbers that overwhelmed him. As more poured in, Malachi lost count of how many he fought. His only thought was to move toward the exit, drawing them away from Ava.

"One of her. Thousands of you, Scribe."

Protect Ava.

He ducked under the water, crouching down, only to burst up, blades flying, catching two Grigori under the chin and throwing them back as their blood sprayed the slick pillars of the cistern.

He slashed again and again until the muddy water was black with spilled blood. And still the corner where Ava hid was silent.

SHE WATCHED, LIP CLENCHED BETWEEN HER TEETH, BITING BACK the screams as she watched him battle. Four Grigori were on him, one slashing his back, another diving for his neck, only to trip over something in the water and fall down, taking out another who approached him.

He fought like a raging beast, his muscles straining, his *talesm* glowing in the harsh light and shadows of the underground cavern. Blood poured from a gash at his temple and she cried when a soldier pierced his side.

Still he fought.

But he wasn't healing.

She'd seen him. Seen the cuts heal in Kuşadası. Seen the unflagging energy. But she knew as he wavered after throwing off an attacker…

He was going to lose.

There were too many. No help came. And a seemingly endless stream of attackers approached. No sooner had he dusted one than another fell on him.

Ava bit back a sob. He was going to lose. He wasn't strong enough.

Because of her.

Furious music pulsed in her head. Ancient songs beat at her.

A low humming chant echoed in a latent part of her mind.

Ava opened her mouth just as shouts echoed from the top of the cistern.

"Malachi?"

She let out a cry of relief when she heard Damien's voice, and two soldiers turned to the dark corner where she hid. Their eyes lit up with predatory glee as they turned to her, and Ava raised the crowbar again.

"Get to Ava!" Malachi shouted, still throwing off his attackers, some of whom had turned to the door. Ava's eyes scanned the darkness. She moved back and forth, trying to see beyond the forest of pillars.

Where was Brage?

The pale Grigori with the angel's blade was her greatest fear. She had no idea what would happen to Malachi if he was hit by the weapon in his condition. Would he be able to hold on as long as Leo had?

"Do you see her?"

"I think so."

The two soldiers drew closer. There was no avoiding them. They were headed straight for her. Ava didn't wait.

Throwing herself into the light with a guttural shout, she flung herself at the first one, swinging the crowbar down where his neck met his shoulder. She felt the bar sink in as the man's eyes went wide with shock; then she pulled. He tumbled forward with a splash, and Ava gasped at her own strength. A chunk of flesh ripped from the man's neck, and his collarbone was slick with blood, sticking out from the top of his chest as he flopped in the water like a wounded carp.

The other Grigori stood still for a moment, then raised a sword, only to look at it with wide eyes and lower it again.

They aren't supposed to hurt me, Ava realized with grim satisfaction.

She plunged forward, eyes focused on the man's neck, but he dodged to the side and grabbed her, tearing the crowbar from her hands as he tried to lift her from the water. She resisted for a few moments, her boots stuck in the thick mud, but eventually he tugged again, and her feet came free.

"No!" she screamed as he threw her over his shoulder. "NO!"

"Ava!"

Malachi saw the Grigori lift her, tossing her over his shoulder like baggage. He started trudging toward the exit, moving as quickly as he could in the heavy water. He was fighting two soldiers, feeling weaker by the moment, but he saw Max spot Ava as Damien sliced his way through the Grigori who swarmed them.

"Max, get Ava!" he yelled as loud as he could. The cistern was filled with the sounds of splashes and grunts, blades ringing against the stone pillars and men crying out in pain. Through it all, Malachi didn't think. He kept going, his single focus to move toward the soldier with his mate.

Get Ava. Escape the cistern.

Something tugged at his leg, but he kicked it away, losing one of the boots and a shoe at the same time. Sharp stones dug into his foot when he set it down again, and he could feel them pierce his flesh.

Damien moved toward him, throwing off the soldier who had attached himself to Malachi's back and was trying to grab his weapons. Most of the Grigori had lost their knives in the fight, the blades falling into the water as they struggled.

Malachi held on.

"Max, she's there!"

"I see her!"

He saw his brother head toward Ava, slicing through two Grigori, dusting one and throwing another into the darkness with a roar.

Almost there.

The lights flickered. Went out.

Ava screamed.

On again.

She'd been stabbed in the fighting. Blood poured from her belly, and he saw her face pale.

"Ava!"

Their eyes met in the flickering light as Malachi raced toward her as fast as he could, his heart beating out of his chest and blood dripping into his eyes.

"Hold on!"

"Malachi, no!"

Just then, a large soldier tackled him from behind a pillar. He knocked Malachi down. The water enveloped him as a painful scream filled the air.

. . .

THE MAGIC RAGED THROUGH HER, CLOSING THE WOUND ON HER belly, and Ava's soul rose in fear and fury. Through the pain, her voice lifted, echoing against the ancient stones.

The songs rang in her mind. The magic called her.

Speak, the seductive voice whispered.

More. Higher. Louder.

Ava's voice rose in pain and anger. She screamed out against the voices in her mind.

The soldier holding her faltered. One hand came up to his ear as he stumbled. She saw others clutching their heads. Blood poured between their fingers.

The lights went on. Then off. On again.

Finally, the one holding Ava dropped her, and she splashed in the water as the soldier ran. Everything was dark and silent for a moment before she surfaced, spitting out the foul water that had filled her mouth. She blinked her eyes, looking for danger. The Grigori who had captured her was pushing for the exit even as Max cut him down. She couldn't see Malachi, but she saw Max. Blood ran from his eyes and ears, but he kept coming toward her.

More Grigori ran past, two scrambling up the stairs as she brushed the damp hair from her face and blinked the mud from her eyes. Max finally reached her.

"You're fine, Ava. You're all right."

"Where's Malachi?"

A voice from the darkness. "I'm here, Ava." He emerged from the shadows, wading through the waist-deep water with a crooked smile. "What was that, love?"

Ava burst out with a sobbing laugh. "I have no idea."

She saw Damien and Malachi on the other side of the cistern. Damien smiled, even as he killed another Grigori with a dagger to his spine. The dust hung like a fog over their heads, wafting toward the exit where the rest of the soldiers had fled. Malachi stood, clutching his side, leaning against a pillar and panting. Blood ran from his eyes and nose, but he smiled anyway, staring across the water.

Come to me.

For a split second, she could hear the thought in his mind.

Ava stood and started running toward him as fast as she could, barely noticing the shadow moving in the corner of her eye.

The shadow rose from the water, blue eyes gleaming in the darkness and blade glinting in the light.

Ava's heart stopped.

Silence.

Malachi stilled as the blade pierced his spine, his eyes locking with hers.

Grey eyes wide in the darkness.

She fell. Her knees gave out.

Cold water rose to her chest.

Her mate's mouth dropped open with a silent cry as Brage's blade plunged in, then his face shone gold.

"NO!" Max's voice behind her.

Gold. He was gold. Shimmering in the darkness. Beautiful. Radiant.

Malachi's visage flickered as the dust began to rise.

Ava's heart beat once, then she heard another long scream.

Silence as her eardrums burst. Her vision went black as the gold dust rose like a ghost in the darkness.

Then the water enveloped her and everything was gone.

CHAPTER
TWENTY-TWO

Blackness. Silence.

She heard groans and knew they came from her throat.

Her chest ached. Her ears hurt. Everything hurt.

Someone was carrying her, but it wasn't him.

"What happened? *What happened?*"

"Gone," she whispered when she heard his brother's voice.

She saw it again. Her mate's radiant face before it dissolved into gold dust and drifted to the sky. The hollow feeling in her chest rose and enveloped her.

She closed her eyes.

AVA RAN THROUGH A DARK FOREST, THICK WITH FOG. HE WAS there. He had to be.

Where was he?

She tripped over roots in the path and the ground rushed toward her. Black leaves slapped her face.

Darkness.

"Do not fear the darkness."

. . .

SHE SLEPT.

She was in Cappadocia. She didn't know how. They put her in a bed that smelled of him, and she slept.

Warm, wrinkled hands forced her up in the bed.

"Drink. You must drink."

No.

"Please, Ava."

SMALL HANDS LED HER THROUGH THE FOREST. SOFT HANDS clutched her fingers. Childish voices whispered in her mind.

"Come back."

No.

"We need you to come back."

CHAPTER

TWENTY-THREE

Ava woke in the blackness, in the cave where they'd first made love. She was wrapped in his scent, but not his arms.

Everything was gone.

She lay still, staring at the chisel marks in the ceiling, wishing the mountain would close in and crush her.

"I know you're awake."

It was Rhys. She turned her head to the side and he was there, sitting in a corner of the room, staring at her with blood-shot eyes. They filled with tears as he watched her.

"Ava."

He reached over and caught her when she started to sob. The cries wracked her body, wringing her out as he held her. She shouted into his shoulder, beating at his back, but he only gripped her closer, rocking back and forth.

She cried for hours, and then the blackness enveloped her again.

DAMIEN WAS THERE THE NEXT TIME SHE WOKE.

"You need to eat, sister."

"I don't want to."

"He wanted you to live." Damien continued, even when she curled into herself, trying to shut out the words. "More than anything, he wanted you to live."

"Go away."

"Not till you've eaten."

"No."

"It's been over a week. You're dehydrated. Evren is hours away from putting you on an IV if you don't drink something."

"I don't care."

Damien knelt beside her, holding out a soft roll and a cup of water.

"Do not let his sacrifice be in vain."

She started to cry again, silent tears rolling down her cheeks, but she sat up. Damien helped her, placing more pillows behind her back after Ava took the roll from his hands. She bit down, and it tasted like dust.

WHISPERED THOUGHTS CIRCLED HER MIND AS SHE STARED AT THE mural in the library, the bucolic scene of families in the village. The ancient scribe she remembered sat across from her, staring silently with pale blue eyes.

She was his companion now.

Ava sat in the library for weeks, staring at the painting as the scribes fed her, forced her to drink. Her body grew strong again.

She slept in the bed she and Malachi had shared. The sense of him lingered for a time, and when it started to fade, Rhys showed up at the door with a blanket that held her mate's scent. Ava silently took it and wrapped it around her before she shut the door.

"YOU GRIEVE," THE ANCIENT SCRIBE SAID ONE AFTERNOON AS the sun lit the rich colors on the wall.

"Yes."

"As do I."

She glanced over. "How long?"

He shrugged. "Just a little while longer."

"You're immortal."

"She was supposed to be, too."

Ava whispered, "We're all immortal, as long as our stories are told."

The old scribe smiled, nodded, and turned back to the painting.

SHE STARED AT THE FIRE SOMEONE HAD STARTED IN THE SITTING room. It didn't warm her. She was cold to her bones.

"Brage?"

"Gone," Max whispered. "You fell in the water, and you didn't come up. He escaped when we ran for you. He's not in Istanbul. We don't know where he went. But we have his weapon. He lost it in the fight."

"I want to kill him."

"Good."

"YOU DON'T SOUND FINE," LENA SAID.

"I am. Or maybe I'm not." She twisted the phone cord around her finger as she sat. "But I will be."

"I want you to come home."

"No, I'm fine here. I like it here. I'm staying with friends."

"Do you need—?"

"I'm not the only woman in the world who's had her heart broken, Mother." She didn't try to stop the tears, knowing her mother believed the lie. "Give me some time. I'll be fine."

It wasn't a lie. He'd left her.

She told the truth. Just not all of it.

. . .

DAMIEN CAME TO HER ROOM ONE NIGHT. SHE WAS LOOKING through the pictures on her laptop, which had miraculously survived the fire at the scribe house in Istanbul. Pictures from her time with him before. When she'd still been human, and he'd still been her bodyguard.

There weren't enough.

He knocked on the door she'd left cracked open, then slipped in the room, sitting in the corner chair where Rhys, Maxim, Leo, and he had all watched over her.

Like brothers. His brothers.

Damien sat and watched her in silence until she spoke.

"What's up?"

"I'm going to take you to my mate. To Sari."

Ava swallowed the lump in her throat. "I don't want to leave yet."

"You need to."

"Are you going to force me?"

Damien took a deep breath and leaned forward. "Ava, when you screamed in the cistern, you burst your own eardrums, along with Max's and mine. Blood was pouring from your nose when we dragged you out. We were crying blood. The only reason you survived the wound to your abdomen and healed yourself was because Malachi performed the mating ritual. Otherwise, I know you'd be dead."

She choked back the cry. "I told him he was an idiot for doing it."

"Even now, I can tell you struggle to control the power. The songs press against your mind, don't they?"

She could do nothing but nod. The music had grown louder each time she slept. The whispering voices more persistent. Ava worried that she cried in her sleep, that she said the words that haunted her, but she didn't know what she said.

Damien ignored the tears that dripped down her nose. "Your magic is growing stronger, but you have no outlet. You must learn how to control it. You could hurt yourself or someone else without even meaning to. I can't teach you, but Sari can. You must go to other Irina."

For some reason, the thought of leaving the scribes angered her. "So you're just going to dump me with strangers?"

"No," he said. "I will not. I will stay with you. Though Sari might be angry, my mate will not turn me away. Malachi was my brother, and you were his mate. From this day, I vow to protect you." He paused and took a deep breath. "As a brother guards his sister, Ava, I will watch over you. You will *never* be alone."

Her shoulders were shaking when Damien crossed the room and closed the computer on her lap, taking her in his arms as she cried in loss. Relief. Confusion.

You will never be alone.

He finally whispered, "Will you go, sister?"

"I'll go."

CHAPTER
TWENTY-FOUR

S
he packed her things in a bag Max had found for her.
Leo would drive Damien and Ava to the airport, but even
she didn't know where they were going. Damien trusted
no one. He only told Max to find warm clothes for her, and
somehow, the clever scribe delivered, even at the end of a
Turkish summer.

She had new documents, a new name, and a new mobile
phone with an untraceable number, according to Rhys. She was
Ava Sakarya, the name Malachi used on documents when he
needed them.

The dreams still haunted her. She stumbled over and over
through the dark forest, trying not to be afraid. On the wind,
whispers in the Old Language teased her.

But one refrain, the mourning cry, echoed over and over
again.

It was the cry she'd heard since childhood. The voice of
every heart who had lost. Only now, it was her soul that spoke it.

The day before she and Damien were supposed to leave, she
wrote it down as best she could on a piece of paper and went
looking for Rhys in the library.

Ava found him working on the computer. She stood behind

him, watching as he typed an e-mail in some language she didn't recognize. Farsi, maybe. It didn't matter.

She placed her hand on his shoulder, taking comfort from the contact. She'd learned not to hold back. Malachi's brothers needed to hold her hand. To hug her. To offer her whatever comfort they could. She knew their hearts ached, too.

Rhys leaned over, pressing his cheek to the back of her hand before he turned. He pulled over a chair, taking her hand as she sat in it, and pushed up her sleeve. With soft fingers, he brushed them over her forearm to reveal the glowing gold spells Malachi had written on her during their mating. They lay hidden in her skin until the touch on another Irin made them visible.

Weeks ago, the very sight of them caused her to burst into tears, but now, looking at the soft smile on Rhys's face, she forced herself not to cry.

"Malachi always was messy about that letter," he said, rubbing his thumb over a twisting character near her wrist. "Never practiced enough. Always in a hurry to go beat something with a sword."

"I think it looks perfect."

"So do I."

He kept her hand in his until she tugged it away and reached into her pocket for the slip of paper where she'd written the words. She knew writing the letters wasn't dangerous for her, only speaking them. Still, she felt like she'd done something forbidden when she handed them over.

He took them with a frown. "What's this?"

"I just…" She cleared her throat. "I need to know what this means."

He looked at them, then he cocked his head. "Why?"

"I hear it." She swallowed the lump in her throat. She wouldn't cry. She was out of tears. "This phrase. All the time, I hear it now. I've heard it for years. When I pass a funeral. When I hear someone who's grieving." She lowered her voice as she nodded toward the old scribe who still sat in front of the mural.

"I think it's the only thing I've ever heard from his mind. I just... I need to know what these words mean."

"Ava, I'm not your teacher."

"But you are my friend." She forced out a smile. "Please? Please, just tell me. It's not that long, right? And it's driving me crazy."

Rhys shook his head. "You're right, of course. There's no reason you can't know what it means. It's not even complicated. It's just..." He cleared his throat. "*Vashama canem.* In the Old Language it means 'Come back to me.'"

"That's all?"

"That's all." He squeezed her hand and tossed the paper in the wastebasket under the desk. "I guess that makes sense for someone who's lost someone."

She nodded. "Yeah."

"Still leaving tomorrow?"

"Like you said, you're not my teacher." She smiled. "But I know I need one."

Rhys knit their fingers together, palm pressed to palm. "I'll see you again someday, Ava."

It wasn't a question.

DAMIEN AND AVA DROVE TO NEVŞEHIR THE NEXT DAY, LEAVING the last pieces of the familiar back in Göreme with Evren and the remnants of the Istanbul scribes. She stared at the twisting rock formations as they drove, then closed her eyes as the plane took off, trying to imagine Malachi's arms wrapped around her as she slept.

That night, Ava stared out the window of her hotel room near Atatürk Airport, watching the moon shine over the city. She draped herself in the blanket that barely held his scent and remembered the night they'd watched the moon rise behind the Galata Tower, huddled under the blanket on the roof of the old wooden house.

"There's no going back. I know that. I…I don't even want to. You were right about what you said before, even if the truth hurt. I was alone."

She wasn't alone anymore. No matter what. She knew that.

"Plus, I'm stupidly in love with you… so I guess we'll have to figure this out together."

"I love you, Ava."

Then the whisper from his mind. From his heart.

Reshon.

Ava buckled over, and sobs wrenched from her gut as the pain hit her again. She was walking through darkness, having lost the one love she'd ever dared to trust. Rage battled with grief as she knelt on the floor of the sterile hotel room, clutching the last piece of him she had.

"I hate you tonight, *reshon!*" She sobbed and curled against the bed. "How could you leave me like this? How?"

Ava beat her fists against the floor, pressing her tears into the rough blanket that had wrapped around them in the garden that night. The scent of her mate filled her nose, but he wasn't there. No arms held her. No touch soothed her. No familiar voice filled her mind.

"I love you," she choked. "I hate you. I love you. Come back to me, Malachi. What's the use of all this if you're not with me?"

His spells glowed in the darkness, and Ava stared at them, the old words whispering in her heart. Her soul wept, reaching for its other half.

In the darkness, Ava cried out. The words slipped from her lips, reaching up to the heavens.

"*Vashama canem, reshon. Vashama canem.*"

COME BACK TO ME.

CHAPTER
TWENTY-FIVE

Hundreds of miles away, he woke with a gasp, his lungs filling with the night air as he lay cold and naked on the Phrygian plain. Grey eyes gazed into the heavens, staring at the full moon, and grass pressed to his back on the deserted riverbank. Night cloaked him, bare and unmarked as the first night he'd been born into the world.

He knew nothing and no one.

But a million stars danced over him, and a familiar voice whispered in his mind.

"Come back to me."

• • • ❖ • • •

Continue reading for a preview of
THE SINGER: Irin Chronicles Book Two
NOW AVAILABLE

PREVIEW: THE SINGER

EDITOR'S PICK: BEST ROMANCE
NOW AVAILABLE!

The Fallen appeared on the summit of Mt. Ararat. Golden eyes reached west, settling on some point unseen by the hawks circling overhead. The wind whipped past him, brushing the black hair that fell to his shoulders. Jaron wore his human form, content to cloak his true nature and enjoy the sharp pleasure of the sun on his skin. Ancient *talesm* covered his shoulders and chest, gold against bronze. He was a vision of glory, resting on the mountain peak.

His brothers appeared beside him, Barak with his wolf-grey hair, gold eyes watching the birds overhead. Vasu, already pacing, his lean human form dark against the snow.

"You gave up your city, brother." Vasu stared down as he spoke, seemingly mesmerized by the tracks his bare feet made in the frost. The angel chose to reside in warm climates, though none of their kind were truly bothered by either heat or cold. They commanded their senses at will.

"You imply defeat. I simply chose not to fight for it. It no longer interested me."

Barak murmured, "And the rest of your territories? Are they secure?"

"Volund knows better than to become too brazen. I allowed his child to overrun Istanbul because it served my purpose. No doubt, he was confused to find my people withdrawn."

"Where are they?" Barak asked. "And do not underestimate Volund. I thought the same about him until he attacked. Now my children think me dead. They hide, afraid of their own shadow." Barak's lip curled. "I would cleanse this realm of their presence if doing so wouldn't give away my continued existence."

"I am watching," Jaron said. He couldn't take his eyes off the city. Something was churning there. The sun fell in the west, slipping below the clouds to shine pink over the plains and mountains of Asia Minor. "I am always watching."

"But for what?" Vasu asked. "I hope your visions sing true."

"Have they ever not? I warned you of Galal's attack, didn't I?"

Gold eyes flashed from behind Vasu's curtain of black hair. His *talesm* sparked gold. Black and gold, the Fallen glared at his brother. "And I allowed you to persuade me. Now my children think their father murdered by a foreign god. They fight to remain true to me, even as Galal's soldiers slaughter them."

"Tell them to be more careful, then." Jaron shrugged. "When the time comes, you will breed more."

Vasu curled his lip. "I have not consorted with human women for a millennium. You know I tire of their attention."

"I hear sorrow," Barak growled, rising to his feet and looking west to the ancient city. "What is this? I thought the female was unharmed."

"She formed a bond with one of the Irin scribes. He sacrificed himself for her." Jaron's voice held a faint note of admiration. "She mourns."

"Does this change anything?" Vasu asked.

"No."

Barak cocked his head. "Why did you allow the sacrifice? Did you foresee it?"

"I did. I was... curious."

"And she mourns him?" Barak's voice held no pity. His eyes were impassive as he stared into the distance, the evening sun flushing his pale skin a gold-tinted rose.

"She does."

"You were curious?" Vasu asked, his voice holding more judgment than Jaron expected. Vasu was younger than his brothers, a mere boy when the Fallen had left their home. He had lived longer in the human realm than the heavenly. "Toying with humans is beneath you."

"His sacrifice was incidental. Still, it is curious how she mourns."

The three angels rested at the peak of the mountain, the hawks circling above them, screaming at their intrusion. Jaron relaxed, bronze and gold in the light, eyes watching the distance, seeing beyond time and space. His children, when it served him, bore traces of his foresight. Vasu stood slightly behind him, dark and brooding. His physical presence dwarfed his brothers. Not in size, for the tall, lean human form he donned was not imposing, but his energy, the tightly chained physicality of his presence, marked him as different, more terrestrial, than his brothers.

Barak sat silently next to Jaron, his brother's mirror in eternity. While Jaron saw, Barak heard, his solemn presence the eternal and constant punctuation of Jaron's curiosity. The two friends had existed in tandem for millennia. And now they struggled to attain what others thought was lost.

"Do you truly think it possible?" Barak asked, rising to his feet. "After all this time?"

Jaron narrowed his vision. Something was stirring in the distance. "Seven years or seven million, brother. He does not see time as we do. It must be possible."

A flicker. A wavering in the heavens as the stars danced above. Jaron stood and walked to the edge of the cliff.

Barak asked, "What is this I hear?" His eyes sought Jaron's, which were wide and filled with a long-lost emotion.

Wonder.

"A complication."

Vasu darted to his side. "What do you see?"

"Look, my brothers."

Then Jaron opened his vision, sending it to the two angels at his side. All three watched as the woman crouched in a hotel room. All three heard the words she uttered, then the tearing of the heavenly realm.

Vasu blinked. "Unexpected."

"Indeed."

"Does this change anything?" Barak asked.

"No. He was necessary to keep her alive. Other than that, he is incidental."

"The female did this," Vasu said.

"So it would seem."

Barak said, "We always knew her powers would be unstable."

"They all are."

Vasu lifted an eyebrow, a decidedly human gesture that Jaron wondered if he was aware of. "Is it any wonder our sons fear them?" he murmured.

"She is a means to an end," Jaron said. "That is all."

Barak and Vasu exchanged a look but did not argue with their brother.

Vasu and Barak asked in unison, "Does this change our course?"

"No," Jaron said, his eyes focused on a dark riverbank. "We do what we always do. We watch."

THE SCRIBE

THE SINGER IS NOW AVAILABLE IN E-BOOK, PAPERBACK, AND
AUDIOBOOK.

Now experience the entire Irin Chronicles series! Read all seven bestselling novels for hours of reading enjoyment and find out why reviewers are raving.

The Scribe (Ava and Malachi pt.1)
The Singer (Ava and Malachi pt.2)
The Secret (Ava and Malachi pt.3)
The Staff and the Blade (Damien and Sari)
The Silent (Leo and Kyra)
The Storm (Max and Renata)
The Seeker (Rhys and Meera)

A fascinating new series. Definitely recommended.

— NOCTURNAL BOOK REVIEWS

Loved this book!!! It was sexy, well written and suspenseful. Just like with the *Elemental Mysteries* series, I was gripped from the very beginning.

— VILMA'S BOOK BLOG

AFTERWORD

Countless individuals helped me with the research for this series, and the month I spent in Israel and Turkey was one of the most rewarding times of my life.

I'd like to thank the Telerant-Faith family, who made my time in Israel so wonderful. Experiencing a country as a tourist or student is nothing like experiencing it with a family. So many thanks to you.

Also, I'd like to express sincere gratitude to the staff of the American Colony Hotel in Jerusalem and the staff and volunteers at the Israel Museum. To all the knowledgable guides who I had the pleasure of meeting, thank you.

To my best friend, Kelli, who took the time to travel with me, enabling me to visit many places I wouldn't have been able to on my own. A great friend and a fantastic research assistant. Many, many thanks.

To the entire country of Turkey!

There are few places I have visited where I have felt more welcome. Your tradition of hospitality shines through your people, your businesses, and your whole culture. Thank you for making my visit such a wonderful experience. I can't wait to return.

AFTERWORD

To the staff of the Ibrahim Pasha hotel in Istanbul, thank you so much. Your guidance and suggestions never steered me wrong. You were my home away from home for the time I was in your beautiful city, and I can't wait to visit you again.

To my amazing guide in Cappadocia, Rüya Kivrim. I was so fortunate to have your knowledgable and fun guidance through the rich history of the region. You truly were a dream(!) to work with.

And to all the people I was fortunate to meet—shop owners, drivers, guides, fellow travelers, and so many more—thank you, thank you, thank you.

Finally, most of you know how important music is to me as an individual and a writer. It was especially inspirational for this book and this series. Thanks in particular to the amazing Loreena McKennit, the brilliance of Sigur Rós, and the inspiring Dead Can Dance for providing the writing soundtrack for this book and ongoing series. Your music touches my soul.

Thank you.

ACKNOWLEDGMENTS

After a while, it seems repetitive to thank the same people over and over, but truly, my work would not be what it is without the support of my incredible family.

Thanks to my pre-readers, Kristy, Sarah, Kelli, Gen, and Natalie. You are my first line of defense.

Thanks again to all the reviewers and bloggers who promote my work and spread the word online and in person. Getting to know so many of you has been a blessing I never could have anticipated.

Thanks to my editing team, Anne and Sara. True professionals who make my work shine. And thanks to the incredible artists at Damonza for their vision and talent. You took a simple idea and brought it to life.

Many thanks to my agent, Jane Dystel, and all the team at Dystel and Goderich Literary Management.

Thanks to my girls. (You know who you are.)

And thanks, always, to my readers. Thank you for being enthusiastic about this new world. Thanks for your encouragement and kind words. I hope I will always do justice to the confidence you place in me as a storyteller.

ABOUT THE AUTHOR

ELIZABETH HUNTER is a *USA Today* and international best-selling author of romance, contemporary fantasy, and paranormal mystery. Based in Central California and Addis Ababa, Ethiopia, she travels extensively to write fantasy fiction exploring world mythologies, history, and the universal bonds of love, friendship, and family. She has published over thirty works of fiction and sold over a million books worldwide. She is the author of the Glimmer Lake series, the Elemental Legacy series, the Irin Chronicles, the Cambio Springs Mysteries, and other works of fiction.

ElizabethHunterWrites.com

To sign up for her newsletter, please follow this link and receive free short fiction and news about sales, specials, and new releases.

ALSO BY ELIZABETH HUNTER

The Bronze Blade

The Scarlet Deep

A Very Proper Monster

A Stone-Kissed Sea

Valley of the Shadow

The Elemental Legacy

Shadows and Gold

Imitation and Alchemy

Omens and Artifacts

Midnight Labyrinth

Blood Apprentice

The Devil and the Dancer

Night's Reckoning

Dawn Caravan

The Bone Scroll

Pearl Sky

The Elemental Covenant

Saint's Passage

Martyr's Promise

Paladin's Kiss

Bishop's Flight

(Summer 2023)

Vista de Lirio

Double Vision

Mirror Obscure

Trouble Play

Made in the USA
Las Vegas, NV
20 March 2024

87510219R00174